W9-BQL-917

Dear Reader,

Some people wonder why anyone would keep a journal. After all, why should the tiniest details of our lives hold any interest for anyone else but us? Sometimes we may even have trouble finding the meaning or the story in the details of our own lives by ourselves.

In this book, Sadie discovers a journal in which a woman has recorded the simple details of her own life—not realizing the importance that they'll have for future generations.

In some ways, it's a unique situation, which is what makes it a good story. But in other ways, the author of the journal in this book isn't all that different from any of us. The details of our grandparents' lives, our great-grandparents' lives, even our parents' lives, can be a great source of curiosity and comfort for us, even if those details might have seemed unimportant to the people who lived through them. We don't just learn about the individual lives of the people who kept the journal—we learn about the broad history of the world, on a very personal level.

But we learn an even more important lesson when we keep track of the seemingly unimportant details of our lives, as well. Just like in this book, when we look back at all the things that we didn't understand or couldn't make sense of at the time, sometimes beautiful patterns emerge. We can see the way God was forming us, and the way our own character was being revealed. And it turns out, the most important things in our lives aren't usually introduced with a bang or a choir or angels. They're revealed slowly, in the seemingly unimportant details—that later we realize were actually the most important things in the world.

Vera Dodge
writing as Carole Jefferson

Mysteries of Silver Peak

A Mountain of Mystery
Nobody's Safe
Silver Surprise

MYSTERIES
of SILVER PEAK

Silver Surprise

CAROLE JEFFERSON

New York

Mysteries of Silver Peak is a trademark of Guideposts.

Published by Guideposts Books & Inspirational Media
110 William Street
New York, NY 10038
Guideposts.org

Copyright © 2014 by Guideposts. All rights reserved.

This book, or parts thereof, may not be reproduced, stored in a retrieval system, or transmitted in any form or by any means, electronic, mechanical, photocopying, recording or otherwise, without the written permission of the publisher.

The characters and events in this book are fictional, and any resemblance to actual persons or events is coincidental.

Acknowledgments

Every attempt has been made to credit the sources of copyrighted material used in this book. If any such acknowledgment has been inadvertently omitted or miscredited, receipt of such information would be appreciated.

Scripture quotations marked (NIV) are taken from *The Holy Bible, New International Version*. Copyright © 1973, 1978, 1984, 2011 by Biblica, Inc. Used by permission of Zondervan. All rights reserved worldwide. www.zondervan.com

Cover and interior design by Müllerhaus
Cover art by Greg Copeland represented by Deborah Wolfe, Ltd.
Typeset by Aptara, Inc.

Printed and bound in the United States of America
10 9 8 7 6 5

Prologue

WITH COLORADO'S FAMOUS SILVER MOON AND THE ENTIRE GALAXY of stars hidden beyond a rare cover of low clouds, Main Street in Silver Peak was an eerie sight: scattered pools of light, separated by long swaths of deep darkness. Nikolai Tesla had brought electric light to the streets of nearby Colorado Springs almost half a century ago, in the 1880s, but tonight Silver Peak's streets were lit by only a handful of modest lights atop poles felled from the lush pine forests outside town. And since the town had begun to struggle in earnest from the effects of the Great Depression, only half of those were lit now, to conserve the town's limited resources.

The street outside the theater was warmed by a circle of warm orange light from the lamp fizzing high overhead. But the bank, and the storefronts on either side of it, were cloaked in darkness.

From the bank, into that darkness, a man emerged. He checked up and down the street, confirming with a glance in each direction that it was deserted, except for him. Then he stopped to listen for voices, or traffic, anywhere out of sight.

After a moment, satisfied, he drew a key from an inner pocket of his coat and carefully locked the front door of the bank. He stood there for another moment, as if waiting for some kind of signal from within. If there was one, it wouldn't have been visible to anyone but him: the bank with its large plate-glass windows remained just as dark and silent as the street it stood on.

The man walked down the wooden sidewalk that ran between the Main Street establishments, into the next pool of light, where he peered down into the hard-packed dirt street. After a moment, he knelt to retrieve something: a good-sized rock, about the same as an apple.

He carried it back into the darkness that obscured the bank window. Then he wound up with all the coiled energy of a pitcher on a mound in front of a crowd of thousands. The rock sailed through the bank's plate-glass window with a *crack*. An instant later, the entire window shattered, raining down onto the wooden slats of the sidewalk, and jangling dully on the hard-packed dirt, gravel, and stones of the street.

The Colorado night air poured into the bank through the breach.

The man stared into the darkness inside.

Then he took a deep breath, turned away, and walked off, whistling, into the night.

1

———

"SADIE, HI!" LUZ VIDAL SAID WITH A WELCOMING GRIN WHEN she saw Sadie appear in the small doorway that connected Sadie's antique shop, the Antique Mine, with Arbuckle's, the charming coffee shop that Luz ran with her husband, Hector. "Just popping in for your regular?"

Sadie gave a rueful smile. It was bad enough to have a coffee shop next door, especially one with treats as tempting as the ones at Arbuckle's, the delectable baked goods created by Maggie Price. Before she met her husband, Lou, Maggie had been a big-time pastry chef in New York City before moving to Silver Peak to enjoy some of life's simpler pleasures, but she hadn't lost her touch: both the Market and Luz's pastry cabinet at Arbuckle's were always full with a rotating selection of inventive, and delicious, temptations, like maple blondie brownies, grasshopper sandwiches with mint buttercream smoothed between chocolate cookies, and red-velvet bar cookies frosted with the best cream-cheese frosting Sadie had ever tasted. But to have a door directly between her shop and Arbuckles, with the delicious scent of coffee and hints of sweet things pouring through it all day, was too much for Sadie to resist.

She tried to go light on the treats, although she didn't always succeed. And anyway, she figured all her long walks with Hank helped ward off the calories. But she did love her coffee, and Luz usually started to set up Sadie's standard order the instant she saw Sadie come through the door.

Today, however, Sadie shook her head.

Luz, who had already bent down to pull a clean coffee cup, looked up in surprise, a questioning expression in her eyes.

"I'm meeting a friend," Sadie explained. Even as she said the word, she felt a little pang. Edwin Marshall was one of her oldest friends. She'd known him even longer than she'd known T.R., her husband, before she was widowed. In fact, she couldn't remember the first time she had met Edwin, who sometimes liked to joke that they might have made their first acquaintance as babies in the Silver Peak maternity ward, although that was a stretch—they'd been born in the same year, but not the same month. But they'd both grown up in Silver Peak, and Edwin had been such a familiar part of life there that he seemed like part of the town itself, just like the streets Sadie knew so well, or the peaks of the mountains outside of town, which Sadie had memorized without trying, simply from gazing up at them so many times over so many years.

But Edwin had never really been only a friend, not since the romance they had shared as teenagers. They'd been young, of course, and they'd had lots of fun together—but neither of them were flighty, even as teenagers, and the feelings they'd had for each other then had been more serious than a fleeting teenage crush. That romance had ended when Edwin went off to college. Their feelings had been serious, but both of them were also sensible, even as kids, and they'd agreed that it made sense to let their relationship end when Edwin left Silver Peak. Of course, part of Sadie had hoped that Edwin might come swooping back to claim her—and maybe part of Edwin had secretly hoped to do that as well. But that wasn't where life had taken them. When Sadie had gone off to college, she'd met T.R., and Edwin had married and moved to Chicago, and their paths hadn't crossed for decades, until Edwin moved back to town, a widower, after his retirement.

He'd already made it clear that he would like to rekindle their romance, but Sadie still wasn't entirely sure she was ready for that. She'd spent most of her life believing she would never love anybody but T.R., and for a while after he passed away, she hadn't even wanted to live without him. But Edwin had continued to be a good friend to her since he moved back, always there for her, but never too insistent—and a few times, more and more recently, she'd wondered if the little thrill of pleasure she sometimes felt when he stepped into the Antique Mine, or called her on the phone, was more than just friendship itself.

"How are you doing today, Luz?" Sadie asked, covering the uncertainty she felt.

Luz smiled again. "It's been a good day so far," she said. "Marisol called from school last night. It's always so good to hear from her."

Marisol was Luz's daughter, whom Sadie had gotten to know during her visits home from college. She shared her mother's thick brown hair, dark eyes, and beauty, and to Sadie, it was obvious that she had a crush on Josh, a handsome young man who was gaining a national reputation for his innovative woodwork. Sadie had gotten to know him when he started supplying interesting pieces of his carpentry to her shop, and she liked him. He was unfailingly kind, and patient, but not because he didn't have any spirit. He could also get incredibly excited about the intricacies of his work. And at twenty-six, he was really only a few years older than Marisol, who was twenty. Sadie had always liked the idea of Marisol's crush turning into an actual romance, but for now, Josh just seemed to think of Marisol as a college kid.

"Any big news?" Sadie asked.

Luz's eyes lit up. But as she began to speak, she hesitated. After a minute, a smile spread over her face again. "I guess not," she said. "Not really. I mean, not anything that would really be news to anyone who's not her mother. She's doing well in classes. She seems happy."

"That's great," Sadie said. "If you ask me, that sounds like news. Just good news. And there's not always enough of that."

"I guess to me," Luz said, "the biggest news is that she still wants to talk with her mother, even though she's all grown-up. I'll tell you, there were years when she was a teenager when that was the last thing I'd ever have expected."

"Well, that's how you know she's growing up," Sadie said, and winked.

As she did, the chime above the front door from the street rang merrily, and Edwin stepped into the shop, leaving a swirl of wind and aspen leaves on the sidewalk behind him. After a cold snap that had brought a fair amount of snow, the capricious Colorado autumn had brought back bright sun and warm, crisp air that had many of the locals trading winter coats for shirtsleeves.

Edwin glanced around for a moment, dressed as always a bit more formally than other Silver Peak natives, in a collared shirt, vest, and neat khakis: a formality that was probably a remnant of the decades he'd spent as a Chicago judge. His salt-and-pepper hair glowed briefly in the sun that fell through the window. Then he caught sight of Sadie, and his face lit up.

This time, the little thrill Sadie had gotten used to feeling when she saw him was tinged with nervousness. The conversation she had had with Edwin, where she told him that she wasn't ready for anything more than friendship, had been coming back to her more and more frequently recently. She'd started to wonder if she had said the right thing—and if she hadn't, what she ought to say to him, and when. But she still wasn't sure how she felt. And it could have been her imagination, but something had seemed different to her about the way that Edwin had asked her to meet him today. Usually, he was more casual, dropping in to her store, or calling to ask her advice on his never-ending restoration of his father's house, which was a source of many of both his joys and frustrations.

But this time, he had called her a few days before, and asked if she would be willing to meet him at Arbuckle's. He'd sounded a little nervous himself—almost the way he had decades ago, when they had first started to go out. Sadie had told herself time and time again over the past few days that it wasn't a date. Edwin knew better. But she couldn't help realizing that, along with her nervousness, there was a growing hope that it might be one.

It didn't help that, as soon as Edwin came in the door, Luz turned away like a knowing mother, trying to give two awkward kids the space to work things out among themselves.

Feeling for all the world like a gawky teenager, she somehow managed to cross the store to greet Edwin.

"How are you?" she asked.

"I'm happy to see you," Edwin told her, and gave her a quick kiss on the cheek.

Sadie tried to remember whether he had done this before or not in the past, but for some reason she had trouble organizing her thoughts. Hoping to collect them, she started to sit down at the nearest table.

"Don't you want anything?" Edwin asked.

Despite the fact that Sadie usually couldn't resist Luz's coffee, she had completely forgotten about ordering a drink.

Sadie pushed her chair back to stand again, but Edwin gestured for her to stay put.

"I'll get it," he said with the same tone of generosity and confidence that Sadie had always liked about him.

"Your regular?" Luz asked from the nearby counter.

Sadie nodded, then offered up a quick prayer while Edwin placed his own order, and paid for the two of them.

Lord, she prayed. *I have no idea what I'm doing. That's probably true more often than I know, but I sure know it right now. Please guide me. I don't want to try to live in the past, but I don't want to miss whatever You have for me in the future.*

A moment later, Edwin was back with both drinks, and a fruit bar balanced on top of his own: pale yellow, with ribbons of deep red.

"Lemon with raspberry," he told Sadie with a quick smile. "Luz assured me it's the best."

"I think they're all the best," Sadie said.

Edwin's smile broadened at her joke. "You might be right about that," he said. He took the cup in his hands, leaned back in his chair, took a sip, and looked across the table at her.

Sadie held his gaze for a moment, but it seemed to last so long that she became embarrassed and looked down. "What?" she said.

"Pardon me," Edwin said, with his slight courtroom formality. "I just like to look at you."

"Oh, there's not much to look at," Sadie said.

"The two of us are just going to have to disagree on that," Edwin said, and took another sip of his drink.

Then he put it down on the table between them. "Sadie," he said. "I wanted to talk to you about this race for Silver Peak mayor."

A wave of—was it relief or disappointment?—washed over Sadie. So that was why he'd made a special appointment with her—the Silver Peak mayoral election, in which he was running as a candidate. Edwin had put himself forward for the position.

Just like Sadie, Edwin cared deeply about history and restoration, while James Morgan, his opponent, seemed more interested in leading Silver Peak forward into some kind of progressive future that even he didn't seem quite clear on. Both Sadie and Edwin liked James, who had graduated from school in Silver Peak several years before they had. And everyone else in town seemed to like him too. But Edwin was worried that, without strong leadership, much of Silver Peak's history could be lost or tainted—and with tourists and new residents pouring into town, if growth wasn't managed carefully, it could compromise Silver Peak's future.

"I'm up for anything," Sadie said. "You just let me know, and I'll do it."

Edwin gave her a wry smile. "Well, you might want to hear what I'm asking, first."

"It doesn't matter," Sadie said. "Whatever you need, you've got it."

"I'm not going to hold you to that," Edwin said. "But I want you to remember you said it."

He pushed the lemon bar across the table. "Try a bite?" he said.

Looking down at the delectable treat, Sadie realized that her usually reliable appetite had also fled. But she took a bite anyway, to give her a chance to clear her head.

Edwin stared down at the confection thoughtfully. The campaign hadn't seemed to worry him much before: like everything, he just seemed willing to give it his best, and let the chips fall where they may. But now his face had turned serious, and he seemed to be choosing and weighing his words.

"We have our first events for the campaign starting this week," he said.

Sadie already knew this, and not just from talking with Edwin. Just about everybody in town followed the brief season of the mayoral election. It only lasted a few weeks, but between the debates between the candidates, the ensuing debates among Silver Peak's citizenry, and the whirl of barbecues and stump speeches each candidate was expected to offer, election season was always some of the best entertainment Silver Peak had seen since Sarah Bernhardt, Collin Malloy, and Mark Twain had graced their historic opera house's stage.

But there was no point in interrupting Edwin, Sadie knew, or in trying to get him to cut to the bottom line. Edwin had a lawyer's patient, logical mind, and nothing would stop him from starting at the beginning, and carrying it through, point by point, to whatever he thought of as the end.

"The campaign is going to take a lot of my time," he said. "And if I win, being mayor may take even more. It'll take a significant commitment."

Sadie nodded, still uncertain what all of this had to do with her.

"But seeing you is important to me too," Edwin said. He looked up as he said it, and his eyes locked with hers for a moment before he glanced away. "I probably won't have the time to call you up for advice on the house in the near future. Or to drop by the store and find you there."

"I'll be there anytime you stop by," Sadie offered.

Edwin grinned. "I know you think that," he said. "But it's not really true. You spend a lot of time out and about, Sadie Speers. Believe it or not, I only catch you about every other time I come by."

Sadie felt a flush come up in her face. Did Edwin really come by to see her twice as often as she knew?

"Sadie," Edwin said. "You know how I feel about you."

"Well," Sadie said, "I know what you said before."

"I still feel that way," Edwin said. "I've been trying to take it slow. We've got time, and I don't want to push you. But I don't want to have to pretend I'm always just dropping by or stopping in. I'd like to be able to call you up and hear how your day went, and know that I'm going to get to see you sometime soon. I know what you said the last time I brought this up, and I respect that. Nothing's changed for me since then. But I can't help hoping that something might have changed for you. What do you think, Sadie? Is there any chance you'd ever consider..." He locked eyes with her again, uncertainty playing with a certain mischievous look on his distinguished features.

"...going steady with me again?"

The last time Edwin had asked her, Sadie had known her answer immediately. This time, she felt even more uncertain than he. She still felt a strong sense of loyalty to T.R. and their life together. She still couldn't imagine what a future with Edwin might look like. But under it all, she felt a deep happiness. Why, she wasn't sure. And she was even less sure about what to say.

She reached for her coffee and took a sip, then looked over her cup at Edwin.

He looked back at her, waiting. Once he'd said his piece, Edwin was a man who knew how to bide his time. But he would want an answer eventually. And Sadie couldn't even begin to put all of her thoughts, let alone her feelings, into words.

A footstep fell behind her. Sadie started, suddenly mortified at the idea that Luz had been nearby, listening to all of this. But before she could turn, a familiar voice called out.

"Grandma!" her grandson, Theo, cried. "Wait'll you see what I found!"

Sadie twisted in her seat to smile at Theo. He was seventeen, lanky, with thick dark hair that tended to fall into his eyes, especially when he was excited. It was drooping so far down over his eyebrows right now that she could barely believe he could see through it, which must mean he'd found something he was pretty excited about.

But then she remembered Edwin, and glanced back at him. Instead of the frustration she'd been afraid she might find on his face, she saw amusement.

"I'm sorry," she mouthed.

Edwin shrugged. "It's been decades," he said. "I can wait another day."

By this time, Theo had reached their table, breathless with excitement. "You're going to love this," he said, pulling up an empty seat from a nearby table and sitting down. "I was just at a yard sale in Denver. I wasn't actually looking for antiques. I was hoping to get a bike to use in Silver Peak, since I keep my good one at Dad's so he and I can go biking on the weekends we're together. They had a bunch of them advertised, but by the time I got there they were all gone."

"You have to get there early," Sadie told him.

Theo nodded, somewhat impatiently. "I know," he said. "I've staked out plenty of early morning yard sales with you before. But I hit rush-hour traffic, and got there ten minutes after it opened, and—" He made a noise like a rushing wind.

"Sounds like bikers are about as enthusiastic as antiquers," Sadie said.

"I guess I wasn't the only one," Theo admitted. "But then I'd already driven all the way out there, so I decided to poke around. They didn't have much that was too interesting to me, just a lot of kids' clothes, and some power tools. But then, in with the knick-knacks, I found this."

He pulled a slim green bank ledger out of his pocket, slightly larger than a piece of standard letter paper.

Sadie couldn't help eyeing it appraisingly. Paper ephemera—books, ledgers, notebooks, and photographs—were some of her favorite antiques. They weren't as highly prized by decorators, who tended to gravitate toward furniture and other large elements that could be used in design, but Sadie loved antiques not just for their beauty, but for their history, and ephemera tended to offer a wealth of details that the mysterious initials cut into a desk, or the wear patterns on an antique chair, simply couldn't give. In terms of history, ephemera was often a gold mine.

"I know how you like paper ephemera," Theo rattled on. "And I thought there might be some interesting Colorado history in it, probably something about Denver..."

As he spoke, Sadie took in the details of the cover. She'd spent an interesting day a few years ago, in a pole barn on the property of an avid ephemera collector who had converted it into a personal library for his cache of antique bank ledgers. They weren't just full of out-of-date numbers, he'd taught her. They were a fascinating glimpse into changes in accounting practices, but also into the stories the numbers themselves told: like the patients recorded carefully in a doctor's ledger, which held stories of suffering and hope, or the decades represented by the careful columns of names and payments for a local bank's mortgage holders. And the ledgers reflected changes in the business of printing itself—more lush during times when the American economy was flush, more spartan when times were hard. This one was so simple that Sadie suspected it might even be Depression era, and the simple design on the cover seemed to match the austerity of that time as well.

"But then," Theo said, breaking into her thoughts, "I looked at the frontispiece of this ledger, and it said Silver Peak!"

Even Edwin leaned forward at this. Excitedly, Theo opened the ledger, and pointed to the front page, where "Silver Peak Bank" was carefully printed. He pushed it toward Sadie, who stared down at it in fascination.

"Well," she said. "I wonder how this wound up at a yard sale in Denver. And I wonder what kind of stories the numbers will tell us."

"Well, that's the thing," Theo said.

"What?" Sadie asked.

Theo caught the upper corner of a page, and turned it for her. "There are no numbers," he said. Across the neat columns, ribbons of text ran, the neat lines of a standard diary entry. Mary had seen ledger-keepers take notes in the margins before—sometimes impassioned or hilarious ones. But it was uncommon to see a ledger used as a diary.

"Well, I wonder who…" Sadie began.

"I searched through it pretty well. There might be clues in the entries, but I couldn't find a name or any identifying information for the author," Theo said.

At this, Edwin, who had crowded around to get a better look at the page, jabbed his finger at an entry, which contained a name in the course of the description.

"The writer mentions a 'Jules M,' " he read.

Sadie met his gaze, recognition in her eyes.

"Do you think that…" Edwin began.

"I don't know who else it could be," Sadie said.

"Jules Morgan," Edwin said, finishing her thought for her.

"Who's that?" Theo asked.

Edwin let the ledger fall closed on the table between them. "The father of my opponent in the mayoral election."

2

THEO FROWNED, CONFUSED. "HIS FATHER? HOW DO YOU KNOW that? Are you friends with your—opponent?"

Edwin smiled. "I'd say I've been friendly with James Morgan for most of my life. There's something about growing up in a small town—even if you aren't close with someone, you can't help knowing things about them—and getting to care about what happens to them."

"But Jules Morgan is another story," Sadie added.

Theo turned to her. "What do you mean?"

"Well," Sadie said. "It's true you do get to know some things about the people you grow up with in a small town. But in a small town, if you've got a big personality, then *everybody* knows you."

"And Jules Morgan had a big personality," Theo ventured.

"That's one way to put it," Edwin said dryly.

"Well, so what do you know about him?" Theo said, trying to hide his impatience.

Edwin raised his eyebrows at Sadie, as if to ask for permission to share the old stories about Jules Morgan with her grandson. Sadie gave a slight nod, to let him know it was all right with her if he went on.

"As a former judge," Edwin began, "I feel like I need to make it clear that most of what anyone in Silver Peak thinks they know about Jules Morgan wouldn't necessarily rise to a standard that might be admissible in court. The vast majority of it would fall into the category of 'hearsay'."

"But people did have a lot to say about Jules Morgan," Sadie said.

Edwin gave a vigorous nod. "They certainly did," he said.

"What did they say?" Theo pressed.

"Well, one thing that a lot of people in Silver Peak had seen for themselves was that Jules Morgan had a strong taste for drink," Edwin said. "I remember I saw him once, drunk as a lord, walking home on a Sunday morning around 6:00 AM when I'd gone out to do my paper route. He was singing 'Clementine' at the top of his lungs, but he was using some lyrics I know my mother never taught me. And he had a stray dog with him that he was feeding fried potatoes to, out of his pockets. He kept trying to get it to come close enough to pat its head, and I think the dog might have been amenable to that after enough of the potatoes, but every time Jules tried to reach him, he missed."

"There were a lot of stories like that," Sadie said. "I remember Rose telling me she saw him once with a car full of ladies she thought he must have brought down from Denver. We were just girls, so this must have been sometime in the 1950s, but she said they looked just like the old pictures of dance hall queens from the real Wild West, with corsets and feathers. She wasn't sure how many there were, but she said she counted at least three of them, all piled into his sky-blue convertible, with fins the size of wings."

Edwin gave a rueful smile. "He did have quite a reputation with the ladies."

"He sounds like a real character," Theo said. "I think I would have liked him."

"He was," Sadie said. "And a lot of people in town did like him. But it wasn't quite that simple."

"Why not?" Theo asked.

"Well, Edwin's story might sound charming if you're just a paperboy looking for amusement on your Sunday morning route. But it might feel a little different if that was your father. And Rose never forgot the sight of all those ladies piled into Jules's car. But that sight might feel a lot different if you were his wife."

"Or if you were the husband of one of the women in town whom he gave his attentions to," Edwin added.

"Or if you were a woman who didn't want the attention you were being given," Sadie added.

"Was that a problem?" Theo asked. "That he had affairs?"

"I'm not sure I ever knew that, one way or another," Edwin said.

"It was more about whispers and rumors," Sadie said. "I never heard of a marriage breaking up over him, which will happen from time to time, even in a place the size of Silver Peak. But he was the kind of man you could believe might do just about anything."

"So what did he have to do with the bank?" Theo asked.

"He was the bank president," Sadie told him.

"And so is his son, James," Edwin added. "The other mayoral candidate."

"How did a guy like that get to be president of a bank?" Theo asked, incredulous.

Sadie grinned. "Well, this did used to be the Wild West," she said.

"But this wouldn't have been that long ago," Theo said.

"No," Sadie said. "He started the bank back in the early part of the century. Until then I think people mostly kept their cash in their boots, or buried in a tin can out back. Folks with serious money dealt with bankers in Denver. But during the boom after the First World War, Jules saw the opportunity in lending to our own community. And to do that, he had to take on deposits."

"Why would folks trust a guy like him with their money?" Theo asked.

"By all reports," Edwin said, "he was actually a good banker. Sure, he had his foibles. But he was likable too, so he was able to get some good investors. And he hired some good people. And it seemed to be a good business. He might have been a bit of a rake, but, in general, I think the town believed he was always on the up-and-up when it came to the bank."

"Until that business with the robbery," Sadie said.

Theo leaned in. "What robbery?"

Edwin sighed and sat back in his chair. "There was a robbery at the bank that was never solved," he said. "It was the late 1930s, just after the FDIC was formed, so all the deposits were insured. Officially, nobody lost anything. But this was the heart of the Depression, and there was a lot of red tape to work through. There was an investigation, and then the town had to wait for the federal government to cover the deposits. And this was a time, you have to remember, when people didn't typically have a lot of big reserves to dip into. The money came through eventually, but it was a hard winter for a lot of people. Just about everyone in town had to cut back somehow. My mom tells the story of making dolls for all her younger siblings that year, instead of buying anything from the store. But some folks had it a lot worse than that. Some farmers couldn't afford to place orders for seed in time, because they didn't have any ready cash. And by the time the money came through, there wasn't any seed to be had."

"Did people think Jules Morgan took the money?" Theo asked. "Why would he do that?"

"People weren't sure what to think," Edwin explained. "But like I said, Jules Morgan was the kind of man you might believe could do just about anything. And whether it was fair or not, some folks who were close to the investigation got the impression that it might have been an inside job. Rumor had it that Jules wasn't all that cooperative in the investigation. And then, like I said, although everyone got their money back in the end, there was a good long winter there where a lot of people were having a very tough time, and they had a lot of time to sit around and think about who might have been at the bottom of it. The investigators never did solve the robbery. So in the absence of the truth, it became another rumor that swirled around Jules Morgan."

"But this one was a lot more damaging than the others," Sadie said.

Edwin nodded in agreement. "Yep," he said. "A lot of people took their deposits back out of the bank, even when the federal insurance did come in. And it wasn't until James took over, decades later, that people really began to feel some goodwill for it, instead of just patronizing it because it was the only bank in town."

"So people must have trusted James, I guess," Theo reasoned. "Is he a lot like his dad?"

"He couldn't be more different," Sadie said. "James Morgan may just be the most reliable man I ever met. It's as if he built his life by looking at everything his father was, and doing the opposite."

"Except he's the bank president too," Theo pointed out.

"But he's a very different kind of bank president than his father was," Sadie said.

"How do you two know so much about this story?" Theo asked. "You wouldn't have even been born yet." He paused for a moment, to check himself on this, apparently uncertain due to the great age of his grandmother and her friend. "Were you?"

"In 1937?" Edwin said. He laughed and shook his head. "Nope. Not quite yet."

"You have to understand," Sadie said. "For the town, at that time, it was a hardship that many, many people went through together. There are a lot of elements of Silver Peak history that I know because I've taken the time to go back and find them out. But the robbery affected the town so much that these stories passed down through the families. Like the ones Edwin just told you. It's still a kind of living history, even now. I don't think there's anyone who was in town at the time that the robbery didn't touch, somehow."

"Wait," Theo said. "Did you say 1937?"

"That's when the bank was robbed," Edwin said. "I know because my father graduated from high school in 1938, and the family still wasn't sure if they'd be able to pay his tuition at college the following fall. He went ahead and applied and even matriculated, and the insurance money came through in August, just before he had to have the deposit in to Sentinel for classes."

"When in 1937?"

"Let's see...," Edwin said. "I think it must have been the fall. Because it was that winter that people really struggled. And I know it took almost a year for the investigation to be closed and the insurance to come through. It's much faster now, but in the early days of the FDIC, they were still working out the details, and apparently this was a complicated case, because of the possibility that it was an inside job. Evidently the authorities were hopeful for quite some time that the thief could be found and the money recovered."

Theo's eyes grew even wider as Edwin explained. Sadie wondered why he should have such a strong reaction to these arcane details of Silver Peak history. He was her partner in crime in antiquing, and delighted in the old stories just like she did, but he seemed genuinely agitated by something.

Then Theo opened up the ledger again, flipped past the front page that identified it as belonging to the Silver Peak Bank, and pointed to the date at the top of the first page: May 1937.

"Well, I'm fit to be tied," Edwin said.

Sadie suppressed a smile. It amused her to hear Edwin, who had gained such an air of dignity during the years he sat on the bench as a judge, slip back into the folksy expressions they had both grown up hearing. But she also felt the little thrill she always did at the prospect of unearthing some new history—or shedding new light on old history.

"It sounds like whoever wrote it must have had a ringside seat to the story of the bank robbery, and how it affected the town," she said. "It can't have been easy to work there in the days and months that followed. May I see it?"

Theo pushed the slim green volume across the table to his grandmother. Sadie glanced at the date on the front page again, then feathered through the rest of the pages. Whoever had written the entries in the ledger hadn't filled up the entire book. Several dozen pages at the end had been left completely blank, so she had to flip back in order to find the final page of writing. When she did, her brow furrowed. "This ends in October 1937," she said.

"That would be right around the time of the robbery," Edwin mused.

"It seems like it," Sadie said, her mind suddenly afire with curiosity. She looked at Edwin, then at Theo, searching vainly for a scrap of small talk to continue the conversation, but it was no use. She couldn't think of anything but how to find out the date of the robbery—and what light this mysterious ledger might shed on that important time in the town's history.

"Your mind's elsewhere, I can see," Edwin said. His lips were smiling, but Sadie thought she saw a trace of something else in his eyes as well. Could it have been disappointment?

When she glanced at Theo, she could see the same excitement and curiosity in his eyes that she knew Edwin must have read in hers.

"Someone in town must know," Theo insisted. "Where could we find that out?"

"I think it might be time for a visit to Kimama at the Silver Peak Library," Sadie told him, then looked apologetically at Edwin. "If you don't mind," she added.

Edwin smiled again. "I wouldn't expect anything less," he said. "All I ask is a full report on the results of your investigation."

"I'll probably tell you more than you even want to know," Sadie said.

"I doubt that," Edwin told her.

Sadie rose, placing the ledger into her purse, while Theo leapt to his feet beside her.

"And don't forget," Edwin said. "I'm still waiting for an answer to my other question."

"What's that?" Theo, always curious, asked.

But Sadie couldn't bring herself to even meet Edwin's parting glance, let alone explain the situation to Theo. Still feeling all the nervousness, and the unfamiliar hope, of a teenage girl, she ducked her head and headed out the door of Arbuckle's, as fast as she could.

3

SADIE SMILED AND GAVE A HAPPY SIGH AS SHE STEPPED FROM the heat of the Silver Peak morning into the air-conditioning of the Silver Peak Library. It was always a pleasure to walk into the spacious, high-ceilinged space, which had been renovated with a gift from a local benefactor. The library stood on the corner of Main Street and First Avenue, just half a block from Sadie's own Antique Mine, in one of Silver Peak's original buildings. But unlike the opera house, which Sadie had recently helped lovingly restore to its original glory, the multi-use building the library now occupied had never been anything particularly special, even in Silver Peak's distant past. So rather than restore the unremarkable storefront, and the offices and storage above it, the library committee had opted for a modern design: in fact, the most modern in town. The architect had taken out entire floors and cut swaths of new windows in the building's old walls, to create an airy, lofted palace of reading full of both books and a bank of computers equipped with powerful search tools and linked with extensive databases. Sadie loved historic design and details, but she also loved the fresh feel of the bold modern space. And she was a friend of Kimama, the Shoshone woman who served as head librarian, who looked up from the light-oak desk and smiled as Sadie walked in, Theo behind her.

"Well, this is a pleasant surprise," Kimama said. "What are you on the trail of today? Or are you just here to explore? I just got a very interesting catalog of Western scrip in. I thought you might find it interesting."

"I would love to see that," Sadie said. At various times in history, when law and order hadn't quite been established yet, people had used all kinds of strange items as currency, everything from privately made coupons to shells. It was where using the expression "clams" in places of "dollars" had originally begun. And of course, in the early days of the west, all kinds of barter and scrip systems had sprung up. Sadie was interested in them, as she was in so many antiques, not just because of the objects, but because of the stories behind them: the fact that beautifully printed coupons, even ones not backed by the government, or even scraps of handwritten promises, could sometimes be exchanged for nuggets of real gold.

But despite Kimama's excellent instincts as a librarian, Sadie couldn't be distracted from the question at hand. She let her bag slip off her shoulder, onto the library's front desk, and pulled out the ledger.

"Theo found this interesting ledger in Denver this morning," she said. "It seems to contain a diary of sorts, relating to the Silver Peak Bank, in the 1930s, right around the time of the robbery."

Kimama's eyebrows shot up. "Well, that would be interesting," she said.

"We're just trying to pin down the actual dates," Sadie said. "Do you have any thoughts about where we might find them?"

Kimama circled around the front desk. "I bet our *Silver Peak Sentinel* archives would be the place to begin," she said, heading for the bank of computers whose chrome and glass gleamed under the morning light that poured through the high windows. Sadie collected the *Sentinel* that she'd laid on the desk, and she and Theo followed.

When they reached the bank of computers, Kimama had already logged in to the scanned archives of the *Silver Peak Sentinel*, which had been publishing in Silver Peak for over a hundred years.

"Do you know the year of the robbery?" Kimama asked.

"Try 1937," Sadie said, and Kimama typed in the date. A slew of issue numbers, sorted by month and day, came up for that year.

Sadie thought back to the final date in the old green Sentinel. "Let's try October," she said.

Kimama's cursor drifted through the October dates, and clicked on one about halfway through the month. The front cover of the Silver Peak Sentinel spread over the computer screen. A giant headline read, ROBBER STILL ELUDES DENVER INVESTIGATORS.

"Good guess," Kimama said, impressed. She stood, and offered the seat she had been using to Sadie. "I'm sure you can take it from here. It looks like this was a big story, so you'll certainly find earlier stories of the original robbery—and probably further articles after this one."

"Perfect," Sadie said, taking the seat with a smile. Theo pulled up the chair from the computer beside her as Kimama drifted back to the front desk. "Let's see, what is this? October 21." She put her hand on the mouse and shook it briefly to bring up the cursor, then went to the back button. "Let's go back a few more days, and see if we can find the actual date of the robbery itself."

"Wait," Theo said. "Let's see what this says, first."

Obligingly, Sadie lifted the finger she was about to click with, and began to read.

"It looks like this is even a couple of weeks after the robbery," Theo observed after a minute.

"I think you're right about that," Sadie agreed. "And it also looks like the Denver investigators didn't come in for just any case. It seems the local police spent several weeks trying to solve it on their own, before they reached out for help."

"This doesn't say much about the robbery itself," Theo said. "Just the investigation."

"My guess is they covered those details in earlier articles," Sadie said.

She clicked over to the previous day's issue. This one announced the fact that the Denver investigators had arrived in town, complete with descriptions of their shiny black 1937 Plymouth, the sidearms each of them favored, and several blustery quotes from the lead investigator about the fact that he expected to have the case solved in a couple of days.

"A couple thousand days, maybe," Theo remarked.

"It's been even longer than that, now," Sadie said.

The articles that preceded the arrival of the investigators were a confusing pastiche of facts, speculation, and editorializing by Silver Peak's local journalists. Because Sadie and Theo were working through the articles backward, the ones they read first were full of both the most inconsequential facts and the wildest speculation. Just before the investigators arrived in town, for instance, the paper reported that, although no fingerprints had been found at the scene other than those of the known employees and officers of the bank, a local woman had identified the tracks of an animal through the crime scene photographs printed in an earlier issue of the paper as those of a raccoon. The editor of the *Silver Peak Sentinel*, perhaps frustrated with the lack of other answers on the story, or perhaps just from a quirky sense of humor, accompanied this article with a photograph of a raccoon, with the caption: *The Silver Peak Bandit?*

Other guesses, in earlier articles, were just as far-ranging. Some people didn't seem to want to believe that such a crime could happen in Silver Peak. One local businessman seemed determined to convince himself that it was all just a kids prank gone horribly awry, and suggested that the police should make an offer of clemency, as long as the missing funds were simply returned. Other citizens, old enough to remember the days when gangs of robbers plagued all travelers through the west, sometimes even stopping whole trains to relieve them of their valuables, hinted darkly that some of the criminal element that was becoming so famous in Chicago might have begun to drift even farther west, to cause trouble for the good people of Colorado again. But through it all, another theme recurred: no physical evidence at all had been found to point to the presence of anyone else in the bank other than its employees. The reporting wasn't accusatory enough to seem biased. But it certainly never let the reader forget the possibility.

Sadie could see how the rumor that Jules Morgan must have had something to do with it got started. It wasn't just rumor. For at least part of Silver Peak's history, it had been news. And the quotes that Jules gave couldn't have helped. He would already have been one of the richest men in town, and he didn't seem to think that the money was exactly real. He kept assuring people, over and over, that the FDIC insurance would come through, and it didn't matter if the money was found or not. And he hardly seemed interested in denying his own possible involvement with the vanished funds. "I wish I did know how to clean out a bank and get off scot-free," he'd said, addressing the rumors about a week after the robbery. "It'd be a darned sight easier than actually running a bank." When they passed the first article that included a photograph of Jules Morgan, Sadie almost gasped.

"What?" Theo asked.

"I'm just surprised by the picture," she said.

"Why?" Theo asked. "Didn't you know him?"

"When he was much older," Sadie said. "More like my age," she added jokingly.

"You're not old, Grandma," Theo protested.

"Yes, but in this picture Jules is so *young*," Sadie said. "He can't have been over thirty when all this happened. And he just looks so much like James. I remember James when he was that age. If you put him in these old-time clothes, you wouldn't be able to tell the two of them apart."

Finally, Sadie clicked back one last date. Beside her, Theo drew his breath in. "This must be it," he said. "Look at that."

The front page of this *Silver Peak Sentinel* was splashed with a giant picture of a stark image: a gaping hole in the plate-glass window of the Silver Peak Bank, with shards and grains of glass still glittering on the wooden sidewalk outside it. A policeman stood, arms crossed, with his back to the window, guarding the scene from a crowd of curiosity seekers that was so big it didn't fit in the frame—at the edges of the picture, Sadie and Theo could see shoulders, hats, and stray limbs that indicated the crowd was far bigger than that pictured. This headline was huge, and straightforward: SILVER PEAK BANK ROBBED.

"The date," Theo said. "What's the date?"

Sadie glanced up at the masthead in the corner, under an eagle with outspread wings, with a nugget of silver in one talon, and a branch of pine in the other. "October seventh," she said.

"And what does the—" Theo began, but Sadie was already flipping open the ledger, which she'd laid beside the computer when the two of them sat down. Quickly, she leafed through the empty pages at the back to the final entry. "October sixth," she read.

"That," Theo said, "is weird. It's got to have something to do with the robbery, right? Why else would a diary someone had been keeping in a bank ledger for months end the day before one?"

4

SADIE DIDN'T EVEN HAVE TO LOOK UP TO KNOW THAT THE NEW customer who had just swept into her shop was her best friend, Roz Putnam. Nobody else came charging into the place as if she owned it. Other customers would stop for a moment in the door, to get their bearings, or distracted by some delightful treasure Sadie had placed to capture their attention just inside the door. But Roz tended to waltz into Sadie's store just as if it were her own living room—which in a way, it sometimes was.

Today, Roz was dressed in one of her signature bohemian tunics, accented with a thick turquoise statement necklace that set off her deep brown eyes behind her stylish glasses, all framed by her shoulder-length gray hair, which she wore, as always, in a long bob. Without even glancing at Sadie's wares, she made a beeline to the antique mahogany desk behind which Sadie sat, on a chair that had, according to the dealer who sold it to Sadie, also served to support the venerable frame of Wyatt Earp.

"Sadie Speers," Roz said. "I hear you have a very interesting artifact here in your shop these days."

Sadie looked up from the ledger, which she was now poring over for the second time since Theo had left it with her earlier in the day.

"I do?" she said.

Roz nodded with conviction. "Something to do with our own Silver Peak history," she said, then leaned over the glass counter to deliver her next line in a dramatic *sotto voce*. "A clue that will finally solve that old bank robbery."

Sadie shook her head, but she was a little disturbed, nonetheless. She couldn't imagine Edwin reporting this news around town, and Kimama wasn't the type to spread idle gossip either—although Sadie knew well how quickly a rumor could take root in a small town—and how long those rumors could last. The suspicion that still clung to the Morgan family from the decades-old bank robbery was proof of that. "Where did you hear that?" she asked.

"Apparently Theo talked with some friends about his find," Roz said with a shrug. "I just came from lunch at the Depot. It's become a topic of conversation there. Especially since James Morgan is running in this mayoral election. Let's face it, there's not really a lot of juicy gossip on James, or on Edwin. So I think it's adding a bit of color to the race, despite the fact that it's almost a century old."

"I don't see why this should have anything to do with the race at all," Sadie said, now with a real frown.

"Well," Roz said, "you have to admit, it was a big deal in the history of this town. My grandmother almost got fired that winter, for sneaking potatoes into her pockets in the house where she was working as a maid. She said she'd never stolen anything before in her life, but she was so tired of seeing her younger siblings go hungry, because money was so tight, and the family she was working for had so many potatoes in the cold pantry that she couldn't imagine they'd miss them. The woman let her stay, but she docked her a week's pay. Which I imagine led to even harder times, at least for a while."

"If she had all that extra food when the town was suffering like that, she should have given your grandmother a whole bag when she realized her family was hungry," Sadie said.

"Well, some people did that, you know," Roz said. "All the stories from that time aren't bad. People might not have had a lot of money, but a lot of them did what they could to help each other. I know my grandfather had had a bumper crop of hay that year. So he gave out what he could, even if people didn't have money to pay. And then they'd come and work for him on the ranch, in exchange. It's how Grandma finally got her gazebo built."

"I guess there's always enough pine in Colorado to go around," Sadie said.

"I hear that," Roz said, with a wry tap at her hearing aid. She grinned and planted both of her elbows on the glass counter. "So," she said, "what have you got there?"

Sadie took a deep breath. "Well, I hardly think it's a single clue that's going to crack the old case wide open," she said. "If anything, it only seems to be more confusing."

"Can you tell who wrote it?" Roz asked.

Sadie shook her head. "Not yet," she said. "I believe it was a bank employee. A lot of what's noted down here seems to be details of events at the bank itself, almost as if it was started as some kind of a record of business days, rather than personal reflections. But then personal reflections begin to creep in."

"What kind of personal reflections?"

"I think it was written by a woman," Sadie said. "Handwriting was more uniform back then, because it was still taught as a skill in school, and an excellent hand was highly prized. But in my experience, even then, women tended to have a slightly more ornate style, which the writer of this ledger does. In the articles about the robbery that Theo and I looked at this morning at the library, there's only one woman mentioned among the handful of employees who worked at the bank at the time of the robbery: Janie Hale. Even from the handwriting, I'd guess it was her. But the reflections in this journal also seem to be a woman's concerns."

Roz opened her mouth, to repeat her question about the reflections, but Sadie held her finger up with a smile, to let her know she was getting to it. "And then there are the reflections," she said. "In the early days of the diary, she's just noting down bank business, the transactions she participates in, any big events at the bank itself, almost as if she's keeping notes in order to have a record for herself, maybe to keep track of her history with customers, or just to have a sense of what she's accomplished."

"Maybe I should try that," Roz said. "I get to the end of a day these days, and I know I'm tired, but I have no idea how I got that way. I'll come home, and Roscoe will ask me how my day was, and I can't remember half the things I did."

"I might worry about that," Sadie joked, "if I didn't know how many things you do in a day. I don't know how anybody could remember them all."

"Still, it's an interesting idea," Roz said. "To write it all down. The last time I kept a diary, I was just pouring all my teenage feelings out. I don't think it worked very well as any kind of sober record of my actual doings during that time. It was probably hopes and fears, more than anything that was really happening. And all those feelings. A whole lot of feelings."

"That places you squarely in the history of the evolution of the personal journal," Sadie told her.

Roz raised her eyebrows, as she always did when she realized she was in for a history lesson. "It does?" she asked.

Sadie nodded. "Yes. People have been keeping journals for thousands of years. But until recently, they always had some kind of purpose, often to record travels, or the history of a crucial time. Fervent religious believers also used journals to record their own spiritual progress. But it's actually a relatively modern phenomenon for people to use them for pure self-exploration."

"The inward-gazing teenager," Roz said.

"Right," Sadie said. "In fact, this diary is an interesting example of the emergence of that phenomenon. I've seen several others like it, usually from around the early part of the last century. What you see is people who are trying to use a journal to record their travels or business, but slowly begin to include personal details, until they start to take up the bulk of the narrative. I handled one set of journals where a traveling singer was simply noting the towns she had played on each date, and the quality of the local hotels and food. But here and there, you'd also get these lovely details, like that she'd missed a train that day, because she was picking violets. And I've also seen a diary of a southern lawyer who begins quite a bit like this, just noting the details of his daily appointments, probably so he can keep track of the progress of his cases. But then he starts to include things like the fur coat he bought his wife for Christmas, and the fact that she went all over town that afternoon, visiting friends to show it off. And later, he begins to vent his feelings about the little spats they've had, right there among the records of which clients have paid him recently, and which are past due."

"So even the respectable lawyers are still teenagers at heart?" Roz said.

Sadie laughed. "I guess so," she agreed.

"Well, but what about this Silver Peak Bank journal?" Roz asked. "What kind of details slip into it?"

Sadie flipped back through the journal to the early pages, and pointed to a column of words and numbers that ran down the side. "I think these are some of the first personal notes," she said. "The rest of the entry is all about bank business. But look at this."

Roz leaned in and squinted to read the cramped but precise lettering. "Eggs. Pharmacy. Rent."

"But this wouldn't have been an employee who was responsible for paying the bank's rent," Roz said.

"I'm guessing the bank was probably dealing with a mortgage, rather than rent," Sadie said. "That's if Jules Morgan didn't own the building outright from the outset. And the bank probably wasn't ordering eggs by the half dozen either." She shook her head. "No, I think this is a list of personal expenses. She's doing her own budget while she's at work. This was the 1930s, after all. How to make ends meet must have been on just about everybody's mind."

Sadie turned a few pages until she came to a new list of names and numbers. "See, here's another one."

"Interesting," Roz said. "Can you tell a lot about her from her weekly budgets?"

"Some," Sadie said. "But even more interesting, in the middle of the summer, she begins to use the journal, just like the old lawyer, as a place to record her personal details. At first it seems to be landmarks, like in the life of her children. See this?"

She pointed to a note scrawled at the very bottom of a day's entry, which otherwise contained nothing but bank business. "A's first tooth."

"You think that's one of her kids?" Roz asked.

"Well, I doubt it was her husband," Sadie said.

Roz grinned. Sadie smiled back, but from the contents of the diary, she knew that Janie's husband probably wasn't really much of a laughing matter. "In fact, she actually seemed to have had a somewhat troubled marriage," Sadie told Roz.

"Why do you say that?" Roz asked.

"She's not very specific about it, but there are several places where she notes that she had a 'bad night' or a 'long night' with B. That could be a reference to a child, but she also makes notes when this same B. finds work for the day. It seems whoever B. was didn't have steady employment like Janie did, so it was news when he found work. And he doesn't seem to find it very often."

"That's too bad," Roz said.

"It's always interesting to look at history through antiques," Sadie observed. "We may think we understand that people around the world went through something terrible during the Depression. But sometimes it's hard to understand what it must have meant for all those people. You really only get the feel of what it must have been like when you see the experience of just one family, like this one, worrying and waiting through day, after day, after day."

Sadie flipped the leaves of the journal as she spoke, rifling through the actual pages of those long-ago lives.

"So it doesn't sound like it really has much to do with the robbery," Roz said, sounding disappointed.

"Well, that's the strange thing," Sadie said. "If it holds any clear clues to the robbery, I haven't found them yet. But it breaks off the day before the robbery."

Roz's eyes widened. "The day *before* the robbery?"

"The timing does seem like more than a coincidence, doesn't it?"

Roz nodded vigorously.

"Of course," Sadie said, "the whole rhythm of the bank would have been disturbed by the robbery. You should see the pictures they posted in the *Silver Peak Sentinel*. The entire front window was broken out, and there seem to have been crowds there for days. The local police were all over the place. And then they had investigators come in from Denver when the Silver Peak police couldn't break the case. Janie may just have given up on keeping the diary in the midst of all the excitement."

"Like my high school diary," Roz observed archly. "I only kept it up when nothing was happening. As soon as anything really extraordinary happened in my life, I completely forgot about writing it down. I was too busy living."

"So perhaps that was what was happening here. Although the situation was probably a bit more intense for Janie after the robbery than it was for us in high school," she teased.

"I don't know about that," Roz said. "It may not actually rise to the level of a bank robbery, but for a high school girl, things can feel *very* intense."

Sadie grinned, giving her the point. "Still...," Sadie said.

"I knew it!" Roz said triumphantly. "You did find some kind of clue to the robbery, didn't you?"

"I'm not sure," Sadie hedged. "But the closer we get to the date of the robbery, the more this B. seems to be getting interested in

Janie's job at the bank. He's not actually asking her for the combination of the safe, but she's making notes like, 'B. walked me to work.' Or, 'B. came in to see the new furniture and safe.' Or, 'B. brought me lunch and stopped to talk with tellers.'"

"So do you think that he...?" Roz said. She trailed off before she finished the thought.

"I couldn't say anything for certain, based only on what we've got here," Sadie said, letting the green cover fall shut again. "But I can't help but be suspicious."

5

WITH A SMILE, SADIE STEPPED FROM THE TWILIT STREET INTO the circle of light provided by the strings of large bulbs that James Morgan's campaign had strung from tree to lamppost to tree, encircling the entire town square. Other western towns had hair-raising stories of public shoot-outs, or at least bandits being chased by lawmen out of town, but to her knowledge, the Silver Peak square had always been used pretty much as it was being used now: as a gathering place for the residents of the town, a place to come to sing carols in winter, eat barbecue in good weather—and sometimes attend to important business, like being part of the conversation over choosing the town's next mayor.

The two candidates in Silver Peak's mayoral elections sometimes had serious differences of opinion, but politics in the town had always kept a friendly tone—largely because, in a town that small, the candidates were likely to have strong con-nections—family members or friends who were also friendly with their opponent. It wasn't even unheard of for the candi-dates themselves to be friends, or at least friendly, as Edwin and James Morgan certainly were. And the elections did serve as a way for the citizens of the town to voice their opinion about any challenges the town faced, and their hopes for Silver Peak's future.

But along with all that, the mayoral elections were always a good excuse for a party. Silver Peak candidates didn't compete based on expensive TV ad buys, but there was a bit of an arms race where entertaining was concerned. And, of course, since neither candidate ever wanted to turn away a potential voter, pretty much the entire town was invited to any candidate party. And because Silver Peak was a small town, pretty much everyone tended to show up.

And from what Sadie could see, the barbecue James Morgan was throwing tonight was no exception. In fact, if anything, the unseasonably warm weather for the November night had brought out even more Silver Peak citizens than usual, bundled up in classic plaids and fleeces against the chill in the air, but still ready to do their best by the feast of barbecue James had spread. She smiled a hello to Josh Ralston, the handsome young woodworker whose Adirondack chairs were some of the most reliable sellers in her shop, and instantly recognized the two men he was in conversation with, Pastor Don Sweeting, and Harry Polmiller.

"Hi, Sadie," Josh said with a big grin, waving her over. Pastor Don also greeted her with a warm smile. He'd been a police captain and a rodeo star before moving to Silver Peak to start Campfire Chapel, and Sadie always thought he still had that sense of power and authority. But he had such warmth that she always felt glad for the undercurrent of command. If something went wrong, she always thought, he would know what to do. And that was a comfort.

Harry Polmiller, who at ninety-four was one of the oldest members of Pastor Don's congregation, just gave her an impish grin.

Sadie smiled back, but she knew from experience that Harry often wore that same grin, even when nothing in particular seemed to be happening. His mind was still sharp as a tack, so his perennial smile wasn't a sign of it wandering. Instead, it always made Sadie wonder about what kinds of memories or antics he was enjoying, although he kept it all to himself.

"Sadie Speers," Pastor Don said. "Maybe you can settle this debate for us."

Sadie held up her hands. "Oh no," she said. "I put my time in settling international incidents when I was the mother of a teenager. I've retired from that business."

"I wouldn't say it's an international incident," Pastor Don said, glancing at Josh with a smile. "Would you, Josh?"

Josh shook his head. "More like a local issue," he said.

"But to be fair," Pastor Don said, "it's the local issues that often lead to international incidents. And this young man has quite a bit of passion about this particular topic."

"What are we talking about here?" Sadie asked.

"Colorado pine," Josh breathed, with the same reverence and enthusiasm another man might have used to describe the world's fastest car, or the world's greatest ball player.

"Josh believes there's no better pine in the world," Pastor Don said, with faint amusement.

"There isn't," Josh insisted.

"I was just asking whether he'd actually sampled all the pine in the world to come to this conclusion," Pastor Don went on. "Like, for instance, the cedars of Lebanon. Which the Lord commanded Solomon to use in the building of the temple." A teasing light came into his eyes. "But maybe that was just because the shipping routes hadn't been established yet to source Colorado pine."

"I don't need to sample them all," Josh said, with a look almost as impish as Harry's. "I already know what's best. Why would I waste my time on anything else?"

At this, Spike Harris's bluegrass-and-country band, the Skylarks, took the stage with a burst of music, cutting off all further discussion.

"I think even God agrees with me on this," Josh shouted above the strains of the trio. "That's why He's giving me the last word."

"Or maybe He's just waiting for another time," Pastor Don parried back. "When you're actually ready to learn."

Sadie smiled her good-byes to all of them, and pushed off into the crowd. But the crowd was full of familiar faces. A moment later, she found herself face-to-face with Julie, who worked part-time for Sadie at the Antique Mine. Julie's long blonde hair was pulled up in a pretty ponytail, and her green eyes were sparkling. She stood between her ten-year-old twins, Brody and Logan.

"You look great," Sadie said, giving her a warm hug. "If I didn't know you were these boys' mom, I'd think you were their babysitter. I doubt you've aged a day since high school."

"It's these two," Julie said. "If I didn't have to keep up with them, it'd be nothing but television and bon bons for me."

"That actually sounds pretty good to me," Sadie said, with a grin. But she knew that what Julie had said was only partly true. It took a good bit of energy to keep up with ten-year-old boys. But Julie was also a hard worker at Sadie's store. And in Julie's spare time, she regularly ran local 5K races.

"There!" Brody said excitedly.

Both Sadie and Julie looked where he was pointing, expecting to see some kind of amazing spectacle because of the enthusiasm in his voice. But there was nothing there.

Logan raised his own hand and pointed out a different spot. "No, there," he said.

"Imaginary friend?" Sadie asked.

Julie shook her head. "We had one of those, but we lost him several years ago. At an amusement park. Apparently he just never wanted to get off the dodge-'em cars. And since he was invisible, he didn't have to. What are you two talking about?" she asked, ruffling Brody's hair.

"Where the line's going to start. We want to be first in line for the barbecue," Logan explained.

All along one side of the square, smoke billowed from giant silver metal barrels, along with the irresistible smell of roasting meat. A quick glance confirmed that Andi Taylor, the town's reigning barbecue queen, was at the helm of the proceedings, busily bustling between a small army of helpers in white chef's jackets and cowboy hats, giving a new instruction here, or a bit of encouragement there. Andi's presence on the scene just made Sadie's mouth water all the more. Andi was the unquestioned Silver Peak barbecue champion, and highly sought after for church events, weddings, and other catering. But her skills also stood up on a grander stage: she had given Denver's barbecue community a run for their money in the past few years, as well, placing high in the big-city barbecue competition.

As understanding dawned on Julie's face, Sadie felt an arm slide around her waist. Then a familiar strawberry-blonde head nuzzled her shoulder. "Hi, Grandma," Sara said.

"Hello, sweetie!" Sadie said, turning away from Julie and the boys with a quick nod good-bye. "It's so good to see you. Theo and I spent some good time together today, but I was starting to miss you."

Sara, who had just turned fourteen this year, gave Sadie a big enough smile that Sadie got a glimpse of her new braces. But Sara was also struggling to play it cool for any other kids—especially boys—who might be in the vicinity.

Not wanting to cause her any embarrassment, Sadie rumpled her hair and released her. "What do you think of the band?" she asked. "They're playing up a storm, aren't they? I'm always amused when I see Spike play with his trio. Since he can play guitar, fiddle, and upright bass, I always tell him he didn't really need to get a band together. He just needed to learn how to clone himself."

Sara smiled gamely, but it was clear to Sadie that she didn't have much interest in Spike's band—despite Spike's evident interest in Sara's mother, and Sadie's daughter, Alice. Maybe if he'd been a fourteen-year-old boy, Sadie thought wryly.

"I'm too hungry to listen," Sara said.

With a grandmother's instincts, Sadie looked around for anything to offer Sara. The party didn't offer any appetizers, just lemonade from a series of giant glass jars. But Sadie could see Andi instructing her staff to remove the aluminum foil and Saran Wrap from the side lined up at the long serving tables. And as she glanced over, the metal drums began to open, and servers began to pile trays high with luscious slabs of meat.

"Well, I think they must be about to serve," Sadie said. "Would you like to get in line?"

"Only if you come with me," Sara said.

Sadie suppressed a smile. This was how it was to be a teenage girl, she remembered with a pang—embarrassed one minute to be seen with your old grandmother, and the next minute too shy to get in line on your own. Sadie wouldn't normally have liked to take up a place in the front of the line, but under these circumstances, there was no stopping her. "Of course, sweetie," she said, resisting an urge to muss Sara's hair again.

They cued up to the old-timey twine that marked off the beginning of the line for supper just as Andi was pulling it aside to let the first "customers" in. Julie gave Sadie a rueful grin as her sons barreled on ahead of her. "I can win some battles," she said. "But against barbecue, I'm helpless."

"I'm helpless against this barbecue too," Sadie said, with a smile at Andi. "I always love to get a taste of your cooking," she said.

"Well, I hope you enjoy this," Andi said, handing her and Sarah each a sturdy paper plate ringed with a fresh blue line. "And don't forget to stock up on the sides. The pumpkin pie is something special. It's got my own homemade maple whipped cream on it."

"Can't wait," Sadie said, passing down the line to heap her plate with sides and receive her own helping of the lusciously prepared meat. It couldn't have looked more perfect: glistening, falling to pieces, and covered with gleaming red sauce. But when Sadie licked a taste from her finger as she and Sara exited the line, back into the crowd, Sadie frowned. The bit of sauce that had strayed onto her finger was incredibly salty. In fact, inedibly salty.

Probably just a little chunk of salt that didn't quite dissolve into the sauce, Sadie told herself, but she was still surprised. She'd never known Andi's sauces to be anything less than perfect. And when she cautiously took her first bite of the meat itself, her whole face screwed up. It was saltier than some anchovies she'd tasted. The taste of salt was so strong that she couldn't even taste any of the other flavors in the sauce.

"Grandma?" said Sara, who was happily munching on one of Andi's featherlight dinner rolls. "What's wrong?"

Sadie choked the piece of meat down out of sheer politeness, then shook her head to get the water out of her eyes.

This was more than just a chunk of undissolved salt. There seemed to be something terribly wrong with the sauce, but she couldn't quite bring herself to believe that things could have gone so wrong on Andi's watch.

Gingerly, she reached a finger out to dab at the sauce on the beautiful chunk of barbecue that lay on Sara's plate. Sara reached to imitate her, but Sadie flagged her away.

"Just let me try this, first, honey," she said. "I—" Before she could finish her sentence, her face wrinkled in disgust again. The piece of meat on Sara's plate was just as briny as the one on Sadie's had been.

Sadie glanced around at the members of the crowd who had begun to cluster around them, stopping as they had to sample Andi's barbecue, because they had been unable to resist a bite before returning to the places they had left to get in line. All around her, she saw the same expressions of surprise—and then dismay.

"There's something not quite right with that meat," Sadie told Sara. "I wouldn't try it if I were you. Excuse me, honey. I'm going to go over and talk to Andi."

With the sound of confusion and consternation growing behind her, Sadie pushed back through the crowd to where Andi was standing, partway down the line, supervising the heating of broad trays of dinner rolls.

"Andi," Sadie said.

Andi turned back with a look that said she was clearly trying to be polite, but she couldn't understand why Sadie would demand her attention twice in one night when Andi was clearly in the mist of such a big production. "Can I talk with you later, Sadie?" Andi said, keeping her voice light with an effort. "We're just—"

"I'm afraid this can't wait," Sadie said, and held out a forkful of the barbecue.

"I'm not sure I—" Andi began.

"Just try it, please," Sadie said.

Apparently resigned to the fact that the quickest way to get rid of Sadie was to give in, Andi took the fork from Sadie, and sampled the taste of barbecue. An instant later, her eyes widened in horror. She took another bite, gave a heroic swallow, then turned, like a woman in a dream, to the large platters of meat that lay beautifully displayed on the serving tables, where the line of hungry Silver Peak citizens passed by, heaping their plates. She tweaked a taste of meat from one of the platters, then the next. Then she began to issue orders. "Remove the meat," she told the nearby servers.

"What?" a teenager with a pretty red ponytail asked, surprised.

"Remove the meat," Andi ordered again. "All of it."

As Sadie watched, Andi turned toward the large drums of roasting meat, half-obscured by the clouds of steam and smoke. She squared her shoulders as if marching to battle, then opened one, pulled a sample of succulent meat from the bone, and tasted it. This time, her shoulders slumped. She turned back to Sadie.

"That's the last of our meat," she said. "There's none that isn't ruined."

"What happened?" Sadie asked.

Andi shook her head, still obviously in shock. But then she turned back, and reached for a large pot, sticky with translucent red sauce. She tasted a fingerful and turned back. "The sauce," Andi said. "There's something wrong with the sauce. And we already put it on all the meat...," she said, looking over the ruined piles of barbecue with a growing sense of despair.

"I can't believe I didn't taste it," she said, almost to herself. "I should have tasted it. But it's a bulletproof recipe. I've done it so many times before."

"Did you make the sauce here?" Sadie asked.

Andi nodded as if this should be obvious. "It was the first thing I did, so the flavors would have some time to blend, before we began to set everything else up," she said.

"Where did you prep?" Sadie asked.

"Over here," Andi said, leading Sadie to a stand of prep tables she had set up with her usual cleverness in a small stand of landscaped pines, out of sight of most of the rest of the activity. As Andi stood before the industrial-sized cans of ketchup, the ten-pound bags of sugar, and the extra-tall shakers of salt, she began to muse. "Maybe they've changed the intensity of the chef's salt," she said, and reached for a shaker. She poured a few white grains into her hand, dabbed at it with her finger, then put her finger to her tongue. Her eyes widened again. A moment later, she reached for one of the large bags of sugar, which she sampled with another finger.

When she looked back at Sadie, understanding had dawned in her eyes, along with the beginning of outrage. "They're switched," she said. "Someone replaced the salt with sugar."

6

SADIE LOOKED FROM THE CANISTER OF SALT TO THE GIANT BAG of sugar. The canister was large, at least twice the size that anyone would use in the course of standard home cooking. But it would still have taken an inordinate number of those canisters to fill up the sugar bag. "That must have been a lot of work," Sadie said. "Can you think of why anyone would want to do that?"

"I can't think of anything right now but what we're going to serve all these people for dinner now," Andi, snapping back into action. "And what I'm going to tell James about how I let this happen."

As she turned around to scan the crowd for James, both she and Sadie caught sight of him, walking up from the line for food, which had now stalled in the absence of the main attraction, the barbecue. He was a tall man with a handsome face under a shock of white hair, dressed in a blue polo shirt and neat but casual jeans. As he came up, Sadie flashed back to the picture of his father in the *Silver Peak Sentinel*. The resemblance was still unmistakable.

"I hope he's not furious," Andi said under her breath.

But when James reached them, he greeted her with a friendly smile. "Andi," he said. "I just noticed there seemed to be some kind of slowdown with the dinner line, so I thought I'd come over here to see what's going on."

"James," Andi said, her face stricken. "I don't know how to tell you this, except to just say it: all the barbecue is ruined. We can't serve it."

James looked back at the heaping plates of seemingly gorgeous hunks of meat that Andi's helpers were now removing from the serving tables, back into the prep area.

"Well, it all looks just fine to me," he protested.

"It's the sauce," Andi explained. "It's much too salty. I'm afraid it's inedible."

James gave her a reassuring smile. "I know your standards are high, Andi," he said. "But a little extra salt never hurt anybody. It doesn't need to be perfect. We just need to feed all these people."

"I think you'd better try it for yourself," Andi said. She picked up a serving fork from one of the rejected plates of meat that a server had just set down nearby, chose a strip of meat glistening with sauce, and offered it to James. He accepted it with a smile, but when he got a taste, his smile vanished.

"My goodness," he said.

Sadie suppressed a smile. Even under this kind of pressure, James still managed to keep up the appearance of a perfect gentleman.

"How in the world did this happen?"

"I'm afraid someone switched the salt and the sugar," Andi said. "But it's still my responsibility. I should have tasted it, but I was so confident in the recipe that I just—didn't."

James laid a comforting hand on her arm. "There's no need to worry right now about whose fault it is," he said. "But we do need to worry about how to feed this crowd.

"Andi," he went on, "I know it won't match your own catering, but would you call the Depot and ask them to deliver an order of spaghetti western large enough to serve this crowd, as soon as possible? I don't imagine they'll be too busy tonight, since I suspect all their regular clientele have joined us for the evening."

"But—" Andi began.

"Please," James said firmly. "Call now. The longer we wait, the longer all these people have before they get anything to eat. And I'm going to go find a microphone to make an announcement."

Andi pulled her phone from her pocket, scrolled through her contacts, then dialed as James pushed away, into the crowd.

A moment later, Sadie and Andi could hear the squeal and thunk of a PA system powering up as Spike's band brought their most recent song to a hurried close.

"Good evening," James's voice boomed over the crowd. "And welcome to our campaign barbecue. This was a little bit earlier than I intended to make any comments. I wanted to make sure you were well-fed and happy before I got up here with the microphone."

A little ripple of laughter washed through the crowd.

"I'm sorry to tell you, it's going to be a bit longer than we thought before we're able to continue serving the dinner this evening. And in place of Andi's famous barbecue, we're going to be enjoying another hometown favorite—spaghetti western, courtesy of the Depot—all you can eat!"

A few cheers rose up from the crowd at this. Nearby, Sadie could see the people who had already gone through the line and received the briny barbecue begin to deposit their still-full plates in the nearby trash containers with expressions of relief.

"Again, folks, we're sorry for the delay, and I wanted to personally apologize to you myself," James said. "I regret the trouble, but I hope you'll see it as an example of how I'd like to lead Silver Peak through any challenges we might face. There's no need for us to get stuck when something doesn't go just the way we'd like. There's always another way. And tonight, that's spaghetti western."

The microphone whined and thunked again as James settled it back into the stand that had been prepared for his after-dinner remarks. Throughout the crowd, applause broke out.

Sadie caught a glimpse of Edwin in the middle of a large group near the gazebo. He was scanning the crowd intently, probably gauging the reaction of Silver Peak's voters to this most recent campaign development, she told herself. But then Edwin caught sight of her. His face broke out into a smile, and instead of scanning past her, over the rest of the crowd, he started over toward where she stood. Had he been looking for her? Sadie thought. But she could hardly believe that. Surely he had more important things to worry about just now.

But before Edwin could reach her, she felt a hand on her elbow. She turned, expecting to see Andi again, but was surprised to see James.

She gave him an encouraging smile. "You handled that very well," she said. "I think the Depot's spaghetti western is about the only thing that could compete with Andi's barbecue in the hearts of Silver Peak."

"I just want to make sure we fill their bellies," James joked.

"It'll be good for us to learn a little patience," Sadie said.

She had expected James to drift back into the crowd, where as the candidate he would be expected to try to greet as many guests as possible, but instead, his face turned serious. "Sadie," he said. "I'd like to talk with you about something."

"Of course," she said.

"I don't know if now is the time or place," James said. "But I hear you're in possession of a diary that may shed some light on the"—he hesitated before finding the words—"events," he finally continued, "at the Silver Peak Bank."

Sadie had been surprised that James would take the time to talk to her in the midst of a campaign event. She was even more surprised that he had already heard about the existence of the journal, but that was small-town life, she guessed. And James was a well-liked man, so if a rumor was circulating that concerned him, it was likely that he'd have friends who cared enough to pass the stories along to him, so that he wouldn't be in the dark about them.

But she was even more struck by the evident emotion in James's face as he waited for her reply. Even as his entire campaign event had seemed to be coming to pieces, in the days immediately leading up to the election, he'd kept his familiar calm and friendly demeanor. Now, however, he seemed to be struggling to master some kind of powerful feelings.

"Well, of course," Sadie said, trying to cover her surprise. "I'd be glad to talk about it with you anytime. In fact, you're welcome to look at it yourself. But I don't want to get your hopes up. I've looked through it a few times myself, and at least at first glance, it doesn't seem to give any clear clues to what might have happened at the bank, one way or another. But maybe, for someone who was more familiar with it…"

"I appreciate that," James said. "But I wasn't even born yet at the time." Despite his distinguished carriage and his shock of white hair, he looked strangely like an unhappy child as he said this, as if he knew he was being blamed for something he hadn't done.

"Of course," Sadie said, feeling a wash of pity that something that had happened so long ago should still affect James like this, long after the robbery itself, and decades after the death of his father. "As I said, you're more than welcome to see it. You really have much more claim to it as the bank president than I do. I just don't want to give you the impression that it will shed any real light on the situation, because my impression, at least so far, is that it doesn't shed much."

"James!" a campaign worker sporting a large "James Morgan for Mayor" button said, striding up. "There you are. I've got some people I'd like for you to talk with."

"Excuse me," James said, with an apologetic grimace.

"No, no," Sadie said. "Of course, please go. I understand."

She glanced around. Edwin appeared to have gotten caught in conversation several yards away, but he caught her movement as James departed, and she could see him begin to make his excuses to the man he'd been talking with. She lifted her hand to her short, wavy salt-and-pepper hair, then let it fall. What was she doing, she asked herself, worrying about how her hair looked like a nervous teenager? She was just as bad as Sara. Even worse—because Sara had an excuse. She actually was a teenager.

But before Edwin successfully disentangled himself from his conversation, Sadie felt another touch on her arm. "Sadie."

Sadie gave a smile of slight surprise to James Morgan's wife, Helen. Sadie glanced quickly at Edwin, who gave a rueful shrug when he saw that she was engaged again. Then Sadie looked back at Helen. In many ways, Helen had always seemed like a perfect match for James. Both of them were calm, gracious, and friendly. And Helen was just as stylish and unfailingly appropriate as James was in her dress, with her white hair swept back from her face in a pair of striking wings, and a neatly-pressed plaid western shirt with emerald-green snap buttons over a pair of crisp blue jeans. Sadie wasn't close with Helen, but almost anyone in town would have been glad to see her.

"Thank you for having us all to this lovely party," Sadie told her. "I don't know how you do it."

"I have to give most of the credit to James's campaign workers," Helen said. "They really do the bulk of it. I'm just glad we didn't try to have this barbecue at our place. That was the original idea. They wanted to give it a real 'homey' feel. But I didn't see how we could possibly serve so many people, even though we do have that big old yard. And really, James's family has been in town for so long, and he's spent so much of his life downtown at the bank, that I tend to think of this square as a kind of home too. Not that we own the town, or anything like that, of course."

Sadie could see Helen beginning to stammer, worried that she had perhaps seemed too entitled, as the wife of the town banker. But nobody but Helen would have worried about that. It was one of the things people liked about both Helen, and James—their deep thoughtfulness about how other people might be thinking and feeling.

"Not at all," Sadie said, trying to put her at ease. "I know what you're saying. When you have deep roots in a place, more than just your own house can feel like home."

"That's right," Helen said, with a grateful smile.

Sadie smiled back at her, but kept quiet. It was clear that Helen had something on her mind other than small talk about the party arrangements. After a moment, Helen's smile faded. She looked down at the tough grass of the Silver Peak square. Then she looked up again, meeting Sadie's eyes.

"I'd like to talk with you about something," she said.

"Anything," Sadie said, although she had more than a sneaking suspicion as to what Helen might be interested in.

"Well," Helen said, dropping her voice. "I can't help having heard about this—document you seem to have found. People seem to think it has something to do with all that nonsense at the bank."

Sadie listened patiently, but she couldn't help but think that, despite the deep roots Helen had formed in town since her marriage to James, the fact that Helen referred to the robbery as "nonsense" made it clear that Helen was originally from out of town. James had met her when they were both in college, and she'd taken to Silver Peak as her own. But nobody whose family had been part of Silver Peak for years would ever have referred to the robbery as nonsense. It had created too much trouble, and too many hard memories, for anyone who had lived through that long-ago winter, or knew anyone who had.

Of course, Helen didn't mean to dismiss all that trouble, Sadie thought. Likely, it was just invisible to her, because it wasn't part of her own history. And Helen's devotion to James was unquestionable, which was probably why she wanted to see the robbery that had haunted his family for so many years as nothing more than nonsense.

"It's a journal," Sadie told her. "Not a diary like something you and I might have kept, but more a record of business dealings, with a few personal observations thrown in. And I'm afraid that its importance as a clue to the robbery may have been exaggerated in the retelling. From what I'm able to see, it doesn't contain anything like a smoking gun. If there are clues to the robbery in it, they're buried much deeper. Although it does correspond almost exactly to the time of the robbery itself."

Helen gave her head a determined shake. "It doesn't matter to me what it says," she said. "As far as I'm concerned, all that is ancient history. James's father was never convicted, and the town needs to accept the fact that there was never enough evidence to tie him to any crime, even after years of investigation. If the police then couldn't find anything, what could some old journal tell us? And even if it could tell us anything, even the government wouldn't prosecute it this late. It's been decades. And in any case, James should never be blamed for anything his father did, even if his father did have something to do with the robbery. I'm just so tired of watching him struggle under this burden. It isn't even his, but he's been carrying it all his life. Silver Peak needs to learn to leave the past in the past."

As a lover of antiques, Sadie couldn't have disagreed more, but at the same time, she understood Helen's fierce loyalty to her husband, and she was touched by it. "I can see how you'd feel that way," she said. "And I don't think anybody is really trying to solve the mystery after all these years. It's more just an interesting topic of conversation."

"Not to James," Helen said. "You have no idea how it hurts him."

Sadie thought back to the haunted look in James's usually friendly eyes when he brought up the diary with her. "I'm sorry," she said. "But I'm not sure what I can do."

"You could sell me the journal," Helen said.

Sadie looked at her in surprise, but before she could say anything, Helen pressed on. "It really should belong to our family," she said. "Of anyone in Silver Peak, it concerns us the most. Obviously, we're in a position to ensure its safety. And of course, money is no object. I have no idea what a piece like that would normally be worth on the market, but because of its value for our family, and because I'd want to make sure that you were paid fairly, I have no interest in bargaining. Should we say, five thousand dollars?"

Sadie's surprise turned to outright shock. Helen's guess at the price for a diary was enormously high. Even far older diaries sometimes sold for less than a hundred dollars, when they had details in them that were far more interesting than those contained in the mundane account of the bank ledger. Of course, the possible connection between the robbery and the ledger might give it slightly more value—but nothing on the order of five thousand dollars. Helen's offer had nothing to do with the price of antiques, but it did show how motivated she was to get it out of public circulation.

"Well," Sadie said. "That is a very generous offer. Of course, I'd want to talk with an outside appraiser about a sale that big, to make sure that you would be getting the value that you paid for."

Helen shook her head again. "Its value on the open market is of no concern to me," she said. "This is an antique that could never have the same value for any other family. And if that isn't enough, I'd be open to making another offer."

It had actually crossed Sadie's mind that it might be nice to simply give the journal to the Morgan family, and she had even thought of mentioning it to Theo, to see how he would feel about it. Yet a sale of the size Helen was talking about would leave her shop on solid footing for months. But even though she'd already thought about simply giving the old journal away, something about Helen's insistence on owning it made Sadie uncomfortable. She could understand why Helen might want it, and even why she might want to bury the story as completely as possible. But Helen's eagerness to possess the journal seemed to Sadie as if it was based on a fear of the truth. Helen didn't seem to care what was in it— just that nobody else would ever find out. And that didn't sit well with Sadie. As Helen had said, nobody should blame James for any of his father's actions, however deeply that had affected the town. And even if something in the journal did point to Jules Morgan as the culprit in the robbery, that might finally give James some closure on the old story, even if that truth stung a bit at first. Sadie had always loved the verse from the gospel of John with the promise, "you shall know the truth, and the truth will set you free." And she believed strongly that real freedom did lie in the search for the truth, and facing it dead-on, not in trying to hide it from the light, no matter what it was.

"Actually," Sadie said, "it's not even mine to sell. Theo is the one who found it, and paid for it. So I'd have to ask him how he'd feel about all of this before we could talk any further." She knew very well how excited Theo would be to hear about an offer of this size for what he thought of as only a somewhat interesting trinket. He'd be overjoyed. And he'd be flabbergasted to think it might be worth even more than that to the Morgan family. But she didn't need to tell Helen that, at least not right this minute.

Helen seemed to take this as a reasonable explanation. "Please do," she said. "I'm very serious about this, as you can see."

Sadie nodded.

Helen reached out and squeezed Sadie's arm. "You understand," she said. "It's not that it's so important to own it as an object. It's about what it might mean to James. Especially with this race."

"I understand," Sadie said.

"Thank you so much," Helen said. "I knew you would."

As they were talking, a small parade of workers dressed in the familiar Depot's server's uniforms began to arrive, bearing giant aluminum pans that Sadie guessed were full of the spaghetti western James had ordered.

Helen stepped back and Sadie shuffled forward to let them pass to the table, where they began to replace the ruined barbecue. Helen glanced unhappily at them as they began to remove the aluminum covers and steam billowed out of them, along with the savory smell of the new meals.

"I really should get back to the party," she said. "But please, have some dinner." She looked down at the plate of barbecue, still in Sadie's hands.

"I appreciate it," Sadie said, and Helen started off into the crowd.

Sadie took a deep breath as she watched Helen go, both impressed by Helen's loyalty to her husband, and Helen's imagination. Sure, there had apparently been some town gossip about the ledger, and it had traveled faster than Sadie might have guessed. But it really took a sensitive and highly loyal wife, Sadie thought, to believe that an almost century-old document could have any effect on a present-day mayoral race. How could Helen think that the people of Silver Peak could let such ancient history sway their behavior on voting day?

7

SADIE STEPPED OUT OF THE WAY OF THE CROWD THAT HAD BEGUN to gather, in search of the newly delivered spaghetti western, and looked down at her own plate. Suddenly, she was starving. She knew the barbecue was inedible, but after a quick sample, she could see why people had been snacking on Andi's sides as they waited for the spaghetti western to arrive. Andi's potato salad was the pure perfection it usually was: with a strong but not overwhelming kick of mustard, and sour pickles that Andi made herself, just for the potato salad.

From where she stood, she couldn't help overhearing the conversation as people shuffled along in line, inching ever closer to the banquet tables. Most of the conversation was just what you'd expect to hear: parents asking kids about their day at school, or what homework they had left to do; kids begging for a new pair of jeans, or permission to see a friend later that week; and plenty of observations about the always-interesting Colorado weather this fall. But to her surprise, she also heard several people mention the ledger. Some of them called it a diary. Some of them referred to it as a journal. Some of them didn't seem to have any idea what the actual antique in question was. But all of them were sure that it contained important new clues in the case of the old robbery. And their feelings about the old robbery were still surprisingly fresh.

Sadie heard one young girl ask her mother, with some youthful impatience, why an old book like that would matter, anyway. And right there in line, the mother took the time to relate how the robbery had affected their family: apparently the young girl's great-grandmother had had to put her plans to go to high school in Denver on hold for a semester, because the family didn't have the funds to pay. When she'd finally gone, the following semester, she'd always felt a little out of place, because she didn't start school with all the other girls. But this story of an interrupted education had a happy ending of sorts: apparently, it was because the matriarch of the family had taken extra classes, to make up for the missed time and graduate with her class, that she met the boy who would later become her husband, and the girl's great-grandfather, who had come over from a local boys' school to help tutor the girls.

Sadie didn't hear any other stories that detailed, but she did hear quite a few scraps of conversation about that hard winter. But even more to her surprise, over and over again, people made the connection between the robbery and the current election. Even as they were lining up to taste the dinner James Morgan had provided for them, she could hear whispers about the Morgan family. Some of them were obviously from gossips who enjoyed bringing up old dirt. Others seemed more sincere—friends just sharing thoughts with each other, mentioning that they'd never been sure if they could really trust the Morgan family. Sadie even heard one old rancher say that it had always been a hard choice between James and Edwin, in his mind, because both of them were good men, but that with this old business about the robbery back in circulation, he was starting to lean toward Edwin, who at least didn't have a history of outright theft in his background. The old rancher chuckled when he said it, meaning it as a joke about the thievery of politicians in general. But Sadie thought he might be telling more of the truth than he knew. People's reasons for voting the way they did were always mysterious. And who knew how much what the old man was joking about now would affect his choice in the privacy of the voting booth?

By the time Sadie had finished her potato salad, and one of Andi's dinner rolls, she was less certain than she had been that Helen Morgan was simply being overprotective of her husband's reputation. It appeared that, even though Helen Morgan had originally come from out of town, she knew a thing or two about how public opinion in Silver Peak worked, after all. But whatever Jules Morgan had or hadn't done, and however much it had affected the town, the people of Silver Peak should know better by now than to blame James for any transgressions his father might have committed. Feeling almost as indignant as Helen had seemed, Sadie shook her head and deposited the remains of the ruined barbecue in a nearby trash bin.

When she turned around, Edwin was standing in front of her, grinning.

"Sadie Speers," he said. "Fancy meeting you here."

"Hello," Sadie said, doing her best to keep the conversation light and casual. She couldn't help thinking about the question Edwin had asked her earlier, about whether she might feel ready to "go steady" with him again. But she just wasn't ready to answer it yet. She knew Edwin better than to know she could put him off forever, even though he'd been patient so far. But that didn't mean she wasn't going to try the best she could to avoid the question until it came up. "How are you enjoying the barbecue?"

"I'm not sure anyone is really enjoying the barbecue," Edwin said wryly. "But I'm very much enjoying the party. The company, in particular."

"Did you get anything to eat yet?" Sadie asked, nodding at the line that still snaked by near where they now stood.

Edwin shook his head. "I have some other things on my mind."

"It is your rival's first big campaign party," Sadie said, quickly steering the conversation out of what she considered might become an uncomfortable topic for her.

Edwin raised his eyebrows and nodded. "Yes," he said. "In fact, Jesse was pretty delighted by the trouble they seem to be having. Of course, I wouldn't wish this on anyone. And in the next few weeks, it could be me, and not him, for all I know. But Jesse was almost gleeful. He was sure that this would have some bump for me in the polls. I had to explain to him that I don't want any bumps in the polls based on the misfortunes of a friend. Also, that there aren't any polls that I know of in Silver Peak, other than the one that really counts, the election at the end. Not to mention that Silver Peak residents become very forgiving when presented with a plate or two of free spaghetti western."

"It sounds like perhaps he was just a little overzealous," Sadie said.

"I hope so," Edwin said. "Still, I wish they hadn't had this problem. Someone was joking with me on the way over that I must have sabotaged the barbecue myself. Of course, it was a joke. But I don't want even a hint of that kind of thing to creep into the campaign. It was just bad luck, is all, I told him."

"Well, actually...," Sadie said.

"What?" Edwin asked, surprised. "You're not telling me someone ruined all that beautiful barbecue on purpose?"

Sadie raised her eyebrows. "I was with Andi when she discovered the sauce was wrong," she said. "And it doesn't seem like
a harmless mistake. Someone switched the sugar and the salt
intentionally."

Edwin's face darkened. "Who on earth would...?" he began.
Then worry appeared on his features. "I hope they don't think I
had anything to do with it."

"I haven't heard anybody even suggest anything like that,"
Sadie assured him.

"But who else would do such a thing?" Edwin asked again.

"I was going to ask you that same question," Sadie asked. "If you
could think of anyone who might have anything against James."

Edwin took a deep breath and spread his hands wide. "It's hard
to say," he said. "When you're a bank president, there are plenty
of reasons people could get angry with you, even if those reasons
aren't good. I happen to know Ginny Friedman isn't a huge fan of
James's, for instance."

Ginny Friedman was the town clerk. Most people knew her
by acquaintance, but Sadie hadn't realized that Edwin was close
enough with her to know that kind of personal information.

"I didn't realize the two of you were such good friends," she
said, with a little pang. *Was she jealous?* she wondered. How could
she be jealous, if she wasn't even sure she was ready to be Edwin's
lady friend?

Edwin shook his head. "I heard the story from her husband.
We've been golf partners a few times. Apparently the bank turned

them down for a loan several years ago. For her husband, it came as something of a relief. According to him, the bank was right, and they couldn't really afford the loan they were asking for. But Ginny had her heart set on the new addition to the house they were hoping to build. And she felt like it was the bank who crushed her dreams, even though all the bank really did was explain the reality of their financial situation to them. And I believe James handled that case himself, which I guess he does from time to time, to keep his hand in the day-to-day business at the bank. So she's held a grudge against James since then."

"And as town clerk, she would have known about this barbecue far in advance," Sadie reasoned.

"Yes, as soon as James's campaign pulled the permit," Edwin agreed. "But I'm not saying I think Ginny had anything to do with it. I'm just saying that the town is probably full of stories like that. You know banking seems like it's all business, but actually, it can be very personal. In a town like this, where everyone knows one another, those kinds of situations can lead to longtime grudges. And when you've got a history like the Morgan family, some of those grudges can go back for years. In fact, it could be a grudge that isn't based on James at all, but on something Jules did, years and years ago."

Sadie frowned, thinking of all the stories she'd just heard, people sharing the way the bank robbery had affected their families' lives—and even taking the time to introduce those stories into the next generation.

"I've been meaning to ask you about that diary you found," Edwin said. "I wouldn't have believed it, but it seems the news of it has really gotten around town."

"I wouldn't have believed it either," Sadie said. "But I think you're right." She sighed. "I wish I had something to tell you about that diary, but I'm afraid there's not much conclusive about it, at least not so far. Theo and I went over the library to check the dates of the robbery, and it does break off the day before the bank was broken into."

"But there could be lots of reasons for that," Edwin said. "For anyone who worked at the bank, the robbery would have been a huge disruption in their lives."

Sadie smiled, thinking how similarly Edwin's mind some-times worked to her own. He was working on understanding the old story, just the way she was. But she didn't tell him that, for the moment. "That's right," she said. "And aside from that fact, it appears to be a quite pedestrian record of bank business, along with some personal notes. We're relatively certain it was written by Janie Hale, the bank's only female employee at the time. But as far as I can tell, it doesn't shed much light at all on the robbery."

"Well, people around here sure think it does," Edwin said. "And I don't like the way that may affect the campaign. I think I'd be a good mayor for the town, or I wouldn't be running. But I want to win in a fair election. And it's not fair to use the emotion the town still has over the events of the robbery against James. Especially not when James wasn't even born yet at the time of that robbery."

Sadie felt a tug at her heart. Edwin could be thoughtful and charming. But the times she felt the most strongly about him were times like this, when it became clear what a good man he was.

"I hate to ask you this," Edwin went on, "but I know you enjoy looking into the history of the antiques that come through your shop. And I wonder if you'd do me a favor, and look into the history of this one. I don't care what that history is, good, bad, or indifferent. I only want to get to the truth, so that we can lay all these rumors to rest, and get on with our campaign based on the real issues Silver Peak is facing, here and now, in the present."

Sadie nodded, looking into his eyes. "I can't make any promises," she said. "But I'll do the best I can."

"That's all I ask," Edwin said.

Sadie smiled. But as Edwin continued to hold her gaze, she began to feel a little flutter of nervousness. "Well, I guess I better—" she began.

"Actually, that's not all I ask," Edwin said.

"Edwin, I—" Sadie began.

Edwin held his hands up. "I'm not asking for an answer to that question I asked you earlier," he said. "Not yet."

Sadie gave a little sigh of relief.

"I just want to know," Edwin said, "if you remember where we're standing."

Sadie looked around. As they'd talked, they'd drifted together away from the crowd that had lined up for the dinner, into the little stand of pines in the corner of the square. The pines had been much shorter when Sadie and Edwin were teenagers, but they'd already become a popular place for teenagers to meet. For all Sadie knew, it might still be a haven for lovelorn kids even now. And she remembered its significance for her and Edwin well: it was the spot where they'd had their first kiss. And not just their first kiss together, but her first kiss, ever. It had been a beautiful Colorado day, about six weeks after they first began to spend time together. They had hiked through some trails outside town together, and then, as night fell and they came back to town, Edwin had suggested they stop for a moment in the park. The cloudless skies that had let the sun shine down on them by day was then full of crystal-clear constellations, and Edwin had pointed several of them out to her: the bear, the hunter, Cassiopeia's crown. Then, as she was staring up at the stars, he kissed her. And from then until the day he went off to college, she'd been his girl.

Surprised by the emotion that welled up in her at those old memories, she nodded. It was all she could trust herself to do in that moment.

But that seemed to be enough for Edwin. A smile lit up his face. "I do too," he told her. "I've had a lot of good times in my life. But that was one of the best."

Then he walked off, into the crowd.

8

"OH, HANK," SADIE SAID, WHEN HER BELOVED GOLDEN RETRIEVER began to circle her legs in anticipation of his morning walk the next day. He knew the drill well: Sadie ate breakfast, spent some time in her morning devotions, cleaned up the dishes, then spent some of her favorite time of the day walking Hank through the nearby forest trails, enjoying the beautiful scenery, and praying.

Hank wagged his tail, the corners of his mouth turned up in what seemed for all the world to be an eager smile.

Sadie bent over to stroke his ears and scratch the soft mane behind them. "I'm sorry, boy," she said. "I don't think a walk is in the cards today. I promised Theo that I'd meet him at the library, first thing."

Hank pranced a bit at the sound of anticipation in her voice, as if to tell her he couldn't wait to join her on the most amazing walk of both their lives. In Hank's world, every walk was the most amazing walk, every bite of food was the most delicious, and every time he saw her was the happiest he had ever been. Sadie wished sometimes that she could see life a bit more like Hank did. He always seemed to enjoy everything to the fullest, and the only thing that seemed to worry him was being separated from the people he cared about.

She patted his head again. "I'm sorry to disappoint you, buddy. But I promise you an extralong walk sometime soon."

A few minutes later, Sadie pulled up to the library. Theo was already there, waiting for her on the front steps.

Kimama greeted them with a smile.

"We're looking for more information on the bank robbery," Theo said.

"Anything in particular?" Kimama asked.

"Actually, I think for the time being, we've brought our own book with us," Sadie said, holding up the old green ledger. "I don't have any illusions that it's going to solve the old mystery, but it's caused such a ruckus in town that we do want to learn everything we can from it, so that we can lay some of these new rumors to rest. But I think it might be helpful for us to have those newspaper archives at our fingertips, to see if we can match some of these characters in the ledger to their actual names. Maybe the ledger will fill in details the newspaper articles don't contain, or the newspaper will help us understand some of the details of the ledger."

"Of course," Kimama said, leading them back to the computers, where she quickly navigated to the relevant sections of the *Silver Peak Sentinel.*

A few moments later, Sadie and Theo were settled comfortably into the seats they had occupied the day before. But to Sadie's surprise, Theo now drew a brand-new notebook out of his own bag. "I have some ideas about how to investigate this, Grandma," he said. "I've thought about it, and the most important thing is to understand our cast of characters. Most of the entries in this diary don't contain names, only initials. So I think the first thing we should do is go through the diary and pull out anyone who is mentioned at anytime. Then we can go through the paper, and see if the initials we have match anyone whom we know was reported as having some involvement with the case. That way we'll at least understand our cast of characters. And who knows—maybe we'll discover there was someone who was closely involved with the bank who never became a part of the official investigation."

Sadie smiled. As a doting grandmother, she would have been glad to let Theo try any harebrained scheme he came up with, within reason. But she also felt a little bit of pride as he described this plan to her. It was a good one—and it was very much like what she had had in mind when she had invited him to join her that morning. "That sounds good to me," she said, smiling.

With a businesslike nod, Theo flipped open his notebook. "Why don't you start going through the ledger," he suggested. "You can read out any names that appear. I'll make a separate page for them, and make notes about the date on which they appear and the activity they're involved in."

This time, Sadie suppressed her smile, trying to match Theo's businesslike attitude with her own. She flipped open the ledger, and began to scan through the first entry for any names or initials. "J.M.," she read.

Theo printed the initials in large letters at the top of the first page of his notebook. "I don't think we even need to look that one up," he said, and wrote "Jules Morgan" beside it. "What does she say he was doing?"

"Not too much," Sadie says. "Apparently he came in late that day."

Jules Morgan's late arrivals proved to be a theme of the ledger as Sadie and Theo continued to sift through it. In fact, the entries often began with a note of his late arrival. But when he was in the bank, he seemed to have a sharp eye. At least once, he caught a mistake that neither teller had noticed in the day's reconciliation, just with a glance over the accounts. And he also seemed to be a caring boss, when he was available. The only place in the ledger where Janie's side notes about her own life intersected with the business narrative she seemed to be trying to record were when "J.M." would ask her about her home, or her children. He even thought to bring a present for "A.'s" birthday, a stuffed rabbit with a blue satin ribbon around its neck.

"That sounds like a present for a child," Theo observed.

"Well, I doubt it was for Janie's husband," Sadie answered, eliciting a brief grin from Theo before he got back down to the serious business of parsing the ledger.

Besides "J.M.," the other major figures in the ledger were also surprisingly easy to identify, based on what turned out to be excellent reporting by the *Silver Peak Sentinel* at the time. Sadie and Theo quickly established that "T.P." was Tom Porter, the bank's day-to-day manager, who apparently offered the kind of steady, reliable leadership that Jules Morgan was unable to, despite his charm and brilliance. But according to the paper, Tom Porter had been out of town at the time of the robbery, celebrating his honeymoon with a trip to California.

"G." was Gavin Anderson, Janie's fellow teller: in the early days of Silver Peak, apparently the bank had only required two tellers to keep up with the steady trickle of customers.

"I suspect the fact that she lists 'G.' as only a single initial indicates that she was on friendlier terms with him," Sadie said.

"A first-name basis," Theo said, as he added a page for Anderson.

"And that's probably the case as well for 'E.,' although he doesn't get mentioned nearly as often," Sadie said.

Theo, by this time, had taken control of the computer, and was blithely flipping between the various screens that contained the newspaper articles regarding the bank as Sadie sifted through the ledger. "I think that's because he's the guard, Ed Walter," he said. "He wouldn't have been her boss, so she might have been more informal with him. But she wouldn't have spent nearly as much time with him as she did with a fellow teller at the next window."

According to the ledger, Ed sometimes came over to joke around with Janie and Gavin, but he appeared to spend most of his time by the door, and to serve more as a greeter than a guard. Frequently, Janie noted that customers had stepped into the bank, only to get embroiled in long conversations with Ed before they made it over to her window. Janie was amused by this, but she also used it to help her in her own customer service—often, when she had forgotten a customer's personal details, she could overhear so much of their conversation with Ed that she was able to greet them with a question about their sick horse, or the singing lessons their daughter was taking, just as if she remembered talking with them about it on their last visit.

Janie's personal notes also frequently cited three other initials, all of them single: "B.," "A.," and "N." Theo's sharp eye found complete names that corresponded to each of these in an issue of the paper in which a reporter had written up brief profiles of all the bank's staff. In Janie's profile, her husband, Ben, was mentioned, along with their two children: an older boy, Nathan, and a younger girl, Agatha. It was this article in which Sadie and Theo found the first conflict between the ledger and the record of events printed in the *Silver Peak Sentinel*. The paper described Ben as a woodworker, but Janie's notes showed him doing very little work. In fact, anytime Ben did find an odd job, it was cause for celebration in Janie's personal notes. And the jobs that Janie noted Ben doing didn't seem to have much to do with woodworking, unless you counted rebuilding the back steps for one of their neighbors. Mostly he seemed to be picking up absolutely anything he could find, including digging miles of postholes for a local rancher, and mucking out stables for a hotel downtown.

"That seems like a lie to me," Theo said. "I just wonder who told it, Janie or Ben."

"I'm not sure I'd call it a lie, exactly," Sadie explained to him gently. "It's possible that Ben thought of himself as a woodworker. It wouldn't be a lie necessarily for him to give that answer, even if he wasn't able to find work in his chosen profession at the time. Or for his wife to describe him that way, especially if she knew that his pride was hurting and that was how he wanted to see himself." Sadie could imagine what it had been like for the two of them, with a young family in the heart of the Depression. And for a grown man to see himself publicly recorded in black and white as doing "odd jobs," or even worse, being "unemployed" would have been a bitter pill. She might have told a white lie or two herself to keep that from happening to someone she loved.

Still, Sadie's sense that Ben had started to spend a lot more time at the bank in the weeks leading up to the robbery turned out to be far more than just her own impression. According to Theo's careful record of when the various figures appeared in Janie's ledger, Ben came to the bank less than every two weeks in May and June, when Janie first began her journal. But by the time of the robbery, he seemed to find some excuse to be there as many as three times a week. To both Sadie and Theo, his reasons for dropping in on Janie seemed a little empty: he just happened to be in the neighborhood, he wanted to know when she might be home for dinner, although according to the ledger, Janie left promptly after the final reconciliation almost every night. Janie didn't seem to mind, though. The visits from her husband invariably seemed to brighten her day, no matter what columns of numbers she had added up that day to reveal their family's growing financial distress. And she carefully recorded each one of Ben's visits, right up to the day of the robbery.

At the same time, Janie's notes about his jobs seemed to drop off. "I wonder if he was spending so much time at the bank because he didn't have any other work to do," Theo mused.

"That's a possibility," Sadie agreed. "But his behavior the week of the robbery doesn't match his regular pattern of visits. He doesn't visit Janie as much as he usually does during the week before the robbery. And Janie notes his working several more jobs than he normally does that week."

"If he really was working," Theo said. "And not planning something."

Sadie took a deep breath. "That's possible too," she said, closing the ledger now that she and Theo had worked through it. "The problem is, everything is possible. It's almost impossible to interpret these entries, or the newspaper, without being able to ask the people who were actually there some questions. The problem is, almost all the people who were there are no longer with us."

"You know whom I'd really like to talk to?" Theo said. "Janie. It's funny, because in some ways we already have the most from her. But I have even more questions about her than I do about anyone else. I just wonder why she started the journal when she did. And what she thought she was doing by keeping it. I wonder if maybe her husband suggested it, so that he could monitor the daily business at the bank. I wonder if she had any suspicions of her husband. She seems like a smart woman. Maybe she did. And I wonder what happened to all of them. Janie, Ben, Nathan. And little Agatha."

"Well, she wouldn't be so little anymore," Sadie observed.

"Do you think any of them are still in town?" Theo asked.

Sadie furrowed her brow, thinking. "I don't know," she said after a minute. "I don't remember growing up with any Hales in school. If any of them were still here, I would have thought I'd have crossed paths with one of them by now."

"Is there any way to find out?" Theo asked.

"You know what I say," Sadie said. "It's always worth a try. Even if you don't find what you thought you were looking for, you never know what else you might run across."

"Let's just try this," Theo said, typing "Janie Hale" into the search box that allowed users to sift through all the indexed issues of the *Silver Peak Sentinel.*

A group of articles popped up, all in the weeks and months surrounding the robbery. Theo scanned through them quickly, reading the samples of text that popped up along with them. "The first break-in...suspects questioned...reaction to external investigators."

He turned to Sadie. "We've already read all these." Then he scrolled down to the bottom of the page, to make sure there were no results they'd missed. "And that seems to be it."

Sadie thought back to all the mentions Janie made of her family in her notes along the margins of the green ledger. "Try just 'Hale'," she suggested.

Theo typed the name in. This time, a new article appeared at the head of the group that mentioned Janie's involvement with the robbery. About two years before, Ben Hale had placed an advertisement in the *Silver Peak Sentinel*. Theo clicked on it, and a handsomely printed quarter-page ad showed up, promising extremely high-quality woodworking from one of the west's best-trained and most experienced carpenters, who had just arrived in town.

"So they had only been in town for about two years when the bank robbery happened," Theo reasoned.

"It looks that way," Sadie said. "And it sounds like, with all the troubles Ben was having finding work in Silver Peak, perhaps they had moved here hoping to find more work for him. A lot of people moved during that time in hopes of a better life somewhere else. But the sad fact of the matter was, during those years, it simply wasn't very good for most people, anywhere you went."

Theo scrolled down through the articles again. "It looks like that's the only new one," he said. "But at least we know when they got to town."

"That's right," Sadie said. "But I'm still curious how long they stayed, afterward. I wonder—" she said.

Theo glanced at her, awaiting further instruction.

"You know what?" Sadie asked. "I know one simple place to start. Let's just run a standard Internet search for Hales in Silver Peak today."

Quickly, Theo backed out of the library archive, pulled up an Internet phone directory, and searched for Hales in Silver Peak. None came up, although the directory did suggest several Hales in nearby small towns. But none of them matched the initials of Janie's children, Nathan and Agatha. "Although I suppose Agatha wouldn't necessarily have the same last name today," Theo said.

Sadie smiled, with a little flush of pride at his deductive skills. "That's right," she said.

"So do you think it's safe to assume that the Hales left town sometime between the time Ben Hale placed that ad, and the robbery?" Theo said.

"I think that's probably true," Sadie said. "But we can't be sure. As you said, it's possible that Agatha married and lives in town under a name we wouldn't immediately recognize."

Now Theo's brow was the one that furrowed. "What if they owned a house?" he asked. "Wouldn't there be a record of when they sold it?"

"That's a great idea," Sadie said.

"Where would they keep that?" Theo asked. "Should we go over to the town office?"

"Not for a record that old," Sadie said. "They have them at the town office too. But they're so useful for historical research that they placed the first hundred years of Silver Peak city records on the library system a few years ago."

She took the mouse from Theo, backed out of the Internet phone directory, and clicked on the search engine for Silver Peak's property records. "It's this one," she said. "And it runs from 1857 to 1957. So if the Hales bought or sold anything during that time, we should be able to find it."

She relinquished the mouse to Theo as the program containing the records loaded. When the search box appeared, he set the search parameter to "Owner's Name," and typed in "Hale."

No records returned.

"Nothing?" Theo said, somewhat incredulous. "They didn't own anything, the entire time they were here?"

Sadie pursed her lips and sighed. "That's not actually all that surprising," she said, "if you think about how much trouble Ben seemed to be having finding work. And Janie wouldn't have made a lot of money at the bank, because she was a woman. Probably not even as much as her fellow teller, Gavin Anderson. The idea was that men had families to support. People didn't think as much back then about the fact that sometimes it was the woman whose job was really supporting a whole family. And given how much she seems to worry about the price of milk and eggs in her journal, it's unlikely they ever got together a big enough chunk of money to make a down payment. It's possible that they were renters the entire time they lived in Silver Peak."

Theo frowned in frustration. Then his face lit up with a new idea. "What about her fellow teller? Or the guard at the bank she was friends with? Do you think either of them still lives in town? Maybe one of them remembers something about the Hales. Or about the robbery," he added, almost as an afterthought.

Sadie suppressed a smile at Theo's youthful exuberance and optimistic math. "It's been seventy-seven years since the robbery," she told him gently. "Anyone who was old enough to be holding down a full-time job at the time is likely no longer with us."

"Well, we could at least check," Theo insisted. Quickly, he returned to the Internet search engine, and ran a search for "Gavin Anderson" in Silver Peak. A moment later, a record did come up, with what claimed to be a permanent address. "Silver Line Road," Theo read. "Where's that?"

"That's the Silver Peak Rest Home," Sadie said. "It sounds like you may have been right, and I was wrong. But if he's still living, he must be at least a hundred."

Theo scrolled down into the collection of guesses the Internet had offered, containing other details that might pertain to a Gavin Anderson in Silver Peak. "He's ninety-nine," he said. "If this record is correct."

"It must be all this fresh Colorado air," Sadie said. "My father always told me how good it was for me, every time I complained about the chilly weather. It sounds to me like it might be worth paying Gavin a visit," she added. "What do you think?"

Theo held up his hand, already clicking away with his mouse in the other. "Let me check just one other thing," he said, and typed in "Ed Walter."

This time the search returned an obituary notice that had been published in the *Silver Peak Sentinel*, and several other news aggregators. It was relatively recent, within the past few years. Ed had apparently enjoyed a long and interesting career after his stint as a guard at the Silver Peak Bank, eventually starting his own security firm, and serving as a consultant for firms in Denver, and a few other Western states. He'd even dabbled in digital security solutions, after he retired. And the obituary noted that, along with a son in Texas, Ed was survived by a daughter in Silver Peak, Jennifer, who now went by the married name of Brayden.

A few quick clicks later, Theo had rustled up a current address for Nicholas and Jennifer Brayden, right in central Silver Peak. They lived just a few blocks from downtown, in a neighborhood of beautiful wood Victorian homes that had been built in a contest of one-upmanship among the newly wealthy mine owners at the end of the nineteenth century, when the mines that surrounded Silver Peak had first begun to pay out. The old houses were a delightful, if sometimes ridiculous, collection of outlandish Victoriana. Old-timers in town tended to look at them with a bit of wry humor, but young people, and retirees, never seemed to get tired of moving in, fixing them up, and adding a new coat of paint or their own personal touches.

Theo took a piece of scrap paper from a nearby pile, and scrawled the address down, along with Jennifer's name.

"Or maybe more than one visit," he said, handing Sadie the piece of paper.

9

———

When Sadie stepped into the door of her own shop, Theo in tow, Sadie's daughter, Alice, was behind the counter. Julie had asked for the day off, and since it was fall break and she was off school, Alice had graciously offered to work in Julie's stead. She had opened the shop for Sadie that morning, just as she had promised, and now sat with her nose in a book, as usual. Sadie felt a surge of gratitude that her daughter had recently moved back to Silver Peak from Denver, even though it had been a result of her divorce with Cliff. Still, Alice was happy here, she knew, as were the kids, and Sadie's heart took great solace in having her child and grandchildren so close.

Alerted by the sound of the door, and footsteps, Alice looked up, ready to greet a new customer. But when she realized it was only Theo, and Sadie, she turned back to whatever scene in her book they had just jolted her out of. Sadie smiled. Alice's love for reading had been a great source of joy to Alice, and a source of pride to Sadie—but also the bane of Sadie's existence, ever since Alice sounded out her first words to a picture book when she was a child.

"I trust that's not the greeting you're giving to an actual customer," Sadie teased, as she and Theo walked over to the counter.

"Actual customers don't have the heart to interrupt me when I'm obviously enjoying my book," Alice said, without missing a beat. She even turned a page as she was speaking.

"Well, that must be why my business is so much better when you're the one who's running the shop," Sadie joked, coming around the corner to give Alice a kiss on the cheek.

Defeated, Alice stuck a bookmark between the pages of her book to keep the place, and gave her mother a little squeeze back.

"So how's it going this morning?" Sadie asked.

Alice shrugged. "Pretty typical," she said. "I sold another one of those Adirondack chairs. There's a woman who's come in a few times to look at that beautiful turquoise cabinet we've got in the back, and she was back in, but I think it's probably going to take her half a dozen more visits before she buys it."

Sadie nodded. "Sometimes this place does seem to function more like a museum than a store," she said. "But I don't mind that. The store is almost the best of both worlds. Some people can come to visit. But some people actually buy things. Which means I've always got an excuse to change my 'exhibits.'"

She bustled back around the corner to straighten the corner of an old quilt whose corner had gotten rumpled by foot traffic passing by the old traveling trunk on which it was displayed.

"Oh," Alice said. "And Edwin was in."

"Oh?" Sadie said. Trying to keep her cool, she pulled the entire quilt from the trunk, opened it, and began to fold it back up again. "Did he leave any message?"

"He said you'd know what he was looking for," Alice said. When Sadie glanced at her, she could see that Alice was watching her closely as she said this.

"*Hmm,*" Sadie said, still trying to sound nonchalant. "Well, I'm sure I'll see him later."

"How was your morning?" Alice asked.

To Sadie's relief, Theo broke in before she had to think of anything to say. The news that Edwin had come by that morning had momentarily scrambled her thoughts so that it was hard for her to even remember their trip to the library. "It was great, Mom," Theo told Alice. "We combed through the diary, and all the articles about the robbery, and we found a couple of leads."

Alice raised her eyebrows. "Leads?" Sadie knew it would take Alice a while to wrap her mind around Theo's plan to become a detective, but her daughter was doing a fine job showing her acceptance.

Theo nodded. "The family of the woman who wrote the diary doesn't seem to live in town anymore," he said. "At least, if they do, we can't find them. But we found the names of two other people who were connected enough with the bank at the time that they might remember something. Or have been told something about the story."

"Somebody who might remember something?" Alice said. "Didn't the robbery happen in 1937? They must have been pretty young then."

"Or be pretty old now," Theo said. "He's ninety-nine."

Alice raised her eyebrows.

"He's over at the nursing home," Sadie explained. "At least, I'm fairly sure that's where his address must be. Over on Silver Line Road."

"Have you talked to him yet?" Alice asked.

Sadie shook her head. "I thought it'd be good to stop in here," she said. "I don't like to leave you all by yourself for too long. You never know when we might get a tough question. Or a rush."

"Mom," Alice said with a smile. "I know it's hard for you to believe I'm not seventeen anymore, because it's hard for me to believe that Theo's not seven. But believe it or not, I can probably handle a little rush at the shop. Or even a tough question."

"Of course you can, sweetie," Sadie said. "I just don't want to depend on your help around the shop too much."

"Are you kidding?" Alice said. "I've still got two hundred and fifty pages left of this book. I haven't even been in the shop all morning. I've been evading English Cavaliers and Gascon bandits in the forest of the south of France."

The chime over the door sounded, and the whole family turned to see the new visitor to the store. It turned out to be more family: Sadie's cousin Laura, who lived in the third-floor apartment above the Antique Mine.

"I couldn't resist," she said. "I saw you all in here when I came down from upstairs. I'm on my way to help do some volunteer gardening in the park. But I thought I'd see how all of you are. You look great."

"Well, we can't help that," Sadie joked. "Don't hold it against us." Alice and Theo both answered Laura's question with smiles.

"What are you planting this year?" Alice asked.

"I'm not sure," Laura said. "But I've been lobbying to plant some Queen Anne's Lace."

"Queen Anne's Lace?" Alice said, her nose wrinkling.

"Well, it's very beautiful," Sadie agreed. "But I have to say, I always thought of it as kind of a...weed."

Laura smiled and pointed at her as if she'd just guessed the right answer in class. "You've got it," she said. "Exactly."

"It grows all over the place," Theo said. "So why would you *plant* it?"

"I think it's gotten some bad PR," Laura said. "The fact that grows it all over just means it will grow even better in our gardens. And you're right, it is beautiful," she added. "So I'd like to have a place where we can pick it, instead of having to pull over on the side of the road, or climb up to find it along a set of railroad tracks."

"Well, if anyone can give it the PR it needs," Sadie said, "it'd be you."

Laura grinned and gave Sadie a quick hug. "Duty calls," she said. "But it's great to see you. I think getting to run into you is my favorite feature of that apartment."

"I didn't factor that into the rent," Sadie joked. "Maybe I ought to raise it."

"Well, good luck figuring out the going rate for love," Laura said. "I hear it's priceless."

With a wave, she went back out the door.

"That reminds me, Mom," Alice said. "Are you still up for Spike's show tonight? Since you're the one who actually promised we'd go."

Spike seemed to play around town at least once a week, and he was always asking Alice to come. But the week before, he'd invited Alice and Sadie both, and Sadie had jumped in and agreed before Alice could protest. It wasn't necessarily that she thought Alice should spend more time with Spike, given his obvious crush on her. It had just sounded like a good time to Sadie.

And Spike had been so excited that now none of them could back out. So Alice had suggested they take Theo and Sara along and make a family night of it.

"Wouldn't miss it," Sadie said.

"You better not," Alice said.

"And you're sure you're all right here at the shop?" Sadie asked.

"Leave me here for the rest of the day," Alice said. "When you come back, I'll have sold every antique in this place."

"Well, in that case," Sadie said, reaching for her purse again, which she'd laid on the counter when she and Theo came in. She looked at Theo. "How would you feel about making a little visit to the nursing home?"

10

THE SILVER PEAK REST HOME, RESIDENTS LIKED TO JOKE, WAS so well designed that tourists sometimes asked locals about "that beautiful hotel" just outside town. Set on a hill, in the midst of a thin pine forest, it was composed of half a dozen large main buildings that housed residents needing a higher degree of care, but was surrounded by condominiums and even free-standing residences where retirees could live relatively independently, but still take advantage of the nursing care, meals, and incredible suite of activities the center offered.

"I hope that Gavin is as healthy as anyone could expect," Sadie told Theo as they drove up. "But I'm going to assume that he probably isn't living in the independent units by this time."

Sadie's deduction about Gavin's whereabouts turned out to be correct. When she and Theo checked at the main building, the receptionist quickly told them that Gavin was on one of the nursing wings—one for high-functioning residents but still not exactly independent living.

"Would it be best if we gave him a call to see if he'd mind a visitor?" Sadie asked.

The receptionist shook her head, laughing, and waved them on. "Oh, Mr. Anderson loves his guests," she said. "He's one of the ones who never met a stranger. And he'll talk to anyone he finds in the halls, even if they're the guests of other residents."

That quality must have served him well as a bank teller, Sadie reflected. Or maybe it was a talent he had developed while working as a teller.

"Well, we're not exactly family," Sadie said. "We're actually doing some historical research on the town, and were curious about some of his memories of the earlier days in Silver Peak."

"I'm a hundred percent sure he'd love to talk with you about that," the receptionist said. "And don't you worry," she added. "If I'm wrong, he won't waste any time in chasing you out. Mr. Anderson isn't exactly a shrinking violet."

"And it sounds like he still has all his...faculties," Sadie said. She'd met older gentlemen who loved to talk, but you couldn't always be sure how accurate all of that talk was, after a certain point.

"I wish I had all the faculties Mr. Anderson has," the receptionist assured her. "Yes, he's clear as a bell. Down that long corridor to the right. It's 14A. Most of the residents leave their doors open by day, but just knock if his isn't."

"Thanks so much," Sadie said.

Theo followed her down the hall. "There's so much history in a place like this," he breathed, in a tone of awe. Sadie's heart warmed again with grandmotherly pride. She wouldn't have blamed Theo at all if he'd felt uncomfortable around so many older people. It was hard for middle-aged people to realize they would ever get old, and for a boy as young as Theo, it was almost impossible. But

Theo walked down the hall, grinning at everyone they passed, just as if he was passing out greetings on a high school corridor. And instead of finding the people there strange, or alien, or sad, he was fascinated by all the history people who had lived so long must have to offer, just as Sadie was. She loved her antiques, because they told her stories. But no antique, however valuable, meant as much as any person—or had more fascinating tales to tell.

They found 14A just where the receptionist had told them, near the end of one of the home's long residential hallways. The door stood open, decorated with a photograph of a young man Sadie recognized with a start as Gavin.

"That's him," Theo whispered, when he saw it. "He looks just the way he did in the old newspaper pictures."

Before they could knock, someone bellowed a hearty "Hello out there!" from inside the room. However else old age might have limited Gavin Anderson, his hearing was still good. A moment later, a man in a wheelchair wheeled himself into view. His face was far more worn and wrinkled than the one Sadie and Theo had just recognized in the old picture, but he still had a shock of white hair, made perhaps even brighter by the navy sweater he wore over a plaid western shirt. "You folks looking for someone?" he asked.

"We were looking for you," Theo said.

Gavin gave a broad smile, and a commanding wave. "Well, don't just stand out there in the hall," he said. "Come on in!"

As Sadie and Theo shuffled into the room, he executed a neat turn with his wheelchair and backed up to allow them to reach the comfortable pair of armchairs that completed the furniture in his room, along with his bed. "There's only two chairs," he said. "But luckily I've got my own." He gave the arm of his wheelchair a vigorous thump. "You two bring any cookies with you?"

Sadie smiled, but Theo shook his head seriously, and looked at Sadie to see how big an error this might have been on their part.

"Or candy?" Gavin went on. "No?" He wheeled over to the nightstand beside his bed and opened the cabinet below it. "Luckily, some other folks did the last time they were here." He poked around the cabinet for a minute, then emerged with a tin painted with images of buttery shortbread photographed on a blue background. But when he popped the top off, it was full of blondies and small pieces of fudge.

"My granddaughter's a world-class baker," Gavin said. "And luckily, a local boy was smart enough to marry her and keep her in town." He held out the tin, offering its contents first to Sadie, who took a small piece of fudge, and then to Theo, who, after significant wavering, settled on a blondie.

"This is wonderful," Sadie said. "Thank you."

Gavin helped himself to a piece of fudge and nodded with satisfaction as he replaced the tin in his bedside cabinet. He leaned back in his chair, savoring it. "So to what do I owe the pleasure of this visit?" he said. "You folks here from one of those churches? Come to see that we're not getting up to too much trouble here at the old folks' home?"

Sadie smiled and shook her head. "Actually, we're here with a few questions we thought you might be able to help us answer," she said.

"Questions?" Gavin said, perking up. "About what? I'm not sure I'm an expert on anything, but that never stopped me from being willing to share my opinion." He chuckled.

Sadie hesitated for just a moment, hoping that his jocular attitude wouldn't vanish when she mentioned the old bank case. But there was no point in putting it off any longer. They hadn't come over just to sample Gavin's baked goods. "I'm Sadie Speers," she said. "And this is my grandson, Theo. I own the Antique Mine, an antique store downtown."

Gavin chuckled again. "We didn't have any of those back in my day," he said. "My wife, God bless her soul, liked to joke that we must have lived very classy lives when we were young, because *everything* we had back then was an antique by the time our own grandchildren came along."

Sadie chuckled, as well. "I guess that's one way to think of it," she said. "To Theo, everything I used to play with when I was a kid would be an antique."

"That's exactly right," Gavin said.

"I guess there must be something in our blood that draws us to old things," Sadie said. "Because Theo's interested in them, as well. And a few days ago, he picked up an old bank ledger at a yard sale in Denver."

She watched Gavin closely when she mentioned the bank, to see if his expression changed at all. It didn't, so she pressed on. "He could tell that it had something to do with Silver Peak, so he brought it home. And when we both started to look at it a bit more closely, we realized it wasn't just a ledger."

"No?" Gavin asked, as if he was just as in the dark as they had been about what else it might be, then.

"No," Sadie said. "It was a diary of sorts. And we believe it was kept by Janie Hale."

Gavin's face broke into a smile. "Janie Hale," he said, and nodded. "I worked with her. Years ago."

"That's what we thought," Theo said, excitedly.

Sadie patted his shoulder, slightly worried that Theo's enthusiasm might overwhelm Gavin, or steer him down the wrong direction, when they might find out far more just by seeing what memories Gavin might share that neither she nor Theo would even know to ask about.

"We just got curious about her, reading the diary," Sadie said. "We did a little research on her at the library, thinking maybe we could learn something more. But we didn't find much. So we thought we'd see if you had any memories you'd like to share."

Gavin nodded, still smiling. "Of course, of course," he said. "Janie." He seemed to fall into a bit of a reverie. "I didn't work with her for very long," he said. "But she was a special girl. The kind you wouldn't forget."

"What was she like?" Sadie asked.

"Oh," Gavin said, his eyes glancing out the window as he reached back into the past. "Sweet. She was sweet. But real smart. She always finished up reconciling her accounts before I was done with mine. Sometimes she'd help me. She never would leave until we were both done, even though Jules always told her get out of there, and go on home."

"Jules Morgan?" Sadie asked.

"Yep," Gavin said. But his thoughts quickly seemed to return to Janie. "She did love going home, though. Her two little ones. And even that husband of hers. Although I never really did care for him much myself."

"Oh?" Sadie said, hoping to prompt him to go on.

Gavin shrugged. "It's always a mystery, I guess," he said. "Love. It is even to me now, and I guess I'm about as old as any person can hope to get. And she sure did love him."

Sadie's mind kicked into a higher gear. If Janie was so obviously still in love with her husband, maybe she would have been too blind to recognize the signs that he was planning a robbery at her workplace. Or even so much in love that she would have been willing to do anything he asked of her, no matter what it was. "What was he like?" Sadie tried.

Gavin sighed, a slight exasperation in his tone even all these years later. "Well, I guess he was a big man," he said. "Not just tall, but square, you know, across the shoulders. Kind of a lumberjack or a miner type. But he thought of himself as almost an artist, I think. Was real careful with his hands. Didn't want to do anything that might crush them. Not that I can blame him," he added. "I can't say I would have liked that either. It's just that there wasn't a lot of work that fit that description here in Silver Peak at the time. I guess he had trained as a carpenter out East, you know, learning how to build gingerbread trims and real nice finishes for those rich folks when times were still good, in the Roaring Twenties. Once the Depression hit, there wasn't much call for that, even out East. And I'm not sure there had ever really been much call for it here in the West. I guess we're just a little bit simpler, in some ways."

Sadie nodded, but her mind was full of questions. "Did Janie ever say why he'd brought her west, then?" she asked. "It seems like there can't have been much call for his type of work out here, like you said. Especially at that time."

"Oh, it wasn't for his work," Gavin said. "They came out here because of Agatha."

"Agatha?" Sadie said, not sure whether to reveal how much she and Theo had already learned about Janie's family.

"Janie's little girl," Gavin explained. "She was real sick. Some kind of problem breathing. So they came out here for the thinner air. Same as Doc Holliday. It wasn't for his job. That was the problem. And Janie was real forgiving with him about everything else, because he'd been willing to come all this way just so Agatha could be a little more comfortable."

"So how long did you work with Janie?" Sadie asked.

"Oh," Gavin said, "it's hard to be sure. A couple of years, I think."

"Just a couple of years?" Sadie asked, calculating. According to the research she and Theo had already done, Janie had taken her job at the bank almost two years before the robbery. So if Gavin was right, that meant that Janie must have left her position close to the time of the robbery. That might have explained why the diary ended around that time, Sadie reasoned. "And then did Janie take some other job in town?"

Gavin shook his head. "Nope," he said. "They just up and left town. I guess Ben finally got some good job. Or one that looked good at first glance. Up in Denver. She didn't even have an address to give me, because it all happened so fast that they were just going to stay in a rooming house until they could find something more permanent. I was always real sorry about that. I'd have liked to have been able to look them up from time to time, when I got up to the big city. And we were real short-handed there for a while, anyway. I mean, after the robbery, working at the bank wasn't the sleepy little job it had been."

Sadie's heart skipped a beat. She hadn't wanted to broach the subject of the robbery too soon, but here Gavin had stumbled into it on his own—and like the end of the diary, Janie's departure from town seemed to coincide eerily with the time of the robbery. "What was it like?" she asked.

For what seemed like the first time, Gavin's face took on a pinched, faraway look. "It was hard," he said. "Real hard. A lot of scared people. A lot of angry people. Maybe those are the same thing. At least that's what it seemed like, a lot of times, to me. And we didn't have any real answers to give them. We kept saying, the money'll come in, the money's coming. But that won't pay your bills today. And it didn't come for a long time."

"I know that was a hard winter for the town," Sadie said.

"It sure was," Gavin agreed. "And I can't say it was real pleasant at the bank, with all those investigators around, trying to get one of us to confess to the robbery. Or to say another one of us did it."

"We could see from the newspaper articles that there was some suspicion it was an inside job," Sadie said. "But I'm not sure I really understood why, from the reporting. I know there was a broken window, so there was at least some sign of forced entry."

Gavin nodded. "Man, I've been over this so many times, I think it may be the last thing I remember," he said. "It seems like they wanted us to talk to a new interrogator every day, for a while. And you're right, if you only read the paper, it might seem like a pretty cut-and-dried robbery. You break the window, you climb in, you take what you want. The problem was with the safe itself. And nobody in town knew much about that except for the bank staff, for obvious reasons."

"What was wrong with the safe?" Theo asked, unable to contain himself any longer.

"Nothing," Gavin said. "That was the problem. When the bank was first built, it had a safe just about anyone with a pick and a bit of determination could crack. And in mining country, just about everyone had at least a pick. That's part of why there were so many robberies in the old west. It wasn't just that we didn't have many lawmen in the early days. It's that those original vaults were more like suggestions than protection. It was just sheer blind luck that the Silver Peak Bank never got turned over in those days. But during the Roaring Twenties, when the bank was flush, Jules had invested in a state-of-the-art vault. There were banks out East that didn't have safes that tough. The walls were made of steel as, so there was no way to blow your way in there even with a man-size pile of dynamite. And the combination to the thing changed every day."

"Before computers?" Theo asked, with the incredulousness of a young person who could barely believe that the sun had managed to come up and go down without digital help.

"A long time before computers," Gavin said, nodding proudly. "It was a mechanical system with moving tumblers that Jules could reset every evening. And the tumblers were absolutely silent, so nobody could have cracked them by sound."

"And only Jules knew the combination?" Sadie asked.

Gavin laughed and shook his head. "That might have worked if Jules had ever been in the habit of getting out of bed before ten o'clock," he said. "But that man, God bless him, didn't even have the stamina to keep banker's hours. No, if he'd been the only one with the combination, we wouldn't have been able to do any business for most of the morning. So he had a—I guess you couldn't really call it a system. But he'd reset the vault, then write down the new combination, and give it to one of us each evening."

"Not always the same person?" Sadie asked.

Gavin shook his head. "I guess this was some kind of security measure he'd dreamed up on his own. He always gave it to someone different, and he liked to joke that it would make it hard for any of us to get tempted, because we'd never know for sure when we'd have the opportunity to pull off a robbery, and he'd always know which one of us had the combination."

"So who had the combination the night of the robbery?"

"I did," Gavin said. "That's why I've been over this so many times. I think some of those investigators are probably still sure I'm the guy who did it. They were sure at least that it must have been one of us. One of the investigators said he'd never seen a safe of that make cracked, in his entire career, although he had seen a would-be robber who managed to blow himself all the way across a two-lane street, trying to blast his way through that steel. They allowed that it was possible in theory that someone could have cracked the combination some other way. But they said it would pretty much have had to be the best bank robber in the world. And nobody could come up with why a thief of that caliber would be spending their time on a safe that tough in a bank that small. Nope, it was a lot easier to believe that one of us did it. And that made things plenty tough around the bank, for a while. I don't think there were any of us who didn't wonder about one of the others.

"And then, of course, everybody in town wondered about Jules. He kept going on and on about how nobody was going to lose anything, that the government had insured it all. But all that time, people were losing things, their time, their dreams. We paid them back their money all right, in the spring. But nothing was really the same after that, at the bank. And nobody would have put it past Jules to line his own pockets with all that extra cash, especially if he really believed he wasn't hurting anybody. He was one of the only people in town who would have had the connections to hide a windfall like that. If any of the rest of us had turned up with a lot of extra money in those days, everyone else in town would have noticed it right away. But nobody was ever really sure how much Jules had—or how little."

Sadie's eyebrows rose. "Did you know of Jules having any financial problems?"

Gavin shook his head. "I didn't *know,*" he said. "But you saw a lot of things, working at the bank. More than once I saw him come in with money that didn't come in through any normal channels, just when we were running short on deposits to cover payrolls, or busy seasons. He never said where it came from, and we never asked. But it sure wasn't part of the regular business of the bank."

That was an interesting possibility, Sadie mused. Perhaps Jules hadn't robbed the bank from greed, but in order to dig himself— or even the bank—out of some kind of financial instability. If that was the case, he might even have believed he was doing the town a favor: keeping the bank afloat, and their deposits secure, at the small price of them having to wait for a short time to have their funds replaced by the federal government.

Gavin's thoughts seemed to mirror her own. "Jules had so much money that he probably didn't feel it much when we had to wait for the government money to come through. But that sure wasn't how it felt to us, working there," Gavin said. "Those were grim times that winter. And times had been pretty grim here in Silver Peak for a few years before that. So that's saying something. To tell the truth, I don't blame Janie for getting out when Ben had that opportunity. In fact, I'm glad she did."

"About how long after the robbery did they leave town?" Theo asked.

Gavin glanced up at the bands of fluorescent lighting in the ceiling, to collect his thoughts. "Not too long," he said. "I guess they were gone before winter really hit. It would have been a hard move otherwise, through the kind of snowfall we get here in Colorado."

"So just a few months?" Sadie said. "Sometime before December?"

Gavin nodded. "Yep," he said. "They were gone by Christmas, I remember that, because I had to take over the Christmas savings accounts from Janie when she left. I guess it might even have been before Thanksgiving. But like I said, that family was in distress, trying to get by just on Janie's salary. I couldn't blame them for jumping at a better situation when it presented itself."

"Did it cause any talk?" Sadie asked. "With the family leaving so soon after the robbery?"

Gavin shook his head decisively. "They weren't the only people to leave town around that time," he said. "A big mine had just opened a few counties over. And people did a lot of moving around at that time, looking for something better. Nobody really thought Janie could have had anything to do with it, so the investigators didn't even really raise much fuss that I remember. They were just like everybody else, I guess, trying to find a way to survive in those days."

"Mr. Anderson?" A pretty redhead poked her head in the door. "I'm sorry to interrupt, but it's time for your physical therapy."

Gavin raised his eyebrows apologetically, but began to twirl his chair around toward the exit. "I'm sorry to leave you two fine people here," he said. "But I've got to keep in training. I'm just doing weight training these days, to keep my arms strong. But Becca here says she's going to have me up on the climbing wall by spring."

Becca raised her own eyebrows, to indicate to Sadie and Theo that she'd never given that promise as a reliable medical prediction.

"Well," Sadie said, rising with Theo beside her. "We're very grateful for your time."

"Yeah, thanks," Theo said. "This helps a lot."

"Well, let me know if you think of any other questions," Gavin said. "I'm glad to tell you anything I know. And if I don't know it, I'm always glad to make something up!"

Becca chuckled, and wheeled him out of the room.

11

———

"WHAT DID YOU THINK OF THAT?" THEO ASKED, AS THEY WALKED out of the double doors of the rest home, into the lot where they'd parked.

Sadie had plenty of thoughts of her own, but she was also interested in her grandson's. And she knew that if she shared her own ideas, he was liable to mold his to hers, instead of voicing his own. "I think it was very interesting," she said. "But what do you think?"

Theo took the few steps toward the car in thoughtful silence. But when they were both comfortably settled in the car, as Sadie nosed out of the lot, he said, "I can see where all the rumors about the Morgan family came from."

Sadie nodded encouragingly.

"I mean, even Gavin seems to think that Jules Morgan was probably the culprit. And he seems to like Jules. If you were someone who didn't like him, I bet it would seem even more suspicious."

"I agree," Sadie said.

"But...," Theo said.

"Mmm?" Sadie prompted.

"I don't have any proof of this," Theo hedged. "It's just an idea."

"We don't have much proof of anything right now," Sadie said. "So ideas are what we have to work with for the time being. And without ideas, we'd have no idea where to look for proof."

"Well, it's obvious that Gavin likes Janie," Theo said. "And he didn't really think much of Ben."

"I think you're right about that," Sadie said.

"So it's surprising to me that Gavin never thought of this," Theo said. "Maybe he just didn't want to. But doesn't it seem like Ben might have had something to do with the robbery? In Janie's diary, he seems to get so interested in the workings of the bank, right around the time the break-in happens."

"Yes," Sadie said. "That seemed suspicious to me too."

"And then for them to leave town so soon after the robbery," Theo said. "I know Gavin wouldn't want to believe Janie did it. And it sounds like even the investigators believed she checked out. But I just wonder—how closely did anybody look at Ben?"

Sadie nodded. "I don't know if it's a good idea or not," she said. "But you're not the only one who had it."

When she glanced over at him, Theo gave a pleased grin. "You thought so too?" he asked.

"It's hard not to wonder," Sadie said. "And if the real culprit left town in the middle of the investigation, that would sure go a long way to explaining why the crime was never solved."

"So how do we—" Theo began, but as he did, Sadie's phone began to ring. Theo fished it helpfully from her purse and checked the caller ID. "It's Edwin," he said, and handed it to her.

If Theo hadn't already noted who the caller was, Sadie might just have let it go to voice mail, to give herself a chance to collect her thoughts, but she didn't want to have to explain to her grandson why she was dodging calls from Edwin. So she took the phone from Theo, and answered.

"Sadie?" Edwin said.

Her heart gave a little flutter at the sound of his voice, but she steadied herself. She still hadn't had the time to really sit down and examine her own heart and thoughts, and she didn't want to risk a friendship like the one she had with Edwin by diving into a romance without some serious consideration. Edwin was a charmer, and he had a lot of drive. His eagerness to be with her, and the way he'd stuck to it, despite the fact that she hadn't always felt as ready as he did, was attractive. And she'd always had a soft spot for him. But for that very reason, she didn't want to let him prod her into anything that they weren't both ready for.

"Hello," she said, trying to keep her tone light and businesslike.

"Have I caught you in the midst of something?" Edwin's tone had none of the teasing, or the tenderness, that had been so apparent the last few times she'd spoken with him. Instead, he sounded far more businesslike than she had. She felt as if she was getting another glimpse of the judge who had ruled a courtroom for all those decades. But along with the sudden professionalism in his tone, he also sounded worried.

"Is everything all right?" she asked, her own voice suddenly full of concern.

In the passenger's side seat, Theo glanced at her.

"I'm not sure," Edwin said, "but I'm afraid not. I hate to bother you, but is there any chance you'd be able to come by the campaign office? I've got something I'd like to talk over with you."

"Absolutely," Sadie said. "I just need to drop Theo off, and I'll be right over."

"Thank you," Edwin said, his tone already relieved.

"See you soon," Sadie said, and closed the connection.

She settled the phone back into her purse just as they arrived in downtown Silver Peak.

"You can just drop me off at the library," Theo said.

Sadie made the turn for the library and glanced at him. "What are you after this time?" she asked.

"I just had another idea," Theo said.

"You have to be careful with those," Sadie said, and smiled as she pulled up at the curb beside the library. Theo jumped out of the car, bounded a few steps toward the old building, then remembered to turn back to wave.

As Sadie pulled away from the curb, her phone rang. She smiled when she saw the caller ID: Roz.

"Sadie's Cab Service," she joked. "How can I help you?"

"Are you opening a new wing of the business?" Roz asked.

"I'm just doing what my clients demand," Sadie said.

"Clients like, let me guess," Roz said. "Theo?"

"You got me," Sadie said.

"And I suppose he's paying heavily for your services," Roz said.

"You can't put a price on love," Sadie said.

"That's true," Roz said. "Speaking of which. I've been meaning to ask you about that date Edwin asked you out on. I know you turned him down, but I thought maybe by now you'd had time to come to your senses."

Sadie felt a little involuntary thrill at the sound of Edwin's name. Along with a twinge. She'd been so wrapped up in the diary that she hadn't found time to tell her friend yet about Edwin's new request. Or was it just that? Maybe she hadn't said anything to Roz because she didn't know yet what she even thought, herself. And as Sadie struggled to put her thoughts into words now, it became clear that was the case.

"Actually...," Sadie began.

"What!" Roz said excitedly. "Is there news on the Edwin front? I can't wait to hear it!"

"Well, you're going to get some practice waiting," Sadie said. "Because I'm not sure exactly what to say."

"The suspense is killing me," Roz said.

"Me too," Sadie said, with a grin. "Listen, I'm about to drive up to Edwin's now."

"Well, I was just calling to check in," Roz said. "I don't think I've been very successful. But at least I know what to bug you about the next time you call."

"So glad to help you out there," Sadie said, and ended the call with a smile.

A few minutes later, Sadie was walking up to the door of Edwin's beautiful old Victorian home, where he had grown up, and where Sadie had first come to visit him during the earliest days of their friendship and teenage romance. Those memories had been buried in the mists of her mind for decades—just a slight, pleasant sensation whenever she passed the place that she never took any time to reflect on during the happy years of her marriage to T.R. But now, with Edwin back in town, living in the same house, and the question of romance in the air again, her girlhood memories came rushing back. She remembered the feel of the clear Colorado nights when she would sit with Edwin on the swing that hung from the wide Victorian porch, overlooking the entire street, and meeting up with him in the very first light of dawn to join him for long weekend hikes, augmented by picnics of ham sandwiches and lemonade. Edwin had a teenage boy's appetite then: she remembered thinking he was crazy when he showed her the eight sandwiches he'd packed for them for a single meal—and then not being sure whether to be worried or impressed when he polished off all seven but the one that she enjoyed for her own lunch. Most of all, though, she remembered the feeling the house had given her during the year that she had dated him: a sense of strength, and warmth, and welcome. The possibility, for the very first time, that the world might hold a home for her besides the one that she had grown up in. The feeling was so fresh when she thought back on it that she couldn't tell whether it was a memory, or whether she still felt it, even now. *Lord,* she prayed, *please help me to see Your way through this. And whatever You do, please let it be a blessing to both of us. And I know You already know what it is Edwin needs. If there's anything I can do for him, please show me what it is. But thank You that all of this is already in Your hands, and You know all the answers.*

She rang the bell.

A beautiful series of chimes rang out inside the house. Then it rang again. And again.

A moment later, Edwin appeared at the door, looking slightly harried. Sadie took a step forward, to come inside, but instead Edwin stepped out onto the porch, the chimes still ringing inside, and began to fiddle with the doorbell. After a few jabs with his index finger, the doorbell finally ceased ringing.

"It's a nice chime," Sadie observed.

"It was nice the first few dozen times," Edwin said. "It's an original, but apparently the fellow who restored it did a bit too good of a job. Now it won't stop ringing. But he's not able to come back until this weekend."

"And in the meantime, you're probably getting all kinds of visitors to your 'campaign office,'" Sadie said, as Edwin led her back through the house to the spare room that was serving as the headquarters for his run for Silver Peak's mayor. "So you've heard a lot of those chimes recently. It's like your favorite song."

"I wish that was the way I felt about it," Edwin said, as they stepped into the campaign office, filled largely by two desks, one for Edwin and one for Jesse, and a long table for volunteers, all cluttered with paper, boxes, phones, and various campaign posters. As Sadie stepped into the room behind him, Edwin turned back with a sigh, and gave her a smile. "I'm glad you're here," he said.

Sadie's heart gave a little tug, and for a moment she wondered if she'd been mistaken over the phone. Had Edwin brought her here to talk over their relationship again? As she wondered about this, he ran his hand back through his shock of white hair and glanced away, the worry evident on his face again. "I just got a strange call from the Morgan campaign," he said.

"Have they learned anything else about the ruined barbecue?" Sadie asked. "I felt bad about it. All that lovely beef and pork."

Edwin shook his head, somewhat grimly. "No," he said. "In fact, something else has happened."

"What?" Sadie asked, feeling genuine alarm.

"All of James's yard signs were destroyed last night," Edwin told her.

"Oh my goodness," Sadie said. "That's terrible."

"Yes," Edwin said.

"And also," Sadie said, "it's a pattern. We could have believed that the ruined barbecue was some kind of mistake. Or that it didn't have anything to do with the campaign, but some error on Andi's part. Or even something to do with Andi, a disgruntled employee, or some personal issue…"

"But to have campaign signs destroyed, the very same night," Edwin said. "This is definitely about the campaign."

"That is awful," Sadie said. "We've never had anything like this happen in Silver Peak politics that I can remember."

Edwin nodded. "That's exactly why I was willing to take part in them," he told her. "I experienced a lifetime's worth of hardball politics when I was sitting on the bench in Chicago. I never wanted to be part of that game again. Whether I won or lost this race, I was just glad to get to take part in an election that was friendly, and fair. It was such a relief, after all the mudslinging and backroom dealing of the big city. But it seems to have followed me here."

"And that's not the worst of it," Sadie said. "From the wrong angle, a person might think you're the one who brought those big-city political tactics back to Silver Peak with you." As soon as she said it, she regretted it. Sadie's mind was great at solving problems—but sometimes she forgot to think just a bit more before she spoke. It was obvious that Edwin might be under suspicion for the troubles in his rival's campaign. But she wished she'd thought of a more delicate way to say it.

Edwin, however, actually smiled. "You get right to the point, as always, Sadie Speers," he said. "That's exactly what I'm worried about. I'm not crazy about finding myself part of a campaign with any dirt at all involved in it. But I'm even less excited about the thought that people might think I had anything to do with it. And I don't know how to convince Silver Peak of that. Of course, I can deny it. But that's exactly what you'd expect someone to do, especially if he was guilty. I can't think of any way to really put the suspicion I had anything to do with this to bed, unless we can find out who the real culprit is. And until we do that, I'm also worried that the campaign won't really be a fair one. It matters less to me that I win than that the people of Silver Peak vote with all the facts, and a clear conscience, for whoever they choose as their next mayor. But with pranks like this in the mix, I'm worried that some voters might turn against James because of the problems his campaign is having, or turn against me because they think I'm responsible for them. And that could sour the genuine outcome of the whole campaign."

Sadie nodded, her mind already jumping into gear. "Where were these signs when they were destroyed?" she asked.

"In James's front yard," Edwin said. "According to James, they'd just been delivered."

Sadie's eyes widened. James and Helen lived nearby, in another one of Silver Peak's Victorian treasures. "There's so much foot traffic through there. Anyone might have done it. And...anyone might have seen it."

Edwin nodded. "You're right," he said. "It was a big risk. But they checked around the neighborhood, and none of the neighbors seem to have seen anything unusual."

"What was wrong with the signs?" Sadie asked, wondering how long the culprit must have stood there, exposed, in the Morgans' front yard. "What did they do to them?"

"They poured paint on them," Edwin said. "Apparently just a very standard house paint. Most of the signs are just smeared and unrecognizable. I guess one of them took the time to draw a little moustache on James's campaign photo."

Sadie looked at Edwin, trying to suppress a smile, but even under the pressures and distractions he was currently facing, he knew her too well. "You can laugh at that," he said. "I guess it is a little funny. And that actually makes it sound like perhaps it was just a bunch of kids."

Sadie's smile faded to a thoughtful frown. "Or someone who wanted to create the impression that it was just a bunch of kids. I suppose it's possible that both these campaign problems were unrelated. But they've come so close together that its hard to believe they're random. And to switch Andi's sugar for salt at the barbecue site would have required quite a bit more patience and sophistication that your average teenager has."

Edwin nodded. Even though he'd shared the bad news of the new campaign sabotage with her, he looked even more unhappy now than he had when she arrived.

"What is it?" Sadie asked. "Was there something else?"

"I hope not," Edwin said.

"But?" Sadie prompted.

"Well," Edwin said. "I hate to say this, but I can't help wondering if Jesse might have had something to do with this."

Sadie took a deep breath and nodded.

"He was there at the barbecue hours before I was," Edwin said. "He told me he was checking out the competition, but he would have had plenty of time to get into all kinds of mischief, if that's what he was set on."

"Although I imagine Andi would have chased him away pretty quickly if she saw him lurking around her stations," Sadie reasoned.

"That's if she saw him," Edwin said. "She had plenty on her hands yesterday afternoon. And Jesse's a smart guy, even if he can be—overzealous. I don't have any doubt he could have gotten away with something like that. I just wish I didn't have any doubt that he wouldn't do a thing like that."

"Well, the fact that he got to the barbecue early hardly makes him the only person who could have sabotaged the food," Sadie pointed out.

"Yes," Edwin said unhappily. "But he also left the party early. Told me he had some work he needed to do back here at the office. But when I got back here, he was already gone. And to tell you the truth, I couldn't see any sign that he'd been here at all."

Sadie surveyed the mess of the makeshift campaign head-quarters. "Well, that would be kind of like looking for tracks in a blizzard," she said.

Edwin gave her one of his wry smiles. "Point taken," he said. "But the window of time is right around when the damage would have been done to James's signs. He's got a neighbor who remembers seeing them about an hour before the barbecue broke up, and they were all still fine. But by the time James got home from the barbecue, they'd all been tampered with. Of course, I don't know for sure that Jesse has had anything to do with it. Most likely, he hasn't. So I'm stuck. I don't want to take even the smallest chance that he has gone overboard in his campaigning for me. But I also don't want to do anything that would give him the sense that I don't trust him. He's been a great campaign manager for me in every other way, and this isn't exactly a high-paid or prestigious position. He's just doing it because he loves the thrill of the campaign, and he believes in me. It'd be a real mess for me to destroy all that, if my suspicions aren't based in fact. Which I very much hope they aren't."

"So what you really need," Sadie said with a smile, "is someone who could look into all this for you. Make sure that everything's on the up-and-up with Jesse, without destroying the trust between the two of you."

Edwin smiled gratefully. "Exactly," he said.

"I'm just not sure," Sadie said. "Do you know anybody like that?"

Edwin's smile turned into a grin. "So you'll do it?" he asked.

Sadie nodded. "Of course," she said. "After all, it never hurts to be on the good side of Silver Peak's next mayor."

To Sadie's surprise, Edwin reached for her hand. He only held it for a brief moment, such a short time that anybody watching might have thought it was a just a friendly greeting. But Sadie was surprised by the warmth of his touch, and by the sensation that ran through her at it.

"Is that all I am to you?" Edwin asked.

Sadie dropped her gaze to one of the stacks of papers and campaign posters. "I didn't say that," she said.

Hope flared in Edwin's eyes. "So then you—?" he began.

Sadie cut him off before he could get any further. "I didn't say that either," she said.

Edwin folded his arms and shook his head. "Yet," he said, with a smile.

Rattled, Sadie took a few steps back. "Well, I'd better get busy," she said. "If we want to stop this person before anything else is sabotaged. I'll let you know if I find anything out."

"I'll look forward to it," Edwin said, as he followed her out.

"Sadie," he said, as she reached the door. "I've been thinking about you."

Sadie didn't know what to say to that. *Thank you*, didn't seem quite right. And although she'd been thinking about him too, she didn't want to give him the wrong impression. Not until she'd made up her mind about him.

Luckily, Edwin went on before she could say anything. "And this is what I've been thinking," he said. "Maybe I've moved a bit too fast. I know how I feel about you, but I know you take your time to think things over. And I know you're thinking over my question about going steady. But I thought it might help if I asked you something else, as well."

"What's that?" Sadie said, not sure whether the lump in her throat was from excitement, or dread.

"It's a simple question, really," Edwin said. "Would you go on a date with me?"

Sadie couldn't meet his gaze for long, so she dropped her own eyes to the floor.

"I'm not sure how that would be any different than just seeing you when I see you," she said.

"Well, you'll have to go with me to find out," Edwin said.

Sadie took a deep breath.

"How about it?" Edwin asked.

"I'll tell you what," Sadie said. "I'm going to see Spike Harris play a show tonight in town. How would you like to go with me to that?"

"It's a date!" Edwin said, elation in his voice. "I'll see you there."

Sadie wondered how he would feel about her bringing her daughter and grandson on a date with him. But they were part of her life, she reasoned. And he'd need to get used to that, from the beginning. Or, something asked, at the very back of her mind, was there some other reason she wasn't quite ready to be alone with him?

"All right," Sadie said, reaching for the doorknob.

"And I'll see you this afternoon too? At the debate?"

Sadie nodded as she went out. Edwin's first debate with James was scheduled for later that afternoon, and she'd promised him earlier in the week that she'd be there to support him. She just hadn't realized at the time that she'd be as nervous as a teenager about going to it. But she still managed to summon some of her grown-up composure as she glanced back at Edwin. "Wouldn't miss it for the world!" she said.

12

SADIE PAUSED FOR A MOMENT ON THE STOOP OUTSIDE OF THE imposing home James and Helen Morgan shared on several beautiful pine-wooded acres just outside Silver Peak, to collect her thoughts. It had been obvious to her that the next stop she needed to make was the Morgan home: it was the scene of the sabotage Edwin had just asked her to look into, and James and Helen were also some of the people in town who would have had the best access to one of the central figures in the old bank robbery that had the town all in an uproar. But before she raised her hand to knock, she bent to pick up the morning edition of the *Silver Peak Sentinel*, which was sitting cockeyed on the Morgans' doormat.

As she picked it up, she had a strange feeling of vertigo. She recognized the picture splashed across the top fold. In fact, she'd seen it in a newspaper in the past day or so. The newspaper she'd seen it in last had been from 1937, and it had been surrounded by the cramped, irregular type of those days, not the bold, digitally produced design of the present day. But the picture was unmistakable: it was one of the first shots the *Silver Peak Sentinel* had published in the aftermath of the 1937 bank robbery, with the window smashed out, investigators and bank staff milling around, and

Jules Morgan featured prominently on the street outside his van-
dalized storefront. From the research she and Theo had done over
the past several days, Sadie recognized most of the figures immediately: Janie, in the far corner of the image, gazing at something
beyond the frame; Gavin, picking his way through the broken
glass of the window; and Ed Walter, who had apparently arrived in
his guard uniform that morning only to discover that there wasn't
much left there to guard, but had taken up a station in front of the
broken window nonetheless. But the only person the paper had
identified in the current caption was Jules Morgan.

"OLD-TIME ROBBERY RECAPTURES TOWN'S IMAGI-
NATION IN MIDST OF CURRENT MAYORAL RACE" the
headline, by Troy Haggarty, blared. And the caption of the photograph continued to drive that theme home. *"Jules Morgan (center)
surveys the damage outside the Silver Peak Bank immediately
following its 1937 robbery,"* it read. *"The culprit was never found.
Morgan is the father of James Morgan, currently a candidate in the
Silver Peak mayoral election."*

Sadie shook her head as she scanned through the opening
paragraphs of the article. She couldn't believe that the rumors
started by Theo's innocent purchase of Janie's diary could already
have landed the old bank robbery story back on Silver Peak's
newspaper's front page. But that was the blessing and the curse
of life in a small town. Because Silver Peak didn't have to deal
with much crime, much smaller events sometimes got reported as
news. That could be lovely when it involved the accomplishments
of local students, or the progress of prize cattle. But it was a little
more disturbing when old rumors were recycled as front-page
news. On the other hand, Sadie reflected, as Edwin had pointed

out, the rumors did seem to be having an effect on the election. And that in and of itself was, she supposed, news.

As she stared down at the paper, the door opened. Sadie looked up, surprised. She hadn't even knocked yet, but there was Helen, staring through the screen door at her.

"Sadie?" Helen said. "What are you doing here?"

"I'm sorry," Sadie said. "I was about to knock, but I'd just picked up your paper..." As she held it out, Helen opened the screen door, took the paper from Sadie, and ushered her in.

Sadie stepped past her. The house was equally imposing on the inside as it was from without, with a sweeping staircase that led up to the next floor and a high ceiling over the entryway, which was still lavishly decorated in a style that had almost certainly been chosen in the previous generation. If James and Helen had been able to choose a home of their own, Sadie reflected, they might have had something much different. But when she tried to think of what that might be, she couldn't imagine anything else. So much of James's life seemed to be about keeping up his family legacy, and so much of Helen's seemed to be about being a good wife to James, that it was hard to know what either of them would really have chosen for themselves. She wondered if even they knew, after all these years.

As Helen looked down at the paper, her face fell. Sadie saw a deep sadness in her eyes as she looked down at the front fold. "Not this again," Helen said. But when she looked up, fire had replaced the sadness in her eyes. "And on the front page? That old robbery happened decades ago. How can they possibly believe this is news?"

"It's not just the robbery," Sadie said gently. "That whole time created an enormous amount of upheaval for almost everybody who was in town then. And it even seems to be affecting the election now."

Helen gave her head an impatient shake. "I can't believe that," she said. "The people of Silver Peak aren't unreasonable. They can't think that has anything to do with an election here and now."

Sadie didn't say anything. She just glanced at the newspaper.

Helen's shoulders crumpled. "You might be right," she said. As she did, she turned away, gesturing for Sadie to follow her out of the hall into a nearby sitting room, where Helen took a seat among a collection of Victorian-era antiques, largely red glass and dark wood, to complement the red flocked velvet wallpaper. Sadie sank down in the next seat. "I just feel like we've been fighting this all our lives," she said. "Or, I guess, James has. But I've been fighting it too, ever since I met him."

"Fighting what?" Sadie asked.

"The stain on the Morgan family name," Helen said. "Oh, I know I pretend nobody should ever think about it anymore. But I know they do. And we do, I think even more than them. And I think James thinks about it even more than I do. Everything he's done, since he was a boy, was to build up the Morgan name again. He wanted to be the best student, the best friend, the best bank president—all to prove that you could be a Morgan without being Jules Morgan."

"Did he not get along with his father?" Sadie asked, assuming Helen was exaggerating the point, but she understood the sentiment.

Helen shook her head and gave a pained smile. "He did," she said. "He adored his father. And his father adored him. I think that actually made the problem worse. If he'd been able to hate him, then maybe he could have gotten some distance. Or if he'd ever been sure about what happened. But he has been. Of course, he doesn't want to believe his father could have been capable of such a thing. But anybody who knew Jules had to know..." She paused, searching for the words. "Well, Jules was capable of doing a lot of things that would never occur to anyone else."

"Did you ever talk with James about the robbery?" Sadie asked.

Helen nodded. "When we first started dating, he told me the whole thing," she said. "Very early in our relationship. I couldn't understand why it was so important, this old story. But later I started to understand why. It had colored everything that mattered most to him in his life. But after that I tried not to ask him about it. It was clear he didn't know, and it only seemed to make him uncomfortable. And I always thought that time was on our side. The longer we waited, the more memories would fade." She rattled the paper in her hand. "I guess I was wrong about that," she said.

"What about Jules?" Sadie said. "Did he ever mention anything about it?"

Helen thought for a moment. Then she frowned, and shook her head. "You know," she said, "I don't remember his ever talking about it. Which is funny, when you think about it. Because there was really no topic that was off-limits for that man. Even things you wished were."

Sadie shifted in her chair. "I know you've been trying to protect James's feelings all these years," she said. "And I understand that's why you were interested in buying the diary. But my grandson and I have been looking into the history, and I keep thinking that if James knew the truth, maybe he'd be able to find some peace on the subject, one way or another. It would certainly be a huge relief to him to find out for certain that his father didn't have anything to do with the robbery. And even if it could be proved that he did, perhaps it would help him if he could learn anything about his father's reasons. Or at least understand what the truth was, so that he could forgive him. I think the not knowing must be the very hardest part, because you simply never know where you stand. You can't move forward, or backward."

"You're just stuck," Helen said, nodding. Clearly, she understood this sensation well.

"Is James around?" Sadie asked, treading carefully. "I know this is a hard topic for him, but he's one of the only people in town who might still be able to shed some light on the old robbery. And it sounds like he's one of the people in town who most needs that light to be shed."

Helen shook her head. "He's out," she said. "Dealing with all this nonsense with the campaign."

"I heard about that," Sadie said. "I guess the signs were ruined last night when you returned home from the barbecue."

"How did you hear that?" Helen asked.

Sadie felt a little prick at the back of her neck. People in town knew she was friendly with Edwin, of course, but she wasn't sure how she felt about linking her name with his. But when she hesitated, Helen grew upset.

"Is the whole town talking about that, as well?" she asked.

Sadie shook her head quickly to reassure her. "No, no," she said. "It's just that I spoke with Edwin, and he had just gotten a call from James's campaign. Edwin was concerned that people might think that he had had something to do with it."

Helen looked incensed. "Who would ever think that Edwin Marshall would do such a thing?" she asked.

"He is James's opponent," Sadie pointed out gently. "And that makes him somewhat of an obvious suspect."

Helen continued to shake her head. "People believe the craziest things," she said.

"When they don't have the truth," Sadie added. "Do you have any ideas of your own about who might have destroyed the signs?"

Helen shrugged. "I don't know," she said. "I guess it was probably just some kids in the neighborhood. We have good neighbors. If they'd seen anything strange, they would have said something. But nobody did."

"That would be the simplest explanation," Sadie agreed. "But do you think it might have had anything at all to do with the ruined barbecue?"

Helen looked at her, genuinely alarmed. "Do you think they had something to do with each other?"

Sadie couldn't quite believe that that possibility hadn't occurred to Helen already, but the shock in Helen's eyes at the suggestion was genuine. And Helen did seem to be a woman who was more than willing to avoid unpleasant truths. It sounded like she had devoted a good part of her marriage to helping James paper over any of the unpleasantness that had haunted his family from the previous generation.

"I think it's a possibility that's at least worth considering," Sadie said. "They're two relatively small pranks to play against James's campaign. Neighborhood kids might be to blame for the signs, although I'm not sure why they'd be interested in campaign signs."

"You can never tell why kids do anything," Helen said.

Sadie nodded in agreement. "But the problem with the barbecue would have required quite a bit more planning and sophistication," she said. "I don't see that as having been done by children. And if it wasn't, and we're right that there might be a connection between the two, then maybe the same person was responsible for the signs."

"Do you think so?" Helen asked, her voice full of wonder, as if she was connecting the two events for the very first time. Sadie could hardly believe the thought hadn't occurred to Helen before. But some people didn't like to see things they didn't want to believe, and Helen was so sensitive about the town's opinion of her husband's family, and so eager to sweep that history under the rug, that Sadie could believe that Helen might just refuse to recognize anything else that was unpleasant or upsetting, like the emerging pattern of sabotage against her husband's campaign.

"I think it's something we should at least consider," Sadie said, gently.

Helen nodded, her eyes still wide.

Lord, Sadie prayed, *please let this be one of the moments when I say the right thing instead of the wrong one. I don't want to cause Helen and James any more undeserved pain. Will You please reveal the truth here? And if I can be of any use, use me.*

"Can you think of anyone who might want to damage James's campaign?" Sadie tried again.

"But why would they want to do that?" Helen asked. Sadie had been doing her best to be tactful, but Helen now seemed to be getting even more upset.

Sadie suppressed a small sigh. She appreciated Helen's love for her husband. And she understood the desire to look away from unpleasant things. Everybody wished they could do that from time to time. But the only way to really deal with them was to face them head-on. Not looking at them didn't make them go away. And if, like Helen, you refused to look at something unpleasant when it faced you, all you could do was wrestle in the dark. Which was what Sadie felt like she was doing right now.

And the truth of the matter was, Sadie had some of the same questions Helen had. She couldn't think of why anyone would be trying to sabotage James's campaign either. The race so far had been friendly and clean. And Silver Peak had a history of friendly, clean politics. So it was just as much of a mystery to Sadie as it was to Helen what kind of motive someone could have for introducing these kinds of mean-spirited tricks into any Silver Peak campaign, let alone against a candidate as universally respected as James.

But Sadie also remembered Edwin's observation, that anyone in a position of power like James, no matter how careful he was to preserve his integrity, must still have made some enemies over the years, just due to the hard decisions leaders sometimes have to make. And, Sadie knew, emotions run especially high, and reason goes out the window especially quickly, around issues of money. Saint Paul had been right when he observed that the love of it was the root of all kinds of evil.

"What about in his work at the bank?" Sadie asked. "Do you know of any cases where people were frustrated by the decisions he had to make? Could he have made any enemies there?"

"James doesn't have any *enemies,*" Helen said, repeating the word as if it were slightly off-color, and she couldn't quite believe someone as refined as Sadie would stoop to using it.

"Of course not," Sadie reassured her. "But not everyone can have been happy with all the decisions James has had to make over the years at the bank. Even if he made the right ones. I know Ginny Pearson, for example, was upset when she was turned down for a loan."

For the first time, Helen began to nod, slowly, but then with increasing vigor. "Yes," she said. "Yes, I do remember that. Ginny was very upset. It was quite unusual."

"So you don't remember very many other unhappy customers?" Sadie prompted.

"Why would James have unhappy customers?" Helen said. "He's only ever trying to do the right thing. He's bent over backward for this town." Her face drew in something that almost looked like pain as she said this. But after a minute, she returned to her train of thought. "But yes, you're right. Ginny was very upset. We'd always been friendly with her and her husband. But after James turned down their loan, I greeted her once at the grocery store, and she walked by as if she hadn't heard a word. Nothing like that had ever happened to me before."

It seemed like a small thing, but Sadie could feel the sting of it. In a place like Silver Peak, which was usually so welcoming and warm, it would hurt even more. And it helped her understand why Helen felt so passionately about town opinion. Both she and James had had a personal taste of what it felt like when it turned against you.

"It even got so that she would cross the street a few times, when she saw James and me out for a walk and it looked like we might have to cross paths. James never said anything about it, but I know it bothered him. I told him that he should just send down someone from the campaign or the bank, when it was time to apply for the permit for the barbecue, so he wouldn't have to deal with her. I didn't see why there should be any unpleasantness surrounding the event, especially from the very beginning. But he insisted on going himself. I think he believed if he just kept at it long enough, he could repair the friendship. Which is what he's been trying to do with this whole town, his whole life, I guess," she said.

"So Ginny did know about the event in advance?"

Helen nodded. "James filed the papers with her himself," she said.

"And do you think she might have had anything to do with the ruined food?" Sadie asked. She was still trying to tread carefully, but Helen drew herself up in surprise at what Sadie had thought was just an obvious conclusion.

"Well, I certainly never said *that*," Helen said. "I couldn't believe that she—I mean, despite everything, do you really think—"

Helen already seemed to be having trouble even completing the thought that Ginny Pearson might have something to do with the tricks against her husband. But before she could finish her sentence, Sadie's phone began to ring.

"Excuse me," Sadie said, fishing in her purse. "I'm sorry."

She extricated the phone from the jumble of her purse on the third ring, and quickly checked the caller ID: a recent picture of Theo, grinning as he held up an antique flag that they'd found together at a local estate sale.

"I need to take this," Sadie said apologetically, and answered the call.

"Grandma," Theo said. "Where are you?" He sounded breathless, as if he'd just run up to tell her some important news.

"I'm just visiting with Helen Morgan," Sadie said. "Where are you?"

"I'm at the library," Theo said. Although he couldn't see her, Sadie smiled, secretly proud that he could get so excited about historical research that he'd call her up as breathless as if he'd just run a race in track and field. "I've got something to show you. Something important. How soon can you get here?"

13

Kimama greeted Sadie with a warm grin as Sadie bustled through the doors of the Silver Peak Library a few minutes later.

"Welcome back," Kimama said. "You and your grandson are becoming some of my best customers."

"It's too bad libraries don't make money based on their customers," Theo said, loping up. He gave his grandmother a distracted kiss on the cheek, then caught her by the elbow and began to steer her toward a long table stacked with dusty antique volumes.

"Don't worry," Kimama called as they headed off toward his research. "I do this job to see the kind of enthusiasm to learn you two have. You can't buy that."

Sadie smiled back gratefully over her shoulder as her grandson guided her to the table and pulled a chair out for her to sit down. She looked over the volumes with a practiced eye. Since they had obviously been handled a great deal, both with love, and carelessly, during their tenure at the library, they probably wouldn't fetch much on the antique market for books and "paper"—documents and even photographs that hadn't been bound but still appeared quite often for sale along with more traditional books. But they were clearly antique: not Victorian, but from the first half of the twentieth century. They probably hadn't been luxury items at the time: if they had, they would have gilt edges and hand-marbled papers, and might even have been bound entirely in thick, exotic silk that likely wouldn't have survived their use as library volumes. But they were still designed with a solidity and a beauty that was rarely seen in books these days, when publishers had mostly given up on beautiful endpapers and edging, and replaced expensive foreign cloths with paper, or rough substitutes.

"So what do we have here?" Sadie asked.

But Theo didn't just want to tell her what he'd found, whatever that might be. He wanted to make sure she understood the work that had gone into finding it.

"Well," he said. "I came back here to go over the Silver Peak Register articles, to see if there was anything at all we might have missed, that might help us shed any light on the diary, now that we had all that new information from talking with Gavin. I went through every single one of them, again. But I didn't really find anything new. If anything, having all that extra information from Gavin only made me realize everything that hadn't gotten covered in those initial newspaper articles. I just wished someone else had been there asking different questions.

"So then I started to wonder…" His eyes lit up as he retold the story of his eureka moment. "If any other papers might have covered the story. So I did a general search for Colorado bank robberies during the months around the Silver Peak robbery, in 1937."

"Was it covered outside Silver Peak?" Sadie asked enthusiastically. "That's a wonderful idea. I suppose something this big might even have been carried in one of the Denver papers."

Theo shook his head, trying to hide his delight at a discovery even his quick-witted grandmother couldn't guess.

"Actually," he said. "It's even better than that. I found a bank robber."

"A bank robber?" Sadie said, leaning forward.

"Yes!" Theo said, flipping one of the old books open with a satisfying thunk. "There were over half a dozen other robberies in Colorado during that month, all credited to this man." He pointed to a grainy photograph of a man with piercing blue eyes that were shaded by a large black hat, a dark bandana tied around his neck.

"In 1937?" Sadie asked. "He hardly looks like the slick crooks who were famous back East around that time. They all dressed like gangsters in the movies, all suits and ties and crisp new shirts."

Theo shook his head. "I know he looks like he's from another time," he said. "That was actually part of his thing. He thought of himself as a descendant of those old desperados, like Billy the Kid and Jesse James. Some of those old bandits didn't like to think of themselves as criminals. They thought they were making a stand for freedom, escaping out into the Wild West as what Easterners thought of as civilization marched across the continent."

"Well, they certainly committed a lot of crimes, for men who weren't criminals," Sadie observed.

"I'm not saying they were right," Theo said. "I'm just telling you what they liked to think about themselves."

"And a lot of times those are two different things," Sadie observed.

"Right," Theo said cheerfully. "In any case, this guy styled himself as an old-time Wild West bank robber. And it sounds like it actually worked to his advantage in a lot of these robberies. He'd walk up to a teller and demand a bag of cash, wearing these old-time clothes, and they couldn't tell if they were dreaming, or going crazy. Then he'd fire at the ceiling, and they'd realize the gun was real. And by then, they were so confused that it looks like most of them just handed over the money without much argument."

"Did he do all his robberies during business hours?" Sadie asked. "Because that's not what we're looking at here in Silver Peak. It wouldn't fit his pattern."

"No," Theo said. "That was just a couple of them. Once they caught him, he confessed to several others. And they were all over the map. One of them, he got a hotel room next to the bank, then drilled through the wall by night. Another one, he apparently befriended one of the tellers, and they just had a couple of shots of whiskey together in the vault, and then walked out with everything that was still in there that night. It was a big deal at the time. I even found some articles about him in the *Silver Peak Sentinel*, when I went back and ran the search for his name."

"What is his name?" Sadie asked.

"Wes Winston," Theo said with a grin.

"With a name like that, you'd almost have to grow up to be a bank robber," Sadie said.

"Or a country singer," Theo said.

"It's a fine line," Sadie answered with her own grin. She pulled the book with Winston's photograph closer. "So what am I looking at here?"

"It's a collection of stories on famous criminals from the time," Theo said. "He was so notorious that I found mentions of him in several of the volumes, just here in the library. And then these are the mentions of him in the Denver paper. There's quite a bit online in a searchable database for the *Denver Post*, because it's still in business. But the tabloid at the time was the one that really had the details of the crimes. And they haven't been put online, because they went under in the 1970s. But Kimama found these bound copies for me."

"That's amazing work, Theo," Sadie said. "I couldn't have done better myself."

Theo beamed, then ducked his head to hide his pride. "So do you think he really could have had something to do with our robbery here in Silver Peak?" he asked.

"Much stranger things have happened," Sadie said. "And of course, I'd love to find an explanation for the robbery that wouldn't cast a shadow on the Morgan family. My only question is, with all of the robberies he committed during that time, would Winston have been able to pull off this one, in Silver Peak?"

"There's only one way to find that out," Theo said, flipping open the book of bound Denver papers. "Take a look at all the robberies."

"Can you tell me what the day the first of September fell on in 1937?" Sadie asked.

Theo flipped quickly to the date and consulted the masthead. "Friday," he said.

As he continued to pore through the pages of news articles, looking for mention of Wes Winston, Sadie pulled a piece of paper from her purse and improvised a calendar for September and October 1937, carefully marking the date of the Silver Peak Bank robbery, on October 6.

"It's a little hard to tell in real time," Theo mused. "Because some of the early robberies didn't get reported in Denver. They would have looked like they were just garden-variety robberies probably, at first. Not part of any big pattern or crime wave."

Sadie thought somewhat nervously of the two nasty pranks the Morgan campaign had suffered in the past week. She hoped the damage to the yard signs was the end of it, not the prelude to an entire spree of mischief to come.

"Here," Theo said. "I think this is the first one where they're pretty sure it's Winston." He read from the page. "Wild West Robber strikes again."

"What's the date?" Sadie asked.

"September 7," Theo told her.

Sadie marked it quickly on her improvised calendar as Theo scanned through the text of the article. "But they mention several others it may have been connected to. Apparently there was one in late August. And then a man fitting his description turned over another bank on September 2."

"Does it say where?" Sadie asked.

"Copper Creek," Theo told her. She noted it down.

"And where was this one?" Sadie asked.

"Thomas Pass," Theo said. "Do you know where that is?"

Sadie made another quick note for the September 7 robbery, then shook her head. "I don't," she said. "Some of these names may have disappeared. And some of the old towns may have disappeared. Colorado is full of ghost towns that died almost as quickly as a mine petered out. Or even when the dream of a mine died."

"Mom got me a book of Colorado ghost towns for Christmas last year," Theo said. "I want to go on a tour of them one day, but she's worried it'd be too far for me to drive, since I just learned."

Sadie looked at him, a twinkle in her eye. "Well," she said. "Maybe she'd feel differently if you were taking your grandmother along."

"Really?" Theo yelped. "That would be *awesome*. When do you—?"

Sadie cut him off with a nod at the book in his hands. "Let's find out what we can here before we start making new plans," she said.

Carefully, the two of them worked through the book of bound Denver papers, noting every robbery that was reported in September or October of 1937. When they finished, they had marked four other robberies: three in mid- to late September, and one in mid-October, about a week after the Silver Peak robbery.

"Well, none of these robberies rule out the possibility that Wes Winston could have broken into the Silver Peak Bank on October 6," Sadie said. "But there's so much space in the timeline that the problem is that he could have been pretty much anywhere else, instead."

"Wait," Theo said, and began to thumb through the pages again, into November. "I know I saw another article, after they caught him. And he confessed to those other ones I told you about. The ones they didn't know were his until they got him. Hang on, I just…" A few more pages rustled, and then Theo stabbed his finger at the page. "Here! I got it."

Wes Winston, according to the article Theo had just unearthed, had become a victim of his own notoriety. Just like Jesse James and Billy the Kid, and, more recently, Bonnie and Clyde, his exploits over the course of that fall of 1937 had earned him fame—and, despite his undeniable crimes, a certain number of fans, who saw

him as a man trying to make his way in a world that for many people no longer made sense, and acting with a freedom and bravado
that they perhaps wished that they had themselves. Ironically, it
had been one of these fans who spelled Winston's downfall. When
he walked into the Beck's Run bank in November 1937, with the
full intention of robbing it, he came face-to-face with a teller
who was, unbeknownst to him, one of his biggest fans, a young
woman whose imagination had been captured by the reports of
his exploits so fully that she believed he'd also earned her heart.
Despite the blue bandana he wore to hide the lower slice of his
face, Winston, with his out-of-date duds and his steely blue eyes,
was still instantly recognizable to her. So when he demanded that
she turn over all the cash in her drawer, she didn't wait for him
to fire into the art-deco ceiling, which the paper noted was richly
decorated with a mural of famous cowboys and lawmen riding
their horses through the sky. Instead, she leapt across the counter
and insisted that he take her with him back to what she referred to
as his "hideout," where she was bound and determined to join in
him a life of crime—and romance.

Unfortunately, she neglected to bring the contents of her
drawer with her. And while Winston attempted to negotiate, aim-
ing to convince her to retrieve the thousands of dollars he had
come to make off with, without committing himself with any rash
promises, the police, alerted by a secret bell the bank owner had
recently installed given the general panic created by Winston's
activities over the past few months, burst in and arrested Winston,
who, seeking leniency through cooperation with the authorities,
promptly confessed to half a dozen other crimes no one had yet
linked him to. There followed a list, which Theo read out to her,

including the hotel wall-breakthrough, and a bank that Winston had completely cleaned out with uncharacteristic lack of drama by pretending to be a representative of the company that built the bank's safe, there to perform a routine inspection to make sure that all of its components were in good working order and up to date. He'd simply carried in two giant bags of "tools" with him, then left the rocks they contained in place of the gold and notes he carried out in the bag.

When Sadie had finished noting down each of Winston's further confessions, and their location, on her quickly drawn calendar, almost all the days in September and October 1937 were accounted for, if Winston's confessions were to be believed.

"Well, that's a bit more conclusive as a timeline," Sadie said.

"But look at this, Grandma," Theo said, pointing to an empty window that still remained in early October. Even with all the information they'd just gathered, they still had no clue where Winston had been between October 3 and October 8, 1937. "That's exactly when the Silver Peak robbery happened."

"You're right," Sadie said, scanning between the September and October calendars. "And look at this. It's the largest span of time in those two months that he goes without a robbery. From the time his spree begins, he's going into another bank every two or three days. But here, he goes almost a week without a robbery."

"If he really went without a robbery for all those days," Theo said.

Sadie and Theo's eyes locked. Then both of them broke out into matching grins. After a minute, Sadie collected herself. "We can't be certain of anything," she said. "This is only circumstantial evidence, at best. And circumstantial evidence that's almost eighty years old. We haven't proved anything."

"But it sure is interesting, at least," Theo said. "Isn't it?"

Sadie nodded, her critical mind going to work now that they'd found the tantalizing possibility that Wes Winston could be the culprit of the Silver Peak Bank robbery, as well. Her finger trailed down to the location of his October 2 robbery, then drifted over to the one on October 8. "I know where Stevens Lake is," she said, looking back at the location of the October 2 robbery. "It's just a half hour outside Denver, and it's still a popular resort town. But I've never heard of Tin Mile before. Have you?"

"Let me just look it up on my phone," Theo said, tapping the name into his map app. A moment later, he looked up, slightly confused. "It says there's no Tin Mile in Colorado," he said.

"Well, this paper certainly thought there was one in 1937," Sadie said.

"Maybe it's one of those towns that disappeared," Theo reasoned. "It does sound like a mining town. Tin Mile."

Sadie nodded.

"Wait, wait," Theo said, shuffling through the books on the table. "I've got something here…" He pushed another book out of the way. "Kimama brought it over. I didn't understand why she'd think I'd need something like that. But I guess maybe she understood more about what I'd need than I did."

"That's a good librarian's job," Sadie said.

A moment later, Theo unearthed a large maroon volume, stamped in black with the title *Colorado Maps and Census 1935*. He flipped through a set of beautifully hand-colored pink, green, and yellow maps, to an index at the back. "Here it is!" he said. "Tin Mile."

"Where is it?"Sadie asked.

Theo was already flipping feverishly to the page number indicated in the index. He slowed, flipped back a few pages, then scanned the snaky lines of mountains and rivers and the tiny dots of towns on a green-tinted map. A moment later, his finger landed on one of the dots, just below a handful of letters that read, "Tin Mile." "Here," he said.

"And where is that?" Sadie asked, trying to get her bearings on the map. The census maps were so detailed that she couldn't find a major city to reckon by. But after a minute, down in the corner, she did catch sight of something familiar. "Look at this," she breathed.

Theo looked to where she had pointed: Silver Peak. "How far away is it?" he asked.

"Check the scale," Sadie told him.

Theo checked the scale at the bottom of the map, using the side of his phone as a ruler. "The phone's about ten miles..." he said.

"...which makes Tin Mile just about twenty miles from Silver Peak," Sadie finished for him.

"And Denver would be up here," Theo said, pointing up, off the map. "So Silver Peak wasn't just in the neighborhood of Tin Mile. It was on the way. It almost seems like Wes Winston would have *had* to hit it, if he was keeping up his past pattern."

"Well, there are several other towns between Denver and Tin Mile," Sadie pointed out.

"But did they have a robbery *that same week*?" Theo asked.

"Well, that's an interesting question," Sadie said. "With all the hullabaloo around Winston, you'd think that he might have come under suspicion for this robbery too. At least when the big-city investigators got to town."

"Sure," Theo said. "But remember what your calendar looked like before we read the article about Winston's confession. It was a lot harder to get a sense of his whereabouts when we were just working from the real-time reports."

"That's true," Sadie reasoned. "And by the time he confessed, the investigators likely weren't trying to tie him to any further crimes. After all, he'd just confessed to half a dozen more than they'd even suspected him of."

"So if he chose not to tell them about Silver Peak, nobody would have gone looking to connect him. Especially with so many suspects right here at home," Theo said.

"The question is," Sadie mused, "if Wes Winston robbed the Silver Peak Bank, why wouldn't he have confessed to that robbery, when he confessed to all the others?"

14

Before Theo could answer, Sadie glanced at her watch.

"Oh my goodness," she said. "I almost forgot. This afternoon is the first debate between Edwin and James. I promised I'd be there."

"When is it?" Theo asked.

"Five minutes ago," Sadie said, sweeping all the possessions that had crept out onto the library table from her bag back into it.

Luckily, the town hall where the debates were held was only a short walk from the library. Sadie found her way into a spot in the back row just a few minutes later. The place was packed, with some people even standing in the back. And the sparring between Edwin and James was lively. Edwin took a strong stance for preserving the history of Silver Peak, and the pristine natural environment that surrounded it. And while James couldn't exactly argue with that, he made a strong case for progress, that Silver Peak had much more to offer than simply looking to its past, and that sometimes moving into the future required change that might seem unfamiliar, or even uncomfortable in the present, but would pay big dividends in the long run.

Sadie was thinking with relief how good it was to see the campaign move back to the essentials that it had always been about, rather than the tabloid-like distractions of unfounded suspicions from the old bank robbery, or the strange events that had dogged the Morgan campaign in the past few days. And in the first few minutes of the question-and-answer period, when Silver Peak's citizens got to raise their own concerns directly with the candidates, it seemed like the population of Silver Peak also agreed. The initial questions were polite and issue-oriented, asking Edwin how he'd feel about making improvements to some of the trails outside town, which Edwin favored, and asking James what limits he would put on growth in Silver Peak, to maintain its identity in the face of progress.

But then a gentleman Sadie didn't recognize took the microphone from Jesse Wilson. He started out with a respectful nod to both of the candidates, but then he turned to James. "This is a question for Mr. Morgan," he said. "I don't think I'm the only one who's heard a lot of talk about the old robbery at the Silver Peak Bank in the past week. I'm just wondering if you've got any comment you'd like to make on that."

It didn't seem to be a hostile question, but Sadie fumed a bit internally, wondering what in the world the gentleman could think the old robbery had to do with the present-day election. And she could see the discomfort spring into James's eyes immediately as he scanned the room, looking for the crowd reaction. But as Sadie scanned the crowd along with him, it was clear that the man with the microphone wasn't the only one with a similar question. He was just the one who had voiced it. All around the room, eyes were fastened on James, with far more interest than they had been when the conversation had focused on hiking trails and growth limits.

Sadie felt a little wash of sympathy for James. After her conversations with Helen Morgan, Sadie suspected that this was pretty close to a living nightmare for him. He'd spent a good part of his life, it sounded like, trying to erase the memory of the robbery from the mind of the town—or at least distance himself from it. But now, decades later, it had still come up. And now he needed to formulate some kind of answer, in front of the whole town.

As uncomfortable as he was, James didn't waver under the pressure. After his quick survey of the crowd, he began to lean toward his own microphone to speak. But before he opened his mouth, Edwin, from his podium, spoke into his own microphone. "I think I'd like to speak to that," he said. "If that's all right with you, James."

James lifted his head, gave Edwin a grateful glance, and nodded.

Edwin placed both his hands firmly on either side of the podium. Silver Peak politics tended to be informal, with not much speechifying. But now Edwin looked for all the world like a judge, handing down his final determination on a weighty case. And he spoke with all a judge's gravitas and command. "With all respect to you, sir," he said, addressing the gentleman who had asked the question, "I can't think of an issue that's less relevant to today's campaign. I've heard some of this talk around town, and I'll admit it's interesting talk. My good friend Sadie Speers runs the Antique Mine in town, and I enjoy hearing her talk about the history of Silver Peak as much as anyone here, I guess. And I understand that that was a time in Silver Peak's history that still touches a lot of us today. But I want to say, once and for all, that it doesn't have anything to do with this campaign. All of those events happened decades ago, before James and I were even born. Neither of us had anything to do with them. So you might find that old mystery intriguing. That's your right. And I'll admit, I find it intriguing too. But the decisions you make about the future mayor of Silver Peak shouldn't have anything to do with that old story. They should have to do with what kind of men you believe James and I are, and what kinds of things you believe we'll do if you give either of us the honor of being your mayor. I know that may not answer your question, sir, but that's all I have to say on the topic. Unless you'd like to add anything, James?"

James shook his head.

"Thank you," the gentleman said, somewhat chastened, as he turned away from the microphone.

Around the room, a few people broke into applause, but as Sadie glanced from face to face, she could see that the crowd wasn't really satisfied. What Edwin had said was absolutely right, and it would be hard for anyone to argue otherwise. But he was fighting a tough battle. He had right on his side, but the town gossip about the old bank robbery was a story with no ending. There wasn't anything in the world that was better food for the human imagination. And until someone came up with the truth, Sadie knew, the rumor mill in the town would run and run, spitting out its own wild tales to fill in the void.

After a few more questions, the debate drew to a close, and people began to rise from their seats, heading out onto the street. Sadie stooped to collect her own things, and when she straightened up, she caught sight of Ginny Pearson, the county clerk who had been disappointed in her dealings with James at the bank.

Other people in the crowd were chatting happily, or discussing what they'd heard, but Ginny charged toward the door with a look of determination.

Sadie stepped into her way just before she managed to escape. She and Ginny weren't great friends, but they knew each other reasonably well, and Ginny wouldn't pass her by without speaking if Sadie greeted her. "Ginny," Sadie said with a friendly smile. "Good to see you. What did you think of the debate?"

Ginny clearly wasn't interested in talking, but Sadie was correct that she wouldn't be impolite enough to brush Sadie off. "It was…interesting," she said.

"I thought James spoke well," Sadie prodded.

"I'm not sure anyone in town would argue that with you," Ginny said. "It sounds to me like the Morgan family have always been big talkers."

"Well, I think James has done a remarkable job with the bank for all these years," Sadie said, trying to keep Ginny on the topic, despite her tight-lipped responses.

"Everyone's welcome to their own opinion," Ginny said. "That's democracy."

The crowd was moving inexorably toward the doors in the back of the hall, drawing Sadie and Ginny with it.

Sadie thought for a moment. She would have loved to have had time to proceed with more tact, but if she waited too much longer, she was going to lose the chance to talk with Ginny at all. "I just feel so awful about what happened," she said. "With James's campaign signs."

She watched Ginny closely for any sign that she had struck a nerve mentioning the sabotage, but Ginny glanced at her with what seemed to be surprise, and genuine ignorance. "What do you mean?" she asked.

"Oh, I guess there was some trouble about James's campaign signs," Sadie said. "They were all destroyed last night."

"Destroyed?" Ginny repeated, a note of what seemed to be actual indignation in her voice. "How?"

Sadie nodded. "Someone threw paint all over them. A few of them are still legible, but they couldn't be used in people's yards in the condition they're in."

Ginny's brows drew together. "Now who in the world would want to do a thing like that?" she asked.

Sadie watched her carefully, but didn't answer. If Ginny had anything to do with it, or with the ruined barbecue, Sadie wanted to give her time to crack. But before either of them could say anything else, another push of the crowd brought one of Ginny's friends within range.

"Ginny!" she cried. "There you are. I was just looking for you. You still need that ride home?"

"I think I needed it about ten minutes ago," Ginny joked, and plowed away from Sadie, through the crowd, to meet up with the other woman.

A few people away, Sadie saw Helen Morgan drifting through the crowd, as well. She caught Helen's eyes and smiled. Helen returned the smile briefly, but then ducked her head as she went out the door. Sadie could only imagine what it must have been like for Helen to have to watch her husband struggle to face the stain on the family name that he'd been trying to erase for their entire marriage.

As Helen slipped out the door with the crowd, someone bumped into Sadie from behind. She turned her head to see Jesse Wilson, Edwin's campaign manager.

"Jesse," she said.

"Oh, Mrs. Speers," Jesse said, "I'm so sorry."

"How did you think the debate went?" Sadie asked.

The fact that they were in a large crowd that had gathered to hear his candidate debate seemed to be the furthest thing from Jesse's mind. "The debate?" he said, as if dragging up a memory of something that had happened long in the distant past. "It was all right," he said. "I think it went fine."

"I really appreciated what Edwin had to say about the old robbery," Sadie said. "But I'm curious what your thoughts were, as his campaign manager."

Jesse's thoughts, whatever they were, were clearly elsewhere. He glanced nervously toward the door. "It was fine," he repeated, as if he were a recording that had gotten stuck on some kind of loop. "I think he did fine."

"Am I keeping you from something?" Sadie said, nodding out the door. "Please, don't let me."

For the first time, Jesse seemed to really see her for a moment. His eyes locked with hers. "I'm sorry, Mrs. Speers," he said. "It's just I'm working on something." He hesitated. "Something big. I guess I'm a bit distracted."

"For Edwin's campaign?" Sadie asked.

Jesse nodded.

"Well, I'm sure I'd love to hear about it," Sadie said. She felt a little twinge of something as she said this. She'd asked Jesse as if she had some kind of right to know the inner workings of Edwin's campaign. But what right did she really have? Edwin had been asking and asking her to be his lady friend; and so far she had refused. If she accepted him, Jesse, and everybody else in town, would expect her to know the kind of details she was asking Jesse for now. Was that what she wanted? Or was she just curious? After all, Edwin had asked her to look into Jesse's involvement with the campaign, whether they ever became more than friends or not.

But despite all the conflicting ideas that swirled through Sadie's head at the thought of Edwin, Jesse wasn't talking. "I'm sorry," he said. "It's private campaign business. I really have to go."

"Of course, of course," Sadie said with a smile. But as he pushed his way past her through the crowd, she followed after him, determined not to lose him—and perhaps to find out whatever this private campaign business was by some means other than simply asking him.

She poured out with the rest of the crowd onto the street just a few moments after Jesse did, but in the confusion that surrounded the reshuffling of the crowd after it had passed the bottleneck of the door, she lost sight of him. Sadie never minded being short in most situations: she liked to think that she more than made up for her small stature in her strength of spirit. And sometimes it was good to be small—when she didn't want to be noticed, sometimes she thought it helped her slip from place to place without attracting too much attention. And sometimes it caused people to underestimate her in ways that proved useful: nobody could believe, for instance, that such a sweet little lady would have as sharp an eye as she did for antiques, or hang on so tenaciously for a good bargain. And by the time they realized what a strong spirit was hidden in her small frame, it was often too late.

But it was infuriating to be a small person in a big crowd—especially if you were trying not to lose sight of someone. Jesse had been there just a moment before, right ahead of her, but now she was lost in sea of backs and shoulders, with very few distinguishing features to tell one from another.

Then, suddenly, a bang like a nearby thunderclap split the air—not from high above, where even low thunder usually rumbled, but terrifyingly close, right on the ground. Sparks and even some small tongues of flame shot up over the heads of the crowd from something in the street. All around Sadie, the individual members of the crowd froze. Then a chatter of alarm rose and the crowd parted, almost as if according to some prearranged pattern, revealing a white sedan with smoke billowing from its trunk. Jesse Wilson stood nearby, regarding the scene with something that might have been shock but looked suspiciously like glee. For a moment, Sadie couldn't understand why Jesse should take any pleasure in the car trouble of some random member of the debate audience. But then she saw Helen Morgan standing beside the car, one hand still on the passenger-side door, a look of shock on her face as the crowd stared back at her. And Sadie realized: this wasn't any random car. It was James and Helen Morgan's. And this was likely yet another act of campaign sabotage.

As Sadie pressed through the ring of people to get a better view, a burly man in a flannel shirt approached the rear of the car.

"Stand back!" someone shouted. "Wait for the police."

"I'm a volunteer fireman," the man said, waving the warning away.

The chatter of the crowd dropped to almost nothing as he approached the car. By this time, almost all the smoke had entirely blown away. He peered into the soot around the trunk. Then he stepped back, shaking his head.

"It's nothing serious, folks," he said, holding his hands up.

"Looks pretty serious to me!" someone shouted.

The man in the flannel shook his head. "Nope," he said. "It's nothing but a bunch of Roman candles. It singed the paint job pretty good." He thumped the trunk, which gave a satisfying ring. "But it's sound. It'll probably even get you home tonight, ma'am," he said, giving Helen a friendly wink.

At this, James pushed his way through the crowd and put his arm around Helen. "Honey," Sadie heard him say quietly. "Are you all right?"

Helen nodded and shrank against him. Sadie saw James's jaw tighten.

"The ruined barbecue was one thing," Sadie heard someone mutter behind her. "But now this? I wouldn't have expected this kind of thing out of Edwin Marshall."

"Now, you don't know Edwin Marshall had anything to do with this," another voice said.

"Well, who else but Edwin Marshall has anything to gain from it?" the first voice asked.

Sadie glanced around the crowd, looking for another glimpse of Jesse Wilson, but he had already vanished.

15

―――

"They're pretty good," Theo said, looking up at Spike Harris and his band, who were tearing through a rendition of one of Sadie's favorites of Spike's: an original he wrote about a wacky carnival family, and all their adventures.

Sadie glanced up at the stage. As she did, she caught Spike looking down at Alice, but she was busy arguing with Sara.

"French fries and key lime pie is not dinner," she was saying. "French fries and a burger is dinner. A burger and key lime pie might possibly be dinner."

"But Mom," Sara said. "I really want the fries. And I really want the pie. And you said we could only spend ten dollars each. So I can't get them both *and* a burger."

"Then you have the opportunity to learn a very interesting lesson about life tonight too," Alice said.

"You don't always get what you want," Sara said, settling back into her chair with her arms crossed.

Alice nodded encouragingly. "You've got it."

"I already knew that," Sara said. "That's pretty much all you learn as a kid."

"It's good practice for being an adult," Alice said, as the waiter came up to the table.

The family ordered burgers and fries all around, until the waiter got to Sadie. "I'll have the burger and fries," she said. "And a slice of key lime pie."

Sara's eyes lit up. Alice gave her mother a sharp glance.

"Good choice, ma'am," the waiter said. "That's one of my favorites. I hate to admit it, but I had a slice of it for dinner."

Sara gave her mother a triumphant look as he walked off to put their orders in the system. "*He* thinks it's dinner," she said.

"His mother obviously isn't here to look after him," Alice retorted. Then she turned on her mom. "You don't always have to get her everything she wants," she said.

"Who said anything about Sara?" Sadie said. "The pie just sounded good to me, that's all."

As she was speaking, she noticed a flurry of activity at the door. Edwin had just arrived, wearing a pair of neat jeans and a slightly newer shirt than she was used to seeing on him. His hair was carefully combed back, and his face looked freshly shaven. She felt a little thrill of excitement as he looked around the room for her, and an even deeper one when he caught her eye and smiled.

Then she felt a twinge of worry. How would he react to the fact that her family was there with her too?

She watched him closely as he took in the situation. His expression did change slightly when he caught sight of Alice and Theo and Sara at her table, but his smile didn't fade. And by the time he reached the table, it was just as bright as ever.

He pulled up a chair from one of the nearby clusters, and set it down beside Sadie. "Is this seat taken?" he asked.

Alice looked up in surprise.

"Hi, Mr. Marshall," Theo said. Sara gave Edwin a shy smile.

"Edwin," Alice said. "What a nice surprise."

"A surprise, huh?" he said, with a sidelong glance at Sadie.

Alice glanced at her mother, but Sadie was suddenly too nervous to say anything.

"Oh," Edwin said, covering for her, "Sadie just mentioned to me that she was coming to this show, so I thought I might come out, too, and see what it's all about."

"They're really good," Theo told him. "This next song's about a runaway train. You can kind of hear the train tracks in the drum, and the engine in the banjo. You hear that?"

Edwin leaned forward, his brows knitting in concentration. "You know, I think I do," he said.

Theo beamed.

The family enjoyed the rest of the set, with Edwin joking and laughing along with the rest of them. Occasionally he put his hand on the back of Sadie's chair, not touching her shoulders, just there. But Sadie could still feel the protective circle of it. And every time he shifted so that his arm was anywhere else, she found she couldn't wait until he reached around to lay his arm over the back of her chair again.

Finally Spike's set wound down.

Almost before the last note stopped ringing, he bounded down from the stage to say hello to Alice.

"Thanks for coming!" he said. "It's so great to have you here. I love seeing all these familiar faces out in the crowd." But the way his eyes stayed on Alice's face, it was clear who he really meant when he said this.

Alice was already on her feet, corralling Theo and Sara toward the door. "Yeah, it was nice," she said. "Good job. Okay, Mom, I think we need to go now. Don't want them up too late."

"I'll see you soon," Sadie said with a wave.

"Bye!" Spike shouted as they retreated toward the door.

Edwin glanced at Sadie as Spike turned back and began to unplug his guitar and roll up the thick music cables.

"What do you say?" he said. "Do you want to stay for the next set?"

"Oh," Sadie said, springing out of her own seat, suddenly very aware that she was out in public on something that looked very much like a date with Edwin Marshall, "I wish I could. I just think I probably need to get back now too."

"Like mother, like daughter," Edwin said wryly, with a glance at Spike.

Sadie felt a little pang. Was she just as oblivious to Edwin's attempts to win her heart as Alice was to Spike's? Then she felt a little offended. She had at least agreed to go on Edwin's date. Maybe he was right. He shouldn't ask for so much from her all at once.

"Can I at least walk you to your car?" Edwin said as Sadie collected the bright scarf she had brought with her to stay warm in case the air-conditioning was too high during the concert.

"That would be nice," she agreed.

They walked back to Sadie's car in almost perfect silence. A few times, their hands brushed against one another, and Sadie thought for a minute that Edwin might try to take her hand. She didn't know how she'd feel about that. It wouldn't be out of line, of course. And even if she let him, it wouldn't have to mean they were getting serious.

But he took her to her car without ever reaching for it.

At her car, he stared into her eyes. Many times before, she'd avoided his searching gaze, but now she stared back herself. She didn't know what she was looking for. Or if she was looking for anything at all. All she knew was that she didn't want to look away.

"Sadie Speers," Edwin said.

Sadie took a quick involuntary breath.

He grinned in the moonlight and executed a little formal bow.

"Thank you for going out on a date with me."

Then, without waiting for her answer, he strode off into the night, leaving her as breathless as if he'd actually kissed her good night.

16

——

Sadie smiled down at Hank's wriggling gold body and bright brown eyes as the golden retriever gamboled at her feet, delighted to see her reaching for the door, which he knew meant they were only moments away from embarking on their morning walk.

"I think I might be just as excited as you are this morning, Hank," Sadie said. "I'm sorry we had to miss the other day."

She open the door and swung it wide, breathing in the fresh smell of a Colorado autumn morning. In an instant, Hank was off like a shot, a streak of golden fur blazing across the yard, up toward the trails that the two of them usually enjoyed together each morning.

Lord, Sadie prayed. *Thank You for this morning. Thank You for Hank. Thank You for these beautiful mountains. Thank You that I can walk.* Sometimes she spent a good chunk of her hikes with Hank just thanking God for all the good things He had placed in her life. If she tacked on her thanks at the end, after giving God a laundry list of her requests, it always seemed too much like an afterthought to her. And she found that, when she began with thanks, somehow the list of things she thought she needed had a way of shrinking. Often, she even discovered in the course of giving thanks that many of the things she thought she needed, she already had. She'd even gotten in the habit of thanking God for some of her problems or worries. And when she did that, she often found that they began to appear in a new light. Of course, some things in life were just hard. But when she thanked God for everything, she sometimes began to see God's gift, even amidst those hard things.

Thank You for Edwin, she prayed. Recently, Edwin had seemed like more of a worry. But it was good for her to remember that he had always felt like one of God's gifts to her. *Thank You for James and Helen Morgan. Thank You for Theo and Sara. Thank You for this election.* Despite all the upheaval it had caused, it was good to remember that free elections weren't a given everywhere in the world. This might not be the kind of election Silver Peak was used to having. But it was a privilege to get to be a part of any election. And Sadie was glad to remember that. *Thank You for the old bank robbery.* Sadie paused for a moment. To thank God for the bank robbery, even though it had been such a big part of her life recently, almost seemed like nonsense. After all, it had hurt so many people. What could there possibly be to thank God for in that? *I'm not sure what that even means, Lord,* she prayed. *But I'm trying to understand how to give thanks to You in all things, as the Bible says. So show me if there's anything to be grateful for about that old robbery.*

By now, she was deep into a trail, Hank trotting along happily in front of her. It took her a moment to recognize the sound of her cell phone when it began to ring. She carried the phone with her for safety—even with Hank along for protection and companionship, it didn't make any sense to go out wandering in the Colorado wilderness without some way to get in touch with civilization if she needed any kind of help. But it always surprised her to hear the ring of the phone out in the pristine air, competing for her attention with the sound of the wind in the trees or the birds welcoming the morning sun.

A moment later, she had pulled it from her pocket, and checked the caller ID to discover it was Theo on the line. She answered. "Hello, honey," she said. "How are you doing? You're certainly out of bed early."

"I've been looking into this Wes Winston character," Theo said, sounding for all the world like a gumshoe in an old movie. Sadie was glad that he wasn't there to see her expression. She wasn't sure she could have successfully suppressed the smile that now spread over her features.

"Oh?" she said. "And what have you found out?"

"Well," Theo said, losing track of his gumshoe persona as he gave in to his native youthful excitement, "I finished looking through all the articles yesterday, but this morning I got up and got on my computer, and I thought, I wonder what they've got about him, just on the Internet."

"That's a good question," Sadie said.

"And they actually have plenty about him," Theo said. "There's all kinds of information out there about Wild West bandits, and he shows up in a lot of it, even though he lived much later than most of the Wild West bank robbers. In fact, many of the sites don't seem to realize that his dates are decades after the people they're lumping him in with. Most of this stuff on the Internet isn't really high quality, and it seems to get recycled."

"That's been my experience too," Sadie said.

"But there is some good stuff mixed in there," Theo said. "So I kept on looking. And I kept on seeing one name over and over. Even when the articles or posts weren't very good, they kept referring to this one guy. Eben Warren. They were always giving him credit for this fact or that about Winston. Like he was some kind of expert. So I decided to look him up. And guess what?"

"What?" Sadie asked. She had been game up to this point, but now she was actually almost as excited as Theo was himself. It hadn't occurred to her that Wes Winston might have been an important enough figure to have experts devoted to his life. But if any expert had studied Wes Winston, he might be a gold mine of information, not just about Winston, but about the gaps in the history of Silver Peak that were currently causing such consternation in town.

"He's written a book!" Theo crowed. "A whole book, about Wes Winston."

"That's wonderful," Sadie said. "Have you been to the library yet? Even if they don't have a copy, I'm sure Kimama can order us one."

"Well, that's the thing," Theo said.

"What's that?" Sadie asked.

"It's not out yet," Theo told her. "It won't come out until August."

Sadie calculated. That was months away.

"But listen to this," Theo said. "I read everything I could get my hands on about it. And it promises new revelations about Winston's life."

"Well, that might be anything," Sadie said, trying to let him down gently. She knew all too well the big claims that antique sellers could make about things when they wanted to make a sale. And booksellers weren't any different. Everyone just wanted to get people interested in their products. That naturally led to a bit of exaggeration. So a lot of times the big revelations they promised didn't seem quite as big once they'd been revealed.

"No, no," Theo said. "Let me read it to you…" There was a series of clicks, presumably as Theo was clicking back through the Web pages he'd been browsing to find the relevant text. "*Warren's book reveals never-before-published details about the crime spree that Winston embarked on in the fall of 1937, and fills in gaps in the history of that time that until now have been lost in the mists of time.*"

"*Hmm*," Sadie said.

"That's exactly what we're looking for, isn't it?" Theo asked. "And we built our own timeline. The only real gap in it is the one around the Silver Peak robbery. So that must be what they're talking about there. Don't you think?"

"It certainly sounds like it might be," Sadie mused. "I guess we'll have to read the book to find out. It's a shame that we won't be able to get a copy yet for months."

"Well," Theo said, "the mystery hasn't been solved for this long. I guess it won't hurt us to wait a little while longer."

Normally Sadie would have been delighted with these signs of maturity and patience in her teenage grandson. They were the signature marks of a true antiquer: somebody who was willing to be patient until they found just the right thing. But it also boded well for the kind of man she hoped Theo would turn out to be— someone who knew how to search for a good thing, even if that sometimes meant waiting—in all areas of his life. But today, she was the impatient one. It was all well and good to wait for a book to come out if the historical question at hand was just a matter of curiosity. But the questions about Silver Peak this new book on Wes Winston might answer was causing real hurt for the Morgan family—and seemed to be becoming a flashpoint issue in the upcoming election. If Eben Warren had answers, they needed to get them well before his book came out.

"You're probably right," Sadie told Theo. "I'm very impressed with your skills as a researcher."

"Thanks, Grandma!" Theo said cheerfully. "I'll call you if I find out anything else."

Sadie ended the connection and replaced the phone in her pocket. Then, with a quick whistle, she called Hank back from exploring what he seemed to find an extremely interesting stand of mountain grass. When he loped up to her, she gave him an affectionate scratch behind the ears. "Sorry to cut this walk short, buddy," she said. "But I've got something I need to check out back home."

Hank looked up at her with a mixture of sorrow, betrayal, and hope that she might change her mind.

"I guess that's the original hangdog expression you're giving me," Sadie told him cheerfully. "But I'll make it up to you another day. And you've still got the whole rest of the way home to explore. Go on." She gestured ahead, toward the path that led back to her home.

Hank immediately seemed to forget all his worries, and bounded off down the path in the other direction.

Lord, Sadie prayed, *teach me to be more like Hank. I want to follow You with the same joy and trust Hank has as he follows me.*

When they got back to the house, as soon as Sadie let Hank in, she went to her own computer. As the screen woke up, she selected a search engine, and typed in "Eben Warren."

As Theo had said, pages of information came up, most of them articles linked with Wes Winston. Sadie tried the hyperlink on one of the articles that linked the author's name to an e-mail address, but when it loaded, a warning came up, noting that that e-mail account had since been closed. It was a university account, so Sadie suspected that he had moved on from one academic appointment to another one, perhaps recently. But the enduring popularity of Warren's articles on Winston, and the number of times they'd been posted and reposted, kept his current employer from coming up, at least in the first several pages of search results.

"*Hmm*," she mused out loud. "Where are you now?"

She tried the search again, this time with the current year in the search. This time, a faculty listing showed up in the first few results, at a university in Denver, along with a picture of a middle-aged, sandy-haired man with round, wire-rimmed spectacles and a friendly although somewhat vague smile. An e-mail was listed. But so was a university phone number, and Warren's extension.

Time was of the essence, Sadie reminded herself. The sooner they could get the facts on Winston, the sooner they might be able to lay all the rumors about the Morgan family to rest. But just as much as her desire to set the record straight, she was also simply curious. She reached for her phone.

Her heart jumped a bit at the first ring, but after the second and third, it began to sink. After the fourth, a voice-mail message kicked in, short and sweet: "You've reached Eben Warren. Please leave a message."

"Hello, Professor Warren," Sadie began, thinking fast. She was sure he was busy, and sharing his research wasn't part of his job. If she couldn't pique his interest in this message, it would be easy for him to ignore it—and ignore any of her future calls. But, she realized, she didn't just want something from him. She had something to offer. If she and Theo were anywhere near correct in their suspicions about Wes Winston and the Silver Peak robbery, she could be providing Warren with yet another new revelation for his upcoming book. "I'm an antique dealer, and I've recently run across some materials that I think might be of interest to you as a Wes Winston scholar. I'd be delighted to talk with you at your earliest possible convenience." She left her number, along with a friendly good-bye, and hung up.

Lord, that's the best I can do, she said. *I leave it in Your hands.*

On the screen, her eye caught the tab for one of her favorite Web sites: *the Chatterbox,* Silver Peak's local news blog. When she clicked on it, a full-size picture of James Morgan's car, with smoke billowing from the rear, came up, covering almost the entire page, with big scare letters that read "Election BOMB?" It was splashy treatment, even for a blog that had been known to treat a garden sale with all the hoopla of a royal coronation. Sadie sighed. She had to admit that it was pretty big news in a town like Silver Peak when someone started tampering with an election. But she knew Edwin wouldn't be happy with the way the blog was blowing it out of proportion. And she hoped that the rest of the town wasn't swept up into the hysteria of the writer of the blog.

She closed the *Chatterbox* window, revealing the university Web site still open below it. Idly, she let her cursor drift across Warren's profile. Along with his e-mail and phone number, it also listed his office hours.

Sadie sighed. If he never responded to her phone call, she supposed, as a last resort, she could actually drive over to Denver and
catch him while he was available in his office.

The thought of Denver triggered something else in her mind,
though. Gavin had mentioned that the Hales had departed for an
opportunity in Denver shortly after the robbery. And Denver was
where Theo had gone to the tag sale and found the diary that had
started it all. She and Theo had done a thorough search for Hales
still living in Silver Peak at the library. But they hadn't searched
for Hales who might have moved elsewhere. What if members of
the Hale family were still living in Denver? Sadie's heart leapt,
then skipped a beat at her next thought: what if Janie Hale was still
alive? She might even be able to answer some of their outstanding
questions about the robbery herself.

Quickly, Sadie typed "Janie Hale" and "Denver" into the
search engine.

With a little pang, she read the first search result that came up:
an obituary in a Denver paper, from about five years earlier. She'd
spent so much time with the diary, and investigating the particu-
lars of Janie's life in Silver Peak, that Sadie felt almost as if she knew
her, so she read through the obituary almost hoping against hope
that it was the wrong Janie Hale, as if she was receiving news of
the death of an acquaintance or friend. But all of the details lined
up with what Sadie already knew of Janie. She was the right age,
and when she first moved to Denver, she had taken work initially
in a bank, although Sadie was pleased to see that Janie appeared
to have eventually taken a chance on opening her own business,
a small bakery in one of Denver's eclectic neighborhoods. Fur-
thermore, all the names of this Janie's relatives matched up: she

had survived Ben by about twenty years, but the obituary noted that she herself had been survived by her two children, Nathan, who worked with agricultural products in Europe, and Agatha, who still hailed from Denver. She had married someone named Jerry Adams, and taken his name.

Sadie substituted Jerry and Agatha Adams for Janie Hale in the search engine. After sifting through a half a page of results, she found an address and phone number appeared for J. and A. Adams, in a part of Denver that was quite close to the neighborhood in which Janie had once run her bakery. Sadie picked up her phone again and dialed. If Jerry and Agatha were still working jobs with daytime hours, which was likely, she didn't expect that they'd be at home. But in this case, it would probably be good for her to leave them a message, so that she wouldn't be a complete stranger the next time she called. And just as she suspected, a message kicked in after the first two rings. "You've reached the Adams family," a booming baritone voice intoned. "Leave us a message. We'll do our best to get back to you."

Sadie smiled at the friendly greeting. "Hello," she said. "This is Sadie Speers. I'm doing some research on the history of Silver Peak, where your mother has roots, and I've recently run across some papers that concern her. I'd love to share them with you, and also to talk with you, if you'd be at all interested." She left her number, then ended the call with a sense of satisfaction. Maybe not everybody would be intrigued to learn more about their mother's history, but most people, she knew, would be. The next time she tried, she was almost certain that Agatha would be willing to speak with her. And who knew? Maybe Agatha would even call her back.

17

THE CHIME OVER THE DOOR OF THE ANTIQUE MINE GAVE A MERRY ring. Sadie looked up with the welcoming smile she always tried to give any customer, grateful for the break in her own thoughts, which had been turning Hales, and Winstons, and Morgans, over and over, without seeming to get anywhere.

But she quickly realized the tall, handsome figure in the door wasn't just any customer. As she recognized Edwin, her smile widened so much that she dropped her gaze to the paperwork she had been absently going over on the counter before her, feeling a little abashed. After a moment, however, she collected herself and looked up as Edwin approached the counter.

"Well, this seems to be becoming a habit," she said.

She caught a clear glimpse of worry on Edwin's face, but at her teasing, it disappeared for a moment in a big grin. "Well, you know I wouldn't mind that one bit," he said. "I'm just not sure how the shopkeeper feels about me hanging around all the time."

"The shopkeeper?" Sadie said. "You know, I actually know her pretty well. I'm pretty sure she doesn't mind."

"Well, I'd feel better about that if I could hear it straight from her," Edwin said. He caught her gaze and held it meaningfully.

Sadie stared into his intelligent blue eyes for a long moment, then looked down at the counter again in confusion. "I'll let you know if I hear anything," she said.

Edwin shuffled on the other side of the counter. "Actually," he said, "pleasant as it is to see you, I'm afraid I'm actually here about the campaign."

Sadie took a deep breath and nodded, her eyes widening as she remembered the explosion outside the debate the day before. "I've never seen anything like that in Silver Peak," she said.

Edwin shook his head. "Neither have the police," he said. "Mac Slattery's working on the case now. Ruined barbecue and campaign signs are one thing, but live explosions in a crowd that size could be hazardous, or deadly—even if they were just Roman candles. He's actually talking about bringing in forensics experts from Denver to have a look at the scene."

Sadie was silent for a moment, musing over the parallel between the present-day Morgan campaign and the robbery Jules Morgan had dealt with decades earlier. In both cases, the problem had been too knotty for Silver Peak's law enforcement to tackle on their own. And it was strange, she thought, that the same family should be at the heart of both.

Edwin lowered his voice. But she was relieved, for a change, that the drop in his tone had nothing to do with her. "Sadie," he said. "I couldn't find Jesse after the debate."

"I saw him in the crowd," Sadie told him. "Right after the explosion."

"Where was he?" Edwin asked.

"Right behind the car," Sadie said. "Not ten steps away. And he looked..." She hesitated. "Happy," she finally concluded.

Edwin winced. "I hate doubting my own campaign manager," he said. "And I hope I'd be the last man in this town to convict someone before they're proven guilty. But I spoke with him this morning, and it was a very disturbing conversation. When I asked him where he'd gone after the debate, he avoided the question."

"It seems like it might be worth going back to him and asking again," Sadie said. "He may not realize how important the issue is to you."

Edwin pushed back his shock of white hair with exasperation. "That's what I thought," he said. "So I told him I needed him to answer the question."

"What did he say then?" Sadie asked.

Edwin shook his head. "He told me that I didn't need to worry about it. He was off the campaign clock, and it was his own private business."

Sadie pursed her lips. "I guess he's technically right about that," she said. "But why in the world would he refuse to answer that question?"

Edwin shrugged his broad shoulders. "I wish I knew," he said. "Or maybe I don't want to know." He sighed. "Jesse's been devoted to this campaign. And with what I'm able to pay him, it's basically a volunteer position. So he's right that I don't have much right to question what he does in his off hours. But I wish I could say I believe for certain that he had nothing to do with that explosion. And I can't.

"It's actually his devotion to this campaign that worries me the most," he continued. "I mean, I'd be glad to be mayor. It'd be an honor. But when you come right down to it, it's just a mayoral election in a small town."

"Silver Peak may be small," Sadie said. "But that doesn't mean it's not important."

"Of course it's important," Edwin said, with a grin. "It's the most important town in the world to me, now. Some of the people I care about most in the world live here." This time, when he caught Sadie's gaze, she held it steadily, staring into his eyes, trying to let herself think about what it would be like to consider him to be anything more than a friend. How would things change? She knew it would be different, but would it be better?

Now Edwin was the one to look away. "But let's face it," he said. "Jesse has been treating this as if it's big city politics, or even a national campaign. I appreciate his taking it seriously. I really do. But he seems to care more about winning than I do."

Sadie nodded. "I understand," she said.

"You know I hated to ask you to look into Jesse for me," Edwin said. "And I was hoping that everything would clear up somehow, so that neither of us would have to have any suspicions of him. But after last night, I just had to come by this morning and see." He shuffled uncomfortably. "Did you have a chance to find anything out? Anything at all that might help me while I'm thinking about these things?"

Sadie took a deep breath, but before she could speak, her phone began to ring. "I'm sorry," she said. "I'm waiting for a few important calls. Can I just—?"

Edwin nodded, and took a step back from the counter. "Of course, of course," he said.

Sadie glanced at the phone as she answered it. It was a Denver number, listed as unknown, and she couldn't tell from the number itself whether it was the university, or even Agatha Hale.

"Hello?" she said. "This is Sadie Speers."

The voice on the other end of the line was a woman's, slightly distant-sounding, and somewhat tentative. "Hello?" she said. "I'm looking for Sadie. Sadie Speers."

"That's me," Sadie said. "Can I help you?"

There was a brief pause at the other end of the line. Then the woman said, "This is Agatha Adams. Agatha Hale."

Sadie's eyes opened. She reached for a pencil and met Edwin's eyes in the same motion. "I need to take this," she mouthed.

Edwin nodded. "No problem," he said. "I can wait."

"Agatha," Sadie said. "It's wonderful to hear from you."

She shook her head at Edwin. "I think it's going to be a while," she whispered, her expression apologetic.

Edwin looked surprised, and then something else passed over his face. Was it hurt that she hadn't made more time for him? Whatever it was, it passed quickly, replaced by his normal affable smile as he gave her a small wave and headed for the door.

"Well, it was a surprise to hear from you," Agatha began. "You said you had some information about our family?"

Sadie hesitated, wondering how much to tell Agatha, and how much she already knew. Families, and the stories that got passed down through them, could both be tricky. Often, children were in a position to know more about their parents than anyone else in the world: after all, almost no one spent as much time with them, or saw them at their most private and vulnerable. But on the other hand, parents often went to great lengths to protect their children from unpleasant truths. Sadie wasn't sure how hard a time the Hale family had had in Silver Peak, whether those stories had ever been told to Agatha, and if they had, how they'd been told. She didn't want to hide anything from Agatha, but she didn't want to surprise or alarm her by telling her a part of the family history she might not have known. And Sadie wanted to keep the conversation going for as long as possible, because while she was glad to share anything she knew about the Hale family with Agatha, what she really needed was for Agatha to share anything she knew that Sadie hadn't been able to glean from the diary and the town records. She needed to tread carefully. And the plain truth was always a good place to start.

"Yes," she said. "I own a little antique shop in Silver Peak."

"Silver Peak?" Agatha said. "I lived there when I was a very small girl."

Sadie nodded to herself. It was a good sign that Agatha already knew about the family connection with Silver Peak, so at least that wouldn't come as a surprise. "That's what I thought," Sadie said.

"You did?" Agatha asked, sounding a little unnerved.

"Well, I've always been interested in Silver Peak history," Sadie told her, trying to sound as light and friendly as possible. "And my grandson is also interested in antiques. He's seventeen. This past weekend, he was at a tag sale in Denver, and he ran across an old diary that was written in Silver Peak. It's actually a very interesting document."

"And does it have something to do with my family?" Agatha asked. She didn't sound impatient, but she was clearly trying to understand what any of this had to do with her personally.

"Well," Sadie said, sending up a silent prayer as she broached the subject she'd actually called about. "I believe it was written by your mother."

"My mother?" Agatha repeated.

"I'm quite certain of it actually," Sadie said. "Most of the figures in it are identified by initials, but they match the members of your family."

To Sadie's surprise, when Agatha spoke next, her voice was full of wonder and excitement. "It sounds like you really did find it," she said. "I can't believe it. And I can't believe you found me."

"I'm sorry," Sadie said. "I'm not sure I understand."

Agatha took a long breath. "Of course not," she said. "Let me explain. About five years ago, my brother got a promotion. It was a big one, but it meant he had to be out of the country. So he sold most of his things, shipped some, and stored the rest of them. Of course, when you do something like that, there's a lot of chaos, and you want to make sure that nothing gets lost. So he had pulled out one box, of all his most important documents, that he planned to take over to the storage unit himself. He didn't even want to risk shipping it internationally. He figured it'd be safest right here, in Denver. All of us were there the day he moved out of his house. I was still packing, he was instructing the shippers, and my husband and son were ferrying stuff all over town—to the storage unit, to the Salvation Army, to the dump."

Sadie gave a little groan as she saw where the story was going. "No," she said.

"My son was trying to be helpful," Agatha told her. "Nathan had set the box of documents to the side by the door, so he couldn't forget it—but Billy thought it was a box his dad missed on one of the trips."

"Let me guess," Sadie said. "It didn't get taken to storage."

"We never could figure out where it got taken," Agatha said. "We went back to the Salvation Army and spent the whole next day there, combing through all their recent donations. You wouldn't believe the things they get there. Old skis. Eight-millimeter cameras. We even found a bear suit."

"But not the documents," Sadie said.

"No," Agatha said. "So we always thought it must have actually gone to the dump. And none of us were going to try to sort through their recent—er, donations."

"I can't imagine how that must have felt," Sadie said.

"Nathan felt terrible," Agatha told her. "I'd given him all the family documents because he was always the responsible one, and especially when I had young kids around and he didn't—well, I just thought they'd be safer with him. Of course, I couldn't blame him, because it turned out my kid was responsible for it after all."

"I'm sure he felt bad too," Sadie said.

"He did," Agatha agreed. "And, of course, none of us really blamed him. But that didn't mean we could get the documents back. I couldn't bear to think about it. We barely had anything from Mom and Dad to begin with. They were so poor when we were young that there aren't even any pictures of us as kids. And then to lose the few things we did have..."

Sadie smiled. She hadn't expected the news that the diary existed would come as such a pleasant surprise to Agatha, and she was glad to hear that Agatha was someone who prized her family history, instead of someone who had let it pass out of her hands because she didn't see the value in it. "I'm so glad to be able to reconnect you with the diary, then," Sadie said. "Of course, I'll have to talk with my grandson first. He's the one who found it at the tag sale, so officially it's his property right now, and I don't want to make any promises for him. But knowing Theo, I can't imagine that he wouldn't want the diary returned to its proper owners."

"That's absolutely wonderful," Agatha said. "Thank you so much."

"Oh, it's a pleasure," Sadie replied. "And I'll get in touch with Theo as soon as possible. But in the meantime, I wonder if you might be able to answer a few questions we had about the time the diary covers. Your mother was writing during a very interesting time in Silver Peak history, and we were curious if someone from the family might be able to shed some light that we weren't able to glean from the historical documents."

"Oh?" Agatha said. "I'm not sure what I'd know about ancient history. But I guess I could try. What time are we talking about?"

"Well," Sadie said. "The diary covers the months that immediately lead up to a robbery at the Silver Peak Bank. I don't know if you would have heard about it. You would have been quite young at the time."

"I was three years old," Agatha said. Her voice had lost its friendly tone, and Sadie noted with interest that Agatha clearly knew at least something about the robbery—and her own exact age at the time.

"That's what I had guessed," Sadie said. "So I wouldn't expect you to remember too much yourself, and I don't know if you were aware that the robbery was never solved. But from her diary, we can see that your mother had a very special perspective on that whole time. In fact, nobody would have been closer to the events than she was, except the other staff at the bank. We were just curious if she ever talked about that time in the family, and what she might have said."

"She never said anything about it," Agatha said, perhaps a little too quickly.

"Well, you had heard of it before I called," Sadie said. "Hadn't you? I can't imagine it would have been big news in Denver." She gave a little laugh, trying to keep the mood light as she pressed the question.

"I knew there was a robbery around the time we moved," Agatha said. "And I know how old I was when we moved. That's all I ever heard."

"Well, that robbery was a big event in the life of the town," Sadie said. "So people around here are still curious." That was an understatement, she added silently. "And Theo and I have made a bit of a project of learning anything we can about it. So if she ever said anything at all, maybe not even about the robbery, but about what it was like to work at the bank, or perhaps the people she worked with there—"

"It was such a long time ago," Agatha interrupted. "I'm sorry. I know that some people find this kind of historical research interesting, but I don't know anything that can help you, and I'm not sure I see how all that could possibly matter much today."

"It does matter here in Silver Peak," Sadie said. "Quite a bit. The story of the robbery is still affecting lives today. So if you have anything—"

"I'm sorry," Agatha said again. "You've caught me at a bit of a bad time. I'm so grateful to you for contacting me about the diary. But I really need to go."

Sadie raised her eyebrows. A few moments before, Agatha had been eager to talk about the diary, and now she was about to get off the phone without even getting Sadie's contact information.

"All right," Sadie said. "I'll give you a call after I speak with my grandson about returning the diary. And you have my number, right?"

"Uh, I did…" Agatha hesitated, obviously rattled.

"Here. Let me give it to you again." Sadie gave Agatha the number. "I'll be in touch," she said.

"All right," Agatha said shortly, still sounding less than thrilled at that prospect, and ended the call.

Sadie laid her own phone down on the counter, thoughtfully. It sounded like Silver Peak wasn't the only place where the story of the old bank robbery still had a strong hold, even on the next generation.

18

SADIE SMILED AS SHE TURNED INTO THE VICTORIAN NEIGHBOR-
hood of Silver Peak, Theo peering out the window in the passenger
seat. Of course, she was familiar with it, and even more familiar
now that she spent so much time at the family home Edwin was
painstakingly restoring. But the profusion of cupolas, gingerbread
trim, and wraparound porches never ceased to delight her—
especially with the backdrop of the Colorado mountains.

"One hundred three," Theo said, reading the addresses as Sadie
piloted her car down the street at a crawl. "One hundred eleven.
One hundred seventeen. There it is!" he yelped with excitement.

One seventeen was the address of Mary Carter, once Mary
Walter—the daughter of Ed Walter, who had been the security
guard at the Silver Peak Bank at the time of the robbery. Theo
had tracked it down at the library that morning, then come
into the shop shortly after Sadie arrived there, to see if she'd like
to go with him to see what kind of light Mary might be able to
shed on the story.

"It's a beautiful house," Sadie said, peering up at the white
brick edifice with a green roof and lavish gingerbread trim. It had
obviously been lovingly cared for: the roof was new, the shutters

were freshly painted a matching shade of green, and the yard and garden were well cultivated and trimmed.

Theo grinned at her and bounded out of the car.

When Sadie finally caught up with him, she reached for the old-fashioned ringer beside the door.

Theo brushed her hand away gently. "I already did," he whispered.

Sadie smiled, impressed by her grandson's gumption.

As she did, the door swung open.

A tall, big-boned woman with a friendly face, blue eyes, and salt-and-pepper hair opened the door, wearing a denim work shirt and blue jeans. At the sight of strangers, the friendliness in her eyes vanished.

"Can I help you?" she asked.

Sadie gave her her best smile. "We're sorry to bother you," she said. "I'm Sadie Speers. I run the Antique Mine, downtown. And this is my grandson, Theo. Theo's gotten interested in Silver Peak history, something your family was involved in, and we wondered if you might have a few minutes to talk with us." She glanced at Theo, who nodded seriously and politely beside her.

"Let me guess," Mary said. "The old bank robbery."

But she stepped aside to let them into the house.

"I don't know that there's much I can tell you," she said. "But you came all this way. I can at least give you a glass of lemonade."

Sadie and Theo shuffled past her. She closed the door behind them, then led them past a staircase that swept up to the second floor from the entryway, down a classic Victorian hall, to a large kitchen at the back of the house where, true to her offer; she pulled a glass pitcher of lemonade from the fridge, then filled three glasses. After handing one each to Sadie and Theo, she took a sip of her own and leaned back against the counter.

"So," Theo said, breaking the silence, "how did you know we were here about the robbery?"

Mary grinned, the corners of her friendly eyes crinkling. "Oh," she said, "we're not a very exciting family. We come from a long line of people who are willing to stay in one place for a long time, and watch the world go by. There's nothing wrong with that. It just means we don't make a lot of history. We're the kind of people who turn out to be bank guards. It just so happens that my father worked at one of the few banks that ever got robbed."

"Had you been born at that point?" Sadie asked.

Mary smiled again. "Well, aren't you sweet," she said. "Thank you for asking. I like to think I look young for my age. But yes, I had been born at the time of the robbery. That doesn't mean I have any memories of it myself, though. I was only two years old at the time it happened."

"Did your family talk about it much?" Sadie asked. "While you were growing up?"

Mary's friendly face darkened. "We didn't talk about it nearly as much as everybody else did," she said.

Sadie held her tongue, waiting for Mary to go on.

"What you have to understand," Mary said after a moment, "is that that case was never solved. It seems like these days, the bulk of the suspicion has fallen on Jules Morgan. I guess maybe that's because he's such a big personality, and he continued to be a big personality for decades after the robbery, so people knew his name, and they knew he was connected with the bank. It was easy for them to connect the two things, if they ever got to wondering. But around the time that it happened, that was a hard winter. A very tough winter. And everyone who had anything to do with the bank was under suspicion. Including my father. And because the case was never solved, it took a long time for that suspicion to fade. Other kids asked me about it from the time I could go out and play. And they were still asking about it when I was in kindergarten, first grade. I used to tell them I wished my father had robbed the bank. But the funny thing was, we never had any money. I remember, when I went to my high school prom, and all we could afford was for me to borrow my sister's old dress, that I briefly considered robbing the bank myself. I didn't want a lot. Just three dollars. That's how much the dress I wanted from the store downtown cost. And I figured the bank had enough money, they couldn't miss it. You should have seen it: it was one of those fifties formals, periwinkle satin bodice, with a cloud of matching periwinkle tulle on the skirt."

Sadie smiled. "It sounds beautiful," she said.

"It was!" Mary agreed. "But I wore my sister's pink chiffon instead. I guess I looked all right in the end. It was a couple of years after prom, but my prom date married me anyway." Her eyes crinkled again in a grin at the thought.

"What about your father?" Sadie asked, carefully trying to work the conversation back to the topic of the bank. "Did he ever say anything about the robbery?"

Mary sighed, and her brows knit. "He felt bad about it," she said. "After all, that was his job, to keep the bank from getting robbed. I'm not sure how anyone could have blamed him, because he wasn't the night guard, and the bank was robbed at night. They didn't even have a night guard, because that possibility seemed so unlikely. They had a real fancy safe there too, one that they figured no one could break into even if someone did get inside the bank."

"A Brenneman One-Fifteen," Theo said. "It was the most secure system in the country, at the time. There were banks in New York that didn't have safes so secure."

Mary raised her eyebrows. "Well, you seem to know even more about it than I do," she said. "Like I said, I don't know if I'm going to be much help to you."

"We can look up the kind of safe they had in the paper," Theo said. "But there's not much in there about what the people who were there really thought about it."

Mary smiled, giving him the point. "Like I said, I wasn't there."

"Did your father ever say anything else about the robbery?" Theo tried.

"Or just about working at the bank?" Sadie added. "Did he talk much about his fellow employees?"

Mary hesitated. Then she sighed. "I don't like to point fingers," she said. "I learned early how that felt, and I never liked it myself, so I don't want to do it to someone else. But I guess most of the people involved now must be dead and gone. I can't see how it could still matter much to anyone."

Sadie had just made the opposite case to Agatha, that the robbery was important because it was still affecting life in Silver Peak. But Mary seemed to be working her way around to talking about the robbery by this line of reasoning, and Sadie didn't want to do anything to derail her. She just nodded, hoping Theo would take her cue and stay silent himself.

"Of course, he never could prove any of this," she said. "But he always thought Ben Hale might have had something to do with it."

"Janie's husband," Theo said quickly.

Mary nodded. "You have done your homework," she said. "Yes, Dad always seemed to like Janie. I think I actually remember meeting her, even when I was that small. Or I'm not so sure I remember meeting her. I just remember someone giving me horehound candy down at the bank. And Dad used to tell me that was Janie. Apparently she liked to keep them in a little jar in her desk, for when kids like me came in."

She smiled at the memory. Then the smile faded. "But Ben," she began. "Ben was another story. Dad said he always felt a little strange, just letting Ben in the door."

"Did he say why?" Sadie asked.

"He was just a bit too interested in the bank for my father's taste," Mary explained. "Always sticking his nose into this or that bank business. When the receipts came in. When they transferred the cash to another bank in Denver, or when the transfers from Denver came in. My dad thought Ben got a lot nosier right around the time of the robbery. He even talked Jules into giving him a complete tour of the vault, how secure the whole thing was, the way the combinations were set, the whole nine yards. Everyone at the bank came under suspicion because it seemed like it must have been an inside job. But my dad always thought Ben Hale could have gotten enough information himself to be considered an inside man. And that's not the only thing," she added.

"Oh?" Sadie prompted her.

Mary shook her head. "No," she said. "I recall his telling me one other thing. The week before the robbery, Dad happened to be downtown after dark. I don't know why, but he was going by the bank. And he said he found Ben Hale there, just staring through that big old plate-glass window. Dad stopped to talk with him, but Ben didn't seem to want to talk much. He just hurried off. Dad always thought that was suspicious, finding Ben there at the bank without an explanation. But then again, I guess Ben could have told the same story about finding Dad there at the bank that night too. And it's true my father always was real loyal to his friends. It would have been hard for him to believe that anyone he liked had anything to do with the robbery. Even Jules Morgan. That man was a character, but my dad knew him well, and he always liked him. At any rate, his take on it was always that Ben Hale might have been good for the robbery. And it didn't help that they left town just as soon as the bank was turned over."

"We talked with Gavin Anderson a little earlier," Sadie told her.

Mary's face lit up. "Oh, Gavin," she said, "I ought to get over there and visit him. He always stayed friendly with my dad, even after both of them had left the bank."

"He seemed to think that move was as a result of a job Ben Hale got in Denver," Sadie said.

"Sure," Mary said. "I'm sure if Ben Hale did rob the bank, they didn't advertise that they were leaving town because now they had everybody's money. Did Gavin say what kind of job Ben got?"

Theo shook his head beside Sadie, then looked at her meaningfully. "No," he said. "He didn't know that."

"Maybe because there wasn't one," Mary said. "Or maybe there was. Like I said, I don't know any of the answers. And a lot smarter people than me have tried to get them, with no luck. But that's everything I've got. I'm sorry if it's not much help."

"I've just got one more question," Sadie said. "Did your father ever mention his suspicions to the authorities?"

Mary gave a brief nod. "I think I remember him saying something about that," she said. "I guess it took him a while to work up to it. Because he liked Janie so much, and he didn't want to cause any trouble for her. So it wasn't until the out-of-towners came in to try to solve it that he said anything. But the man he talked to wasn't real respectful of him. Kind of acted like he was a country bumpkin. I remember my dad got kind of fired up about the way he was treated. So I'm not sure how much of his story he really related to them before he gave up."

"So the new investigators were dismissive of the idea," Sadie mused.

"At least when my dad brought it up," Mary agreed. "They were all excited about the idea that it might be some big-time bank robber. Not some small-town guy they'd never heard of. They couldn't imagine a bank with that fancy safe could have been robbed by someone who usually did odd jobs."

Sadie set down her lemonade glass on the counter. Theo drained his quickly, then raised the empty glass toward Mary. "This was delicious," he said. "Thank you."

"I'm glad I could at least give you a glass of lemonade," Mary said. "Even if I didn't give you any answers."

She led the two of them back through the house and saw them to the door, where Sadie and Theo thanked her and went out.

Back in the car, Theo turned to Sadie as she started it up. "She didn't think she gave us many answers," he said. "But I felt like she did."

"Why do you say that?" Sadie said, trying to give her grandson the chance to think for himself, before she swooped in with her own thoughts.

"Well," Theo said, "we had our own ideas about Ben Hale. But we weren't there. If we had been, maybe we would have been able to tell that all the visits he made to Janie were completely innocent. Gavin wasn't crazy about Ben, but he wasn't there to see much of what happened between Ben and Janie for himself. But Ed Walter was there at the time, and he didn't like the way Ben was acting either. In fact, it sounds like Ben's behavior at the time was even more suspicious than we suspected."

"I think you're right," said Sadie, whose thoughts had been progressing along the same lines.

"I get that from my grandmother," Theo said, and grinned. "What do you think?"

"I'm still interested in the idea that Wes Winston might have had something to do with all of this," Sadie said. "Maybe I just don't want to believe anyone from Silver Peak would be capable of such a thing. I don't know. But I feel pretty certain that Ed Walter and Gavin Anderson aren't strong suspects. If they did rob the bank, there's no evidence that they ever came into the kind of windfall that would have represented. I suppose there's a chance they socked it away somewhere and never used it—"

"But what kind of person would rob a bank and then hide the money all their life?" Theo asked.

Sadie nodded firmly. "That's right," she said. "To me, it doesn't add up. And that just leaves Jules Morgan, and Ben Hale. And I have to say, if we could be sure Winston wasn't the culprit, I'd lean toward Ben. Jules would have had the means to hide the money, that's for certain. But he seemed to have so much money already that it's hard to know why he'd need to steal."

She sighed. "We may not have gotten all the answers from Mary, but she gave us another important piece of the story. And it sounds like it's a piece that couldn't come out until now. During his lifetime, her father didn't want to spread rumors about Ben Hale. And in any case, I think we've talked to everybody in town who might still have any memories about the bank around the time of the robbery."

"Not everybody, Grandma," Theo said.

Sadie glanced over at him. "What do you mean?"

"We haven't talked to James Morgan."

19

SADIE STEPPED INTO THE ENTRYWAY OF THE SILVER PEAK BANK, and paused. The bank occupied the same small storefront it had at the time of the robbery, but it had been much improved over the intervening decades. The second floor had been removed to create a high, airy lobby, and the footprint of the bank had almost doubled, thanks to the purchase of a building on the other side of the block that had allowed for significant expansion. The teller's window where Janie had once welcomed customers was still there, its ornate brass gracing the lobby as it always had, but it was now turned to the side, so that customers could also walk by into an area of offices where the more complex business of the bank was conducted, and where James Morgan's office lay.

Theo had been right, Sadie realized. In her concern for James and Helen Morgans' feelings, she'd developed a large blind spot of her own: she'd traipsed all over town, talking with anyone else who might know even the slightest bit about the old robbery, but never gone directly to James himself. In a way, she thought now, it was almost as bad as the people who had been gossiping about him behind his back. She might not have meant to be malicious, but both she and the gossips had been letting the old robbery isolate

James from the rest of Silver Peak, despite everything he had done for the community over the years. The topic might not be a pleasant one for James, as Helen had so strongly intimated. But the reason it wasn't pleasant was exactly this: that it created a barrier between him and the other residents of Silver Peak.

Sadie didn't want to be part of building, or even preserving, those barriers anymore. Whatever the truth was, it was better than all the uncertainty and rumor, and James probably had better information about his own father's guilt and innocence than anyone else in town. Even if he'd never wanted to take a hard look at the evidence that might lie in his own father's financial history, perhaps, with the new information Sadie and Theo had unearthed, he could find the courage. After all, they now had two suspects besides Jules, who had been in the shadow of the town's suspicion for all these years. It seemed more possible that a closer look into the old robbery could clear Jules's name than it ever had before. But she was still sensitive to James's feelings. And she didn't want him to think that she was digging into the old history on a teenager's whim. So she'd told Theo she thought it was better if she made this visit on her own.

Still, Sadie felt a twinge of misgiving as she walked past the teller's window, heading for James's office. She couldn't shake the memory of Helen's fierce desire to protect her husband. And the last thing Sadie wanted to do was to cause James more pain by bringing up the past, especially after all the trouble he'd been having these days with his campaign.

Outside James's door, she smiled at Angie Rader, his administrative assistant.

Angie smiled back. "Sadie," she said. "Good to see you."

"You too," Sadie said. "I'm here to see James. If he has a minute."

Angie picked up her phone, exchanged a few brief words with James, and then nodded at the door. But before Sadie could knock, James opened it himself.

"Sadie Speers," he said, with a broad smile. "It's always a pleasure. To what do I owe this surprise?"

Sadie waited to answer until the door was closed behind her, out of respect for James's privacy. Then she took a seat in one of the richly appointed brass and leather chairs across from his desk.

"We talked a bit earlier this week," she began. "About that diary that Theo found in Denver."

James's smile faded immediately, but his face didn't harden. Instead, at the mention of the old journal, he suddenly looked both almost boyish, and sad.

"I've been looking into it, as I told you," Sadie said. "And I wanted to share with you some of the things I've found."

"It's such old news," James began.

"But it's still affecting life here in Silver Peak," Sadie said gently. "Even—your campaign. It's not really in the past anymore, is it? If it ever was."

James stared down at the blotter on his desk.

"I know you weren't even born at the time," Sadie said. "So I thought you might be interested in some of the things we've discovered about it, since Theo found the diary. First of all, we've verified that it did belong to Janie Hale. Her daughter remembers it, and it only passed out of the Hales's hands by an accident."

James nodded, but didn't look up to meet Sadie's eyes.

"And I've talked to a few people around town who still might have any firsthand information about the events," Sadie said. "Talking with them has been interesting, because neither of them seems to believe that your father had anything to do with the robbery."

"Why would he have anything to do with the robbery?" James suddenly burst out, looking at her. "It was his own bank that was robbed."

Sadie nodded. "That's a very good question," she said. "And both the diary and some of the eyewitnesses suspected someone else."

"Who?" James asked.

"Ben Hale," Sadie told him. "Janie's husband."

For the first time, something like hope dawned in James's eyes. But then his brows drew together and he shook his head, almost as if he was trying to shake the hopeful thoughts out of it, unable to believe them after years of coping with bad news and trouble.

"And he's not the only other potential suspect," Sadie added. "There was a relatively famous bank robber, Wes Winston, operating in the area at exactly that time. He was on a crime spree that lasted all that fall, and he wasn't caught until long after the Silver Peak robbery."

"That sounds a little far-fetched to me," James said.

"Well, as I understand it, nobody in Silver Peak expected the bank to be robbed," Sadie said. "So the robbery itself was pretty far-fetched. It doesn't seem too much more far-fetched to me that it should be a bank robber who pulled it off."

James tilted his head to show he followed her logic.

"So there are some strong possibilities that suggest your father's name could one day be cleared of the robbery," Sadie said.

"He was never convicted of that robbery," James said quickly, almost as if he wasn't talking to her, but repeating something he'd said over and over again, in his own head.

"Not in a court, maybe," Sadie said. "But I'm afraid that, fairly or unfairly, some people have convicted him in the court of public opinion. That may not be fair to him. But it's definitely not fair to you."

Sadie could tell that she had struck a nerve by the way James's eyes bored into hers as she said this.

"And there's one very big question that only you may be in a position to answer," Sadie continued.

"What's that?" James asked.

"The money," Sadie told him. "I know this has been a hard topic for you, for obvious reasons. And I wouldn't blame you for wanting to leave it all in the past. But if your father did have anything to do with the robbery, he must have put the money somewhere. And now that you're in control of the bank, you would have the best access to any records that show where that money was hidden—or prove that it was never in his hands at all."

James leaned back in his chair, a smile twisting his face. "Don't you think that hasn't occurred to me before?" he asked. "Ever since I was a kid, from the first time other boys started teasing me on the playground, I've wanted to know this answer. Those boys said terrible things. I'd go to school with a pair of new shoes, and they'd shout at me that I could only afford them because my father had stolen from theirs. I didn't want to believe it, of course, but my father was"—his hand stopped in midair with a gesture that was far more eloquent than any words—"my father," he finished.

"So I looked for proof," he said. "I did. Every chance I got. I don't even know what kind of proof I was looking for—that he did it, or that he didn't. I just wanted to know the truth. Even before he died, I was always snooping into various accounts, anything that seemed unusual, anything that had lain dormant for a long time."

Sadie raised her eyebrows expectantly.

James raised his hands in defeat. "I never found anything," he said. "Except carelessness, or forgetfulness, on my father's part. And that was hardly news to anybody. Least of all to me."

He took a deep breath and released it. Even if it wasn't a pleasant topic, Sadie got the sense that it was a relief for him to talk about it. There was a chance, she realized, that Helen had been the only one to have heard this story besides Sadie, for all these years. After all, who else in town would James have felt safe with sharing his doubts about his own father?

"Then, after he passed away and I took over the bank, I went over everything with a fine-tooth comb. I couldn't find anything, so I hired a team of forensic accountants to audit us. A complete historical audit, all the way back to 1937. Two of the members of the team had worked as analysts for the FBI before they joined the firm. One of them had been a history professor at Stanford. It cost a fortune. If my father had hidden the proceeds of that bank robbery anywhere in the bank accounts, or our family accounts, they would have found it—and I would have already spent it, by hiring them."

"And what did they find?" Sadie asked.

James shook his head. "Nothing," he said. "The same things I had always known. My father was eccentric, and erratic. But there's no evidence that he's a thief. At least from what we were able to find."

"So you don't believe he had anything to do with the robbery," Sadie said.

"I don't know if I can say that," James said. "After all, he was the one with the intimate acquaintance with that state-of-the-art vault. And for all his faults, he was not a stupid man."

"Unless what the bank was dealing with was another kind of inside job. Like Ben Hale. Or someone with the skills of a professional criminal. Like Wes Winston," Sadie said.

"I guess so," James said. "But in any case, from what I can tell, that money was never in our family's hands."

"I'm not sure I totally understand," Sadie pressed on. "If your audit made it clear that your family never had that money, why didn't you make it public? It sounds like you could have laid all these rumors to rest a long time ago."

"That's the thing about rumors," James said. "You could say the same thing about the fact that my father was never convicted for any crime. Shouldn't that have laid any rumors to rest? You might think so, but it didn't. And as thorough as the audit was, you can't ever be sure that someone *didn't* do something until you can prove someone else did. Even I knew there could have been some secret account there that never showed up, despite our best efforts. Heck, knowing my father, he might have taken it out and spent it all in one night. Placed it all as a bet in some under-the-table gambling house. Or left it as a tip for some pretty girl or paid off a debt. It wouldn't actually have been the craziest thing he ever did. And I was looking for the truth. But that's not what a rumor wants. A rumor just wants a good story, something juicy to pass along to the next person. Hopefully not too loaded with facts, because those are hard to remember. Especially compared to a good story.

"No," he said, shaking his head. "From the time I was a boy, I knew talking about what had happened there wouldn't do any good. It would just stir things up again. Which is exactly what's just happened. You've seen it."

Sadie nodded. "I have," she agreed.

"Does that answer your question?" James asked.

"It does," she said. "I'm sorry to have to bring it up. I'm just interested in the same thing you are. The truth."

"I'm not sure it's out there," James said. "It may be that we all just need to learn to live with that."

Sadie didn't contradict him, although she very much hoped he was wrong. For her, the bank robbery was still mostly a matter of curiosity. For James, it was an event that had shaped his entire life. And his willingness to accept it after he had done everything he possibly could was just more evidence that he was a very different man than his father had been.

"Well, I appreciate the time," Sadie said.

"Anytime," James said, rising to show her to the door.

"And I'll let you know if I find out anything certain," Sadie told him.

"That would be wonderful," James said. "But could you do me a favor? Unless you've got something you feel is certain proof, please don't mention any of this to Helen. She's very protective of me, and I'm afraid she may find it even more upsetting than I do."

Sadie nodded, suppressing a smile. The love between James and Helen, and their concern for each other's feelings, was touching.

Briefly her mind wandered from that notion to an image of Edwin, but she quickly reined in her thoughts.

She walked thoughtfully through the maze of loan officers' desks, back into the high-flown lobby, but before she reached the main doors, she caught sight of a familiar figure. Jesse Wilson, Edwin's campaign manager, stood near one of the tall marble counters that lined the walls, for customers of the bank to fill out their coupons and arrange their paperwork before approaching a teller.

"Jesse," Sadie said, going over to him, "what a surprise to see you here! Are you here on campaign business?"

But even as she said this, she could see that Jesse didn't have anything in his hands that indicated he was there at the bank to do business: no coupons, no checks, no receipts. If he wasn't there at the bank to do business, what was he at the bank for? Her mind thought back quickly to James, working diligently in his office. Could Jesse's presence here at the bank have anything to do with the campaign?

At the same time, Jesse's gaze dropped to the floor. Then he glanced through a window, and out the door. He seemed to be willing to look at anything, other than Sadie herself. "Sorry," he said, after a minute. "I can't really talk right now."

Sadie looked at him in surprise, but he didn't even meet her eyes to see her expression. He just hurried out. And by the time she collected herself and followed him into the bright autumn sun on the Silver Peak street, he was gone.

20

SADIE TOOK A FEW STEPS IN ONE DIRECTION ON THE SIDEWALK outside the bank, then a few steps in the opposite direction, but it was no use. Jesse had vanished without a trace. With a sigh, she turned to head back to the Antique Mine. But after a few steps, she stopped.

The county clerk's office was just a few storefronts down from the Silver Peak Bank. In fact, the bank's importance in the town could be observed by the fact that the county clerk's office had been situated near the bank, which predated the modern county clerk's office, rather than the other way around.

And through the glare on the storefront window, in the dim office, Sadie could see Ginny Pearson, her head bowed over some kind of paperwork, at the front counter.

A moment later, Sadie swung through the door.

Ginny looked up and gave her a professional smile. "Sadie," she said. "What can I do for you?"

Sadie tried to muster her most winning smile. "I just wanted to finish the conversation we were having the other night," she said. "Before we were interrupted."

Ginny looked genuinely bewildered. "What conversation was that?" she asked.

"At the debate," Sadie prompted. "You were just sharing your thoughts with me on James Morgan's campaign."

At the mention of James Morgan, even Ginny's professional friendliness vanished. She raised her eyebrows. "I'm not sure I've got much more to say on that topic," she said.

"Why not?" Sadie asked.

This question seemed to perplex Ginny, whose raised eyebrows now lowered into a glower. "I don't know why I'd need to explain any thoughts I might or might not have about James Morgan to you," she said.

Sadie smiled to show that she wasn't offended, even by Ginny's relatively barbed reply.

"Of course not," Sadie said. "But it just seemed to me that you had some strong feelings on the subject. And it still seems like that now. And I was curious, because of everything that's happening with the Morgan campaign, if you might know of any reason that might make somebody in town want to create the kind of trouble they've been seeing for the past several days."

Ginny's shoulders dropped at this, and her face smoothed out a bit. "All that is terrible," she said. "I can't say I've always been a fan of James Morgan's. Maybe I even got a kick out of it when I first heard about his ruined barbecue. But those signs you told me about and then the explosion with his wife right there, beside the car—terrible," she repeated.

"You must see a lot in this office," Sadie said, trying to keep her questions neutral, since she was still uncertain whether her suspicions about Ginny were founded or not. As Edwin had originally said, Ginny was clearly no fan of James Morgan's. But she'd seemed genuinely upset by the news of the ruined signs. And Sadie had been standing right there with her just before the Roman candles went off in James's car—although she supposed Ginny might have had enough time to slip out and set a short fuse burning. "Can you think of any reason somebody might want to do a thing like that?"

"I'll admit there might have been a time when I did," Ginny said. "So I guess I can see how someone else might arrive at that point."

"Why did you feel that way?" Sadie gently asked her.

Ginny sighed. "You know, you're the first person who's asked me that in years," she said. "And to tell the truth, I've been mad about it for so long, I hardly know why. Looking back, I see it was probably just as much my fault as his. I'd been dreaming and dreaming of a new wing on our house. Now that I say that, it sounds so superficial, and even greedy. But it had been a terrible year for us. My son was only five years old, and he'd been sick all winter. And Jeff lost his job around that time too. So I was alone all the time, because he was always off trying to find work, and I was at home trying to take care of a sick child. I guess that's when I started to dream about it. We were going to have a big glassed-in room, with a beautiful view of the mountains, and a skylight. I didn't really think we could ever afford it. At that point, it was just a dream to get me through the days, that one day I'd be sitting in this beautiful room, looking out at the mountains, with my healthy child and happy husband, and everything would be fine again. But then Jeff found a job. A great job. Much better than he had ever had. And I thought, well, finally here's one dream that's going to come true. But his job wasn't so good that we didn't still need financing from the bank. And we'd gotten into a tough situation while we were waiting for Jeff to find work. It wasn't really the ideal time to build an addition. But I wasn't ready to hear that. I was still pretty distraught and fragile. From everything we'd been through, I just didn't feel safe. I couldn't be happy that now my husband was happy and my child was happy. I wanted that room too, to prove it, somehow. James Morgan worked on our loan application himself."

She shook her head. "I actually think he did the best he could for us. I suspect he might even have bent a rule or two in our favor. But the numbers just didn't work. My husband had been trying to prepare me for that for weeks, because he could see it coming. But I wouldn't listen to him. James Morgan was always so friendly and polite, I couldn't believe he'd turn us down. But in the end he was the unfortunate soul who had the unenviable job of telling me that I wasn't going to get my dream room. At least not that year."

"I can see how that might have been hard to hear," Sadie said.

Ginny nodded ruefully. "But I didn't make it any easier," she said. "For myself, or for anyone else. I said some things I still regret. And I've been angry ever since. I don't really know whether it's at myself, or at him. I think it might be some of both."

"I know that feeling," Sadie said. More than once, her tendency to speak before she thought had resulted in her not wanting to encounter people who'd seen her put her foot firmly in her mouth. It wasn't their fault; it was hers. But seeing them just brought up embarrassing memories.

"But still, he doesn't deserve what's been happening with his campaign," Ginny went on. "And to tell you the truth, I can't think of anyone who would really wish that on him. Sure, people come in here sometimes, grumbling about the bank. The same kinds of things I've been telling you. Now and then, they might even mention James by name. But I can't say I've ever seen anyone in this town who I believe would really want to do him harm. Not putting explosives in his car-type harm."

"Were you at the barbecue?" Sadie asked.

Ginny shook her head. "I didn't want to eat his food. So I just stayed home."

"With your husband or son?" Sadie asked.

Ginny smiled. "There was nothing keeping them from Andi's barbecue," she said.

So Ginny didn't have an alibi for the barbecue, and she'd been close enough to the car to set a fuse, Sadie calculated. Even though Sadie leaned toward believing Ginny didn't have anything to do with the sabotage, she didn't have any proof.

In her purse, Sadie's phone rang. She pulled it out and checked the caller ID: Edwin. Remembering the look on his face when he'd left the Antique Mine last, she glanced at Ginny. "I'm sorry," she said. "I need to take this."

Ginny waved her hand to show she understood, and Sadie stepped away from the counter and toward the door, answering the phone as she went out the door of the county clerk's office, onto the street.

"Edwin," she said.

"Sadie!" Edwin exclaimed. "It's good to hear your voice."

"How are you doing?" she asked. Whatever else happened between them, she didn't want Edwin to ever get the idea that he wasn't important to her, or to feel that she was neglecting him. And she had been spending a lot of time trying to unravel the mystery of the bank journal recently.

"Oh, I'm fine," Edwin said, almost impatiently, as if that was the furthest thing from his mind.

Sadie quickly guessed that he must be calling about the campaign, or the bank robbery, because of his businesslike tone. "I have been making some headway on the Silver Peak Bank robbery," she reported. "And maybe even on the sabotage. At least I think I may have ruled some things out. That's where I was just coming from, I—"

"That's not what I called to talk about," Edwin said. "In fact, all that is about the last thing on my mind. I just needed to talk with you. I've been thinking, and—"

His next words were drowned out by the insistent beep of call waiting. As Sadie pulled the phone away from her ear to check the caller ID, Edwin's words grew distant, tinny, and garbled beyond recognition. Her eyes widened when she saw the name associated with the call: University of Denver.

Hurriedly, she put the phone back to her cheek. "Edwin," she said. "I am so sorry. I have another call, and I absolutely have to take it."

"But Sadie," Edwin began to protest.

The caller ID beeped again. Sadie knew that if she didn't take it now, it would go to voice mail. And she had no idea when she'd be able to get in touch with Eben Warren again.

"I'm sorry," she repeated, and switched over to take the call. "Hello?"

There was a sound of static on the other line, but then it resolved into another man's voice. "Hello," it said. "This is Professor Warren from the University of Denver. I'm trying to reach Sadie Speers."

"That's me," Sadie said, somewhat breathlessly. "You've got her."

"I believe I got a message from you earlier," Professor Warren went on. "You mentioned something about some new information relating to Wes Winston."

"Yes!" Sadie said. "That's right. I did."

"Have I caught you at a good time?" Professor Warren asked. "Because I'd be very interested to hear anything you think might be of interest."

Sadie took a long breath before she began. Edwin certainly didn't seem to think it was a good time, but she was thrilled to have gotten in touch with the professor so soon. It was certainly much quicker, she thought briefly, than waiting for his book to come out, months from now. But he was calling, she realized, because of the information she had promised him.

"Yes," she said. "This is fine. I may have mentioned this in my message, but I'm the owner of an antique shop in a small town outside Denver, Silver Peak."

"I've heard of it," Professor Warren said.

"That makes sense," Sadie said. "Because it appears to be in the same region as the Wes Winston crime spree that you're currently writing about."

"You're absolutely right," said Professor Warren.

"But what you might not be aware of," Sadie continued, "is that Silver Peak suffered a bank robbery during that same period. A robbery that was never solved."

"Really?" Professor Warren said. A note of interest crept into his voice, but it was still cautious. "Well, it'd be nice to tie every robbery in Colorado around that time to Winston, but I'm afraid he really was just one man. He can't be responsible for all of them."

"I've done a bit research on Winston myself," Sadie said. "My grandson and I have been researching this particular robbery, just as a bit of local history, and when we ran across Winston we realized it was a possibility he might have something to do with the robbery of the Silver Peak Bank. Like you, we realized that was an outside possibility. So we created a timeline of his activities, based on the existing articles we could find on him."

"I'm impressed," Professor Warren said. "Most of those materials are quite obscure. And the ones that aren't are in disarray. Putting it all together, in one place, is the reason I wrote my book."

"I wish we'd had it, believe me," Sadie told him. "But I think we came up with a pretty good timeline anyway. And if our research is correct, there are no robberies attributed to Winston during the time of the Silver Peak robbery. For almost four days."

"Four days?" Warren said. "That's a bit of time for Winston. During the time he was active, he struck much more frequently than that."

"That was our impression, based on our timeline," Sadie said. "And as you said, he was in the area, close enough to travel easily between his two confirmed robberies, both before and after. I know it's a long shot, but we thought perhaps we had stumbled on a previously unrecognized Winston robbery. And one that might actually prove to be quite interesting, given the fact that, for whatever reason, he never acknowledged it. So we thought, along with whatever other facts you've managed to dig up about Winston in your research, that this might prove to be another interesting revelation for your readers."

"That does sound interesting," Professor Warren said. "When did you say the dates were?"

"October 6," Sadie told him promptly.

Professor Warren laughed.

"I'm sorry?" Sadie said.

"No, I'm sorry," Professor Warren said. "Please, don't think I'm laughing at you. It's just that I can conclusively tell you that Wes Winston was not robbing a bank in Silver Peak on that date."

"How do you know that?" Sadie asked.

"I should really make you sign a confidentiality agreement before I tell you this," Professor Warren said. "Because it's the big revelation my publishers have been promising. Can I trust you with it as a secret?"

"I may need to tell my grandson," Sadie said. "Since he's the one who worked out the timeline with me."

"I doubt that will cut into my sales too much," Professor Warren joked.

"If anything, it may increase them," Sadie said. "I think you've probably already sold two copies here in Silver Peak."

"Well, that may constitute half my sales," Professor Warren said. "And that would be pretty good, for an academic title."

"Your secret is safe with me," Sadie said, trying to guide him back to whatever information he had to share about Wes Winston. "I promise. I'd just like to know how you can be so sure he wasn't in Silver Peak on October 6."

"Because he was getting married," Professor Warren said.

"Married?" Sadie repeated, incredulity in her voice.

"Yep," Professor Warren said. "I couldn't believe it either. But when I started studying him, really studying him, I found out all kinds of things about his history. Of course, I worked back into his childhood, looking for clues in where he'd come from, how he'd grown up. None of them seemed to explain why he'd go on a spree like the one he went on. But then I started looking at another area most people had neglected, because they thought the story was more or less over by the time he was put in prison. But I actually went there, like a good academic, and looked up the records. And what I discovered was that he had a visitor. A very consistent visitor, over the course of many years. Who was then the very same person who signed him out after his term was up."

"A lady visitor?" Sadie guessed.

"That's right," Professor Warren said. "A Miss Matilda Jennings. But when I searched the public records for her in Denver, I found that Miss Matilda was in fact a Mrs. She signed papers before a justice of the peace to be joined in holy matrimony to one Wes Winston..."

"...on October 6, 1937," Sadie finished for him.

"Exactly," Professor Warren said.

"Which explains his hiatus from his criminal activities," Sadie reasoned.

"And may explain the criminal activities themselves," Professor Warren said. "At least that's my argument. Miss Matilda came from a family of means, and Winston didn't. One explanation, and the one I favor, is that Winston's robberies were motivated by old-fashioned love. He wanted to get the means to provide for his sweetheart in the manner to which she was accustomed. And there weren't a lot of avenues for a poor kid from a ranch in Colorado to do that, back in 1937."

"But she stuck with him, money or no money," Sadie said.

"She did stick with him," Professor Warren agreed. "But I'm not sure it's accurate to say she had no money. Somehow, all those years, she managed to stay in some of Denver's finest hotels. And the instant he was released from prison, they both vanished without a trace. It would take some means to accomplish that."

"Has your research provided any clues to where they went?" Sadie asked.

"Only clues," Professor Warren said. "And most of those are contradictory. I've heard reports of a couple who match their description living in a kind of castle in the Mexican desert. And of a similar couple who set up house in San Francisco, where the husband became, of all things, a banker. My favorite theory is that they actually did both, one after the other."

"Which came first?" Sadie asked.

"That hardly matters, does it?" Professor Warren said. "Either one makes a great ending for the story."

"That doesn't sound very academic of you," Sadie observed.

"Well, I think there's a bit of the storyteller in every historian. We're not just interested in facts and figures. At least, I don't think the best of us are. We're interested in the story."

"That's what I always tell my grandson," Sadie said.

"Well, it sounds like you're a real historian yourself, then," Professor Warren said.

"I like to think so," Sadie said, smiling.

"And you have done some excellent work here," Professor Warren went on. "If you were one of my students, you'd have a straight A. Even maybe some extra credit. And I'm sorry I can't validate your theory, because I'd love to have stumbled across an undiscovered Winston robbery, just in the last moments before the book had to go to press. But I'm afraid this theory is at odds with the established facts."

"I'm grateful to you for sharing those established facts with me," Sadie said. "They're quite interesting in their own right. And my grandson and I were simply looking for the truth about this robbery in Silver Peak, whatever it turned out to be. So although you haven't proved our theory, you have helped us narrow the field."

"Glad to be of service," Professor Warren said. "I hope I haven't told you so much that you won't buy the book."

"It's just piqued my interest," Sadie said. "I can't wait to read it."

"And good luck on solving the Silver Peak Bank robbery," Professor Warren said.

"Oh, I'm not sure I'll be able to do that," Sadie protested.

"I have no doubt you will," Professor Warren told her. "And keep me updated on what you find. Maybe it'll be my next book."

Now Sadie laughed. "I'll let you know," she said, and signed off.

She stood in the street, still turning over the conversations of the last hour or so in her mind. The thought of Edwin surfaced for a moment, but was quickly replaced by a sort of mental chess game, new pieces moving and falling into place as others were removed from the board. When she and Theo had talked over the bank robbery outside Ed Walter's house, Wes Winston had still been a serious suspect. And they still hadn't known about all the internal auditing James Morgan had done of his family's historical book-keeping. Even if James was right that that wasn't enough to prove him innocent in the mind of Silver Peak, it certainly suggested to Sadie that the guilt for the robbery might lie elsewhere. And of everyone she'd talked to in the past few days, there was only one whom she believed hadn't told her the whole truth: Agatha Hale.

Sadie scrolled back through her phone to Agatha's number, but when she reached it, she hesitated. She hadn't been able to keep Agatha on the phone for long in their earlier conversation, and since Agatha had been so uncomfortable then, she wasn't sure she could even get her to answer the phone if she tried again. And even if she didn't there was no reason to believe Agatha would be more forthcoming in another phone conversation.

But if Sadie showed up on Agatha's doorstep, she'd be much harder to ignore. And if she could see Agatha's face as she was talking about the old robbery, maybe she'd be able to catch some kind of clue that would help her to convince Agatha to tell her whatever else she knew—because Agatha clearly knew something she wasn't telling, or at least had some thoughts she hadn't been ready to share with a stranger.

Instead of dialing the number, Sadie copied it, then pasted it, along with Agatha's name, into the Internet browser on her phone. A single address in Denver flashed up on the screen. Sadie clicked on it, calling up the map program, which quickly located the address in one of Denver's outlying neighborhoods. With another click, she had requested directions from Silver Peak to the address, and they had flashed up on the screen, the first step highlighted.

Sadie strode over to her car, hopped in, and a moment later, she was on the road to Denver.

21

SADIE MADE THE LAST TURN THE MAP PROGRAM INSTRUCTED, and pulled up at the curb outside a trim-looking ranch house with blue siding and a gray roof. It had seemed like a great idea to pay a visit to Agatha Hale when she was standing on the street in Silver Peak, but now that she was here, she felt a bit of hesitation about going up to a virtual stranger's home and knocking on the door—especially since, from the one conversation she had had with Agatha, she could make a pretty strong guess that Agatha might not be exactly thrilled to see her.

She sighed as she shut down the mapping program, then placed the phone back in her purse, and said a little prayer. *Lord,* she said, *it seems like, these days, I can't say anything about this robbery without making someone uncomfortable. I don't want to just make people feel bad. I want to find the truth. And I believe that, even if it stings, the truth will put everything right in the end. So please don't let all this discomfort I seem to have been causing go to waste. Please use it to reveal Your truth. And please use Your truth to set everybody involved with all of this free, from whatever they need to be freed from.*

When she looked back up at the house, she still couldn't say she felt eager to go up and knock on the door, but she did feel a little pulse of hope as she collected Janie's diary, then went up the walk, where she rang the doorbell.

It took so long for anyone to answer that Sadie actually began to feel a sense of both disappointment and relief over the possibility that perhaps nobody was home at Agatha's house after all. But just as she was trying to decide whether or not to ring again once more before she gave up, the door opened.

Sadie would have recognized Agatha anywhere, because she was the spitting image of Janie in the old photographs of the bank robbery, with Janie's same warm, questioning brown eyes, and her same rounded cheeks, although she was now quite a bit older than her mother had been at the time of the robbery.

"Agatha," Sadie said, with the enthusiasm of a person greeting a long-lost friend.

At this greeting, Agatha frowned and took a short step back, recognition struggling on her face.

"Oh, I'm so sorry," Sadie said. "I should have introduced myself. I'm Sadie. Sadie Speers, from Silver Peak. I spoke with you earlier this week. About your mother's diary."

"Oh," Agatha said, her eyes still wary, "did you bring it?"

Sadie held it out. "As soon as I told my grandson the story, he agreed that you should have it," she said. She had been touched by how generous Theo's reaction to the story of the lost family treasure had been. He had agreed that it ought to be returned to the Hale family immediately, and without reservation.

Agatha's eyes lit as she took it, then teared up as she flipped to the first page. "This is it," she said. "It's my mother's handwriting. I don't know how to thank you."

"There's no need to thank me," Sadie said. "We're just glad to bring it back to its proper home. So many antiques seem to be orphans in the world, separated from the people who first used and loved them. I'm glad this diary has a family to come back to."

"Well, you must have paid something for it, wherever you found it," Agatha said. "Could I at least pay you that?"

Sadie gave her head an emphatic shake. She might be making an unwise business decision, but she had no doubt that Theo would have done the same. "But I do have a few questions," she said. "If you'd have a moment to answer them."

Agatha's eyes turned wary again. "I told you on the phone," she said. "That was all a long time ago. I was practically a baby."

Sadie recognized the echo of James Morgan's plaintive refrain, when he spoke about how the events of the robbery had shadowed his whole life, even though he hadn't even been born at the time. But while the problem for James Morgan was his lack of knowledge about the truth of the events that had shaped him, Sadie still had the strong sense that Agatha actually knew more than she was telling, even if it was true that she had been too young to understand the events of the robbery at the time that it happened. But it was still very possible, Sadie thought, that she now remembered things that seemed different when she looked at them with adult eyes, or that Ben Hale had let something about the robbery slip in the years since it happened. Or even, Sadie reasoned, that Agatha had grown suspicious about the robbery because of things that had happened in her family since then—unexplained funds when she was a child, or strange paperwork that emerged long after the death of her parents.

On the phone, Sadie had thought that Agatha began to sound cold when she asked about the robbery, but in person, she could see that, although the warmth had left Agatha's voice, worry, rather than hostility, was the primary expression on Agatha's face.

"I understand that," Sadie said gently. "But I wonder if you might have heard or seen anything later, as you were growing up, that gave you any insight into the events surrounding the robbery."

Agatha just stared at her, without answering.

"I know it seems like a long time ago," Sadie said. "But the consequences of those events aren't really in the past. In fact, they're affecting life in Silver Peak today. The money from the robbery was eventually returned, but until it was, many people in the town really suffered that winter. Those stories are still fresh in people's minds. And some people are still suffering because the mystery has never been solved. James Morgan, the son of the man your mother used to work for, has spent his whole life trying to remove the shadow of those events from his family name. But the resurfacing of this diary in town just seems to have stirred up sentiment against him. In fact, he's running for mayor of the town right now, and there's actually been some violence against his campaign."

"Violence?" Agatha said, her eyes widening. "In a town the size of Silver Peak?"

"Strange as it may seem, it may have something to do with this old robbery. So if you have anything that you could tell us, it could be a great help. It might actually affect people's whole lives."

She could see from Agatha's expression that she was affected by the appeal Sadie had made. But something was still holding her back.

Maybe, Sadie guessed, she was worried about sharing what-ever she knew about the robbery because of the consequences for her own family, or her own family name. "But as you said," Sadie added. "It is a long time in the past. Of course, the case is too old for any official action to be taken. We're just interested in the truth here. But I believe the truth can make a real difference, even all these years later."

Agatha sighed, and stepped out of the door to allow Sadie to enter. "Maybe you'd better come in," she said.

Sadie followed her into the house, to a cheerful sitting room overlooking the front yard, decorated with simple furniture and dozens of family pictures. At Agatha's gesture, she took a seat on the couch, where Agatha also sank down.

But although Sadie waited what seemed like several minutes for Agatha to open the conversation, Agatha remained completely silent, staring at the upholstery of the couch, as if waiting for it to tell her what to say.

"We did read your mother's diary, after my grandson found it," Sadie said. "I'm sorry if that feels like an invasion of privacy, but at the time we had no way of knowing that there was an exist-ing family that was still looking for it."

"Oh, that's all right," Agatha said, still not meeting Sadie's eyes.

"Well, I can see from the diary that your family was having some very hard times around the time of the robbery. They weren't alone. A lot of people were. But it's clear that your mother was quite worried about money from the notes that she makes on vari-ous days. And it also seems clear that your father was quite inter-ested in the workings of the bank. In fact, his visits to the bank become increasingly frequent, leading right up to the time of the robbery. And this might not have been clear to you, if you weren't acquainted with the details of the robbery, but your mother's diary breaks off the day before the robbery occurred. It seems that your family may have been linked to that robbery through more than just your mother's job there. Or that perhaps your mother's job led your father to begin to think about the possibility. I know he had been having some trouble finding work, and I'm sure that was very frustrating to him as a man..." Sadie trailed off, watching Agatha's face to see her reaction.

Agatha shook her head. "You're right about that," she said. "Life was never easy for my father. At first my mother thought it was just the effects of the Depression, but the truth was that he simply wasn't an easy man. And he didn't make life easy for any of the rest of us. Especially my mother."

Sadie nodded, and Agatha dropped her gaze again, this time staring down at her hands. "But I don't believe that he would have robbed the bank. He was never any good with money. When he had it, he spent it. But we never had any extra money, the whole time I was growing up, and neither did he. Especially not when we first moved to Denver. We were in a terrible apartment, without even a bathroom. We had a kitchen of our own, but we had to go down the hall to use the facilities. I was very sick around that time, and I just remember Mama carrying me up and down the hall, over and over."

Sadie felt a wave of sympathy at the hard times she had endured. But she also felt a bit of a letdown at this. Maybe, after all the investigating she'd done, the town of Silver Peak had been right after all, and Jules Morgan was actually to blame for the mysterious events at his bank, so long ago.

"It sounds like she was a very loving mother," Sadie said.

"She was," Agatha said. When she looked up, her eyes were bright with tears. "We never had much, but we always knew how much she loved us."

"Do you remember her ever saying anything about her time at the bank?" Sadie said. "Did she ever tell you stories about what life was like for them in Silver Peak?"

Agatha gave her head a firm shake, no. "It was funny," she said. "My father sometimes liked to talk about her days at the bank. He was especially interested in an old safe they had there. I guess for the time it was like the Cadillac of safes, and he thought it was about the most interesting thing in the world. He especially liked the fact that, even though it had been such a big expensive investment, the bank had been robbed anyhow. He got a real kick out of that. But Mama didn't seem to like to talk about it. I don't remember her ever saying anything about the time she spent there. That's why the diary meant so much, when we found it after her death. It gave us a window into a part of her life we'd never really known about. I guess it might not seem so interesting, just the daily workings of the bank. But to us, it was a way to get to know our mother, just a little bit better, after she was gone."

Sadie nodded, her expression sympathetic. "But she never said anything to you about her time at the bank herself," she said, hoping to elicit something, anything, that Janie might have passed on to her daughter that wasn't already included in the diary she and Theo had combed through so carefully.

Agatha shook her head. "I thought for years that it just must have been such a hard time in the family that she didn't want to relive it. And I could understand that. But then..." She trailed off.

"What?" Sadie said, after a moment.

Agatha rose from the couch in a sudden motion. "I'll be right back," she said.

Sadie watched her leave the room, then waited as she heard her moving through the back rooms of the house. For what seemed like a long time, there was dead silence. Then Sadie could hear Agatha's footsteps, approaching through unseen rooms.

When she stepped back into the front room, Agatha had a letter-size envelope in her hand. Just one line was written across it, where a full address would usually be emblazoned. As Agatha approached, Sadie could read the letters to make out a name: Jules Morgan.

Sadie drew in her breath, but held her tongue, waiting for Agatha to explain.

Agatha sank back down beside her and held the letter out. Sadie took it and turned it over in her hands. It was sealed, but it had never been formally addressed, or mailed.

"My mother gave that to me," Agatha explained. "As she was dying."

"Had she ever mentioned Jules Morgan to you before?"

Agatha shook her head. "Never," she said. "I knew the name, because my father had mentioned him, when I was younger, as the owner of the remarkable bank vault. But I couldn't understand why my mother would be writing to him in her last days. And she didn't tell me. Not only that, she made me promise to send it without reading the contents."

Sadie looked up from studying the envelope. "But you haven't sent it," she said.

"I tried to," Agatha said, with a break in her voice that gave Sadie the sense that she was trying to explain, not just to Sadie, but perhaps to her own mother, why the letter had never been sent. "But when I looked up his address, a few weeks after her funeral, I found his obituary. So there was nobody to send it to. And she had made me promise not to read it…"

"And so you still haven't," Sadie finished for her.

Agatha nodded, her eyes sad. "I tried to honor her wishes," she said. "I just didn't know how best to do that. So I didn't do anything. But I had no idea that the old robbery was still affecting life in Silver Peak. Do you think this might have anything to do with it?"

"There's only one way to know for sure," Sadie said, looking down at the letter.

"Do you think," Agatha said haltingly, "that you could open it? I know it's silly, but that wouldn't violate my promise to my mother."

"I'd be honored," Sadie said. Very gently, she broke the seal on the envelope, and pulled out a single sheet of paper. The handwriting wasn't as sure or neat as the handwriting in the diary, but she still recognized it as Janie's, despite the ways it had changed as Janie aged.

Carefully, Sadie unfolded the page. But before she began to read, she looked at Agatha. "Would you like me to read it to you?" she said.

"I guess that's not the same as my reading it," Agatha said. "Not exactly."

Sadie took a deep breath. "*Dear Jules,*" she read. "*The doctors tell me that I'm not long for this world, and as I face the next life, something has been weighing on my mind. It's funny what weighs on your mind at the end of your life. It's not the things that you* would expect. But one of the things that weighs on my mind is that I never got to thank you. You would think it might be something else. In my case, you know exactly what I mean. But I've never regretted what I did. I would have done anything for my daughter. But we had nothing to give her. And I would have been glad to spend the rest of my life in prison, if it meant that she could have the surgery that saved her life. The problem was, I didn't have anything to pay with. And so I thought I had to take it. Looking back, I wonder if that was really true. From the way you reacted when you found me at the safe and I broke down and told you our story, and why I had to have the money, for Agatha, I wonder now if perhaps I could have just asked you for it. But I was young, and scared, and I didn't think I had any other choice. But you made a choice that night, to let me go with the money that saved Agatha's life, and, in many ways, saved mine. I don't know how much that cost you. I hope it wasn't too much. But the gift you gave us was priceless. And although I don't regret the risks I took to protect my daughter, I've always regretted that I never had the chance to thank you. So I want to do that now, from my deathbed. People around Silver Peak always had all kinds of ideas and things to say about you. I'm sure they still do. But to me, you'll always be the best man in town."

"And she's signed it, here," Sadie finished. She let her hands drop into her lap, taking in the contents of the letter.

"So my mother..." Agatha said, her eyes wide, unable to complete the sentence.

"Your mother robbed the Silver Peak Bank," Sadie said.

"For me?" Agatha said, her voice soft.

"That's what she seems to be saying," Sadie agreed.

"I never even wondered, how they managed to pay—" Agatha said. "I did have a surgery, just after we moved to Denver. But my mother never told me I was sick enough to die."

"That's the kind of thing a mother might try to protect her child from, if she could," Sadie said.

Agatha nodded. "I guess so," she said. "And she did. And Jules Morgan—"

"It sounds like he must have discovered her there," Sadie said. "And let her go."

Agatha's face fell. "But you told me that his son has been suffering for all these years, under the suspicion that his family was responsible for that crime?"

Sadie nodded. "And it sounds like, in a way, Jules was responsible for it. Just not the way some people in Silver Peak might think."

Agatha nodded, her eyes still wide as she took in the huge shift in her family history. But Sadie had another family's history on her mind too.

"I know you've only just now gotten your mother's diary back, years after it went missing," Sadie said. "And I hate to ask you to part with another piece of your family history so quickly. But if I promise to take extremely good care of it until I bring it back to you, would you be willing to let me take this letter with me?"

22

WHEN SADIE SLIPPED INTO THE BIG HALL WHERE THE SECOND and final debate of the Silver Peak mayoral race was being held, it was even more packed than the first debate had been, if that was possible. Sadie had forgotten all about the debate in her eagerness to get to Denver, and she had been glad when she remembered it on her drive back that she still had time to catch the tail end of it, so that Edwin wouldn't be disappointed that she had missed it completely.

The debate was already in full swing, with both Edwin and James vigorously but good-naturedly sparring over the long-standing question of a four-way stop just outside of town. For years, some people had been agitating to put in a stoplight, which they believed would better regulate traffic and make the corner safer, especially for young drivers, or elderly ones. But a lot of people in Silver Peak valued the small-town sense, and there was a considerable amount of local pride in the fact that the whole population of Silver Peak had managed to get along for all these years with only two real stoplights, right in the heart of town. To them, adding another stoplight signaled a dangerous step toward the big-city living that they escaped by residing in Silver Peak.

Sadie wriggled into a small space among the crowd standing at the back of the hall, but as she did, a familiar face looked up at her from one of the benches that lined the rear of the hall. Helen Morgan gave her a brief smile, then scooted over from her seat to create just enough room for Sadie to squeeze into.

Sadie shook her head, and waved her hand no, not wanting to cause any trouble, but Helen nodded insistently, unwilling to take no for an answer.

Finally, Sadie pushed her way somewhat reluctantly through the crowd and took the seat beside Helen. "Thank you," she said.

Helen smiled, and nodded up at the podiums, indicating that her concentration was on the debate, which had now turned to the question of expanded funding for the library that was under consideration by the city council. There wasn't really much to debate about that. Neither Edwin nor James was at all against more funds for the library. But they did have a brief but spirited discussion about the purpose of a library, with Edwin emphasizing the need to introduce readers to the classics, and James stressing the need for libraries to stay relevant in a changing world.

"I don't know why we can't ever try to do both things at the same time," Sadie said to Helen, with a joking tone.

But Helen's gaze was fixed on her husband so intently that Sadie wasn't sure she had even heard her.

The question of the library was apparently the last one that had been prepared by the moderator, a pleasant-looking redheaded woman. When Edwin and James had both finished their statements, she lifted her microphone. "That concludes the formal debate," she said. "But as always, we'd like to spend a few minutes in a more town-hall meeting style, if there are any questions from the floor."

Around the room, throughout the crowd, hands went up.

The debate moderator identified one of them by pointing, a man about Edwin and James's age, wearing a blue and green plaid shirt, his hair still dark, but his face leathery from years of Colorado sun. He nodded his head, and took the wireless microphone that one of the election volunteers scampered to hand to him.

"I almost hate to bring this up," he said. "Because it seems like this election season has taken a real turn this time around."

A murmur of assent rippled through the crowd.

The man waited for it to pass, then went on. "It seems like there have been a lot of rumors floating around town," he said. "And not just about both candidates. About one candidate in particular."

Beside Sadie, Helen stirred. Before Sadie knew what was happening, Helen was on her feet, pushing past her. "Excuse me," she said, after she had more or less climbed over Sadie in her eagerness to leave her seat. She glanced back over her shoulder at the bag that had been sitting at her feet. "You'll watch my bag for me?"

"Of course," Sadie said, and nodded. As Helen headed for the exit, Sadie inched over, to put a little more space between her and her neighbors, and pulled Helen's bag into her lap for safekeeping.

"I don't mean to pick a fight," the man was saying. "I just think sometimes a man likes a chance to face these things head-on, instead of dealing with a whisper campaign where he never gets to say his own piece."

The contents of Helen's bag had shifted when Sadie placed in on her lap, so that Helen's sunglasses, and wallet, and a handful of loose receipts were now hanging precariously out of it. Absently, Sadie tucked the sunglasses and wallet safely back into the depths of the big bag. But when she started to tamp the receipts back in, as well, something caught her eye. She never would have snooped through Helen's purse without permission, but she couldn't help reading the receipt once she caught sight of it, because it was only for a single item: salt. And the sales price was enormously high. Over fifty dollars.

That wasn't so odd, Sadie tried to tell herself. Industrial-size bags of salt, for a water softener or snowmelt, could easily run that high, especially if Helen had bought them in any quantity. It wasn't necessarily suspicious. But just to ease her own mind, Sadie looked at the receipt a bit more closely. When she did, it became clear that the purchase hadn't been for a water softener, or for snowmelt. The receipt was clearly labeled as table salt. And it looked like Helen had bought several dozen containers of it. Quickly, Sadie glanced at the date, and calculated back. Helen had made the purchase the same day as James's campaign barbecue.

"So I just want to know," the man with the microphone was concluding, "what James Morgan has to say about all of these rumors?" Now he was addressing his comments to James directly, instead of the entire crowd. "You've been in charge of the bank for a long time. You've had a chance to look through the books, if you wanted it. And you'd know better than anyone whether these rumors about your family are true. I want to know, what do you have to say about them?"

Behind his podium, Edwin frowned. He started to take a breath, but then stopped. Sadie could guess that his logical lawyer's mind was hard at work. He'd defended James at the previous debate, but it hadn't stopped the question from coming back. Maybe, Sadie guessed he was thinking, it was time to let James answer his own questions, however unfair those questions might be.

Edwin glanced at James, giving him the floor. James acknowledged Edwin's gesture with a grateful nod. He cleared his throat,
then looked out over the gathered crowd, people whom he had
spent his whole life serving, but also trying to convince of his family's innocence—or at least his own.

But he didn't say anything.

The conversation that she had had with him earlier at the
bank flooded back to Sadie. James had a story to tell, but he
believed it wasn't enough to stifle the rumors that had dogged him
since he was a boy. All his life, he'd believed it was best to just let
the rumors lie, and let his actions speak for themselves. But he
couldn't do that anymore. And, Sadie thought, looking around
at all the eyes glued to him, he might be right. This crowd didn't
want to hear about inconclusive audits, and how he'd done the
best he could. Almost everyone in the room had had their lives
marked in some way, big or small, by the Silver Peak Bank robbery. And they wanted an answer.

Sadie knew that she often spoke before she thought, but she
didn't usually find herself doing it in front of a whole crowd of her
fellow citizens. But suddenly, without really choosing to rise, she
found herself on her feet. "Excuse me!" said, waving her hands
in the air to get the attention of the candidates on the podium.
"Excuse me!"

Edwin's gaze immediately fastened on her, but it took James a
moment longer to scan the crowd, and pick her out. By this time,
the only other person standing, the man with the microphone,
was looking at her, as well—along with the rest of the seated
crowd.

"I have a question," Sadie said, pushing her way into the aisle.

The man with the microphone ducked his head to speak into it. "I'm sorry," his voice boomed through the room. "I haven't got an answer to my question yet."

Sadie was halfway down the aisle by then. And before the man with the microphone could protest, she swiped the mic from him as she passed him in the aisle.

"My question is a follow-up to the last question," she said, heading for the front of the hall. "I'd just like to ask a similar question of the candidates. And I have a bit of information I think everyone might find relevant."

As she reached the front of the hall, Edwin looked down from the podium with a questioning glance, but she swept past him, to James's podium, where she stood on tiptoes to hand him Janie's letter.

"What's this?" James asked, his voice low, and away from both mics.

"It's proof," Sadie told him. "That your father didn't rob the Silver Peak Bank. At least not for his own benefit."

James straightened up, staring down at the letter in his hands as Sadie turned to address the crowd. "My question is a simple one," she said. "Mr. Morgan, would you be willing to read us the letter I just gave you? I think it will shed some light on the questions we've all been pondering recently."

Wonderingly, James took the letter and returned to his own podium, where he slowly pulled the sheet of paper from the envelope, laid the envelope to the side, and smoothed out the folds. "*Dear Jules,*" he began to read. "*The doctors tell me...*" His voice trailed off as his eyes scanned ahead, reading silently through the text for himself. As he did, his head drooped lower and lower.

From her vantage point just below the podium, Sadie could see the tears in his eyes. Then he reached the bottom of the page. His eyes stopped their quick scan from side to side, and closed for a moment. Then he put a hand up over his brow, shielding himself from the inquiring gazes of the gathered crowd.

Sadie glanced over at Edwin, and nodded her head toward the letter.

Edwin crossed the short distances between the podiums, and laid a comforting hand on James's shoulder. He spoke quietly to James, out of range of either microphone. James nodded, and, his hand still over his eyes, handed Edwin the letter, which Edwin carried back with him to his own podium.

Without any further explanation, Edwin picked up where James had left off, reading slowly but clearly until the end of the letter. When he finished, a complete hush had fallen over the crowd. Edwin looked down at the man with the microphone. "Does that answer your question about the Morgan family's responsibility for the Silver Peak Bank robbery?" he asked.

Soberly, the man nodded. Then he handed the microphone to the election volunteer, who had stood in the aisle all this time, waiting patiently to reclaim it. Then, slowly, he began to clap. Around him, other members of the crowd started to clap along with him, until the hall was filled with a thunderous sound of applause that drew the members of the crowd, one by one, and then all at once, to their feet alongside the single man who had been holding the microphone.

Edwin smiled and handed the letter back to James, his hand on James's shoulder. Finally, James lifted his head and looked out at the crowd, his eyes bright with tears, but a smile on his face. To Sadie, he looked freer than he had in years.

23

SADIE LINGERED BY THE STAGE WHERE THE DEBATE HAD TAKEN place as the crowd began to file out. Instead of the atmosphere of suspicion and hostility that had marked the last debate, the mood was now buoyant and friendly—almost as if the crowd had been there to celebrate at a victory party, instead of just to hear the final debate of a campaign. And in a way, Sadie thought, it had been a victory party of sorts, both for the Morgan family, and for the truth.

Thank You, Lord, she prayed. *For leading us into Your truth. And thank You for the ways that truth sets us free.*

As she finished her prayer, she felt a hand on her shoulder. She turned, expecting to see Edwin, but smiled when she saw James.

"Sadie," he said, and folded her into a bear hug. "Thank you."

Sadie did her best to hug him back, but he was so much bigger than her that she could do little more than pat his sides and smile. She couldn't remember James Morgan ever having done anything quite so undignified in his life. When he released her, she raised her hand to her thoroughly mussed hair, to pat it down into its customary short curls.

"I know I wasn't excited about your looking into the Silver Peak Bank robbery," James said.

"Well, you had some very understandable reasons," Sadie told him.

"But I was wrong," James insisted. "I think it's important that I tell you that. If you'd listened to me, we never would have found out the truth, not just about the robbery, but about—" he hesitated, his voice breaking slightly as he spoke the words. "My dad."

Sadie patted his arm again as he regained his composure. "All these years," he said, "I thought I was worried about what the town might think of my family. Or even of me. I told myself that was why it was best to let sleeping dogs lie concerning all that old history. But now that I know the truth, I can see that wasn't the reason at all. I was afraid of what I might find out about my own father. I thought I could handle it if he had something to do with the robbery. After all, it wouldn't have been his only foible. But somehow, I guess, hurting the whole town that way seemed like a bigger mark against him than all of the little foolish things I knew for sure he had done. I just couldn't stand to believe he could really have done something like that. And because I couldn't face it, I suppose there was always a little part of me that always believed he probably had. It's such a relief to know he wasn't a thief, and that he did what he did at the bank to help another family, not to enrich our own. It changes everything. It may take me years to understand it all. But I know I owe it all to you."

As he was speaking, Helen came up and threaded her arm through his, her bag hanging from the crook of her other elbow.

"I'm sorry," Sadie told her. "I forgot all about your bag in my rush to share this letter with the crowd."

Helen gave her a warm smile. "That's all right," she said. "It was just fine when I went back to pick it up. And even if something had happened to it, that would have been a small price to pay for the gift you gave us today. I don't know how we'll ever be able to thank you."

Sadie felt another gentle touch on her shoulder. This time it was Edwin, joining the conversation. "That was quite a debate," he said. "I don't remember seeing the likes of that before, not even in those rough-and-tumble big-city Chicago politics."

A shadow crossed briefly across James's face. "Yes," he said. "I wonder if it's too much to hope that whoever has been trying to sabotage my campaign has been satisfied by the evidence of my family's innocence."

Sadie glanced at Helen, who glanced away from her husband's face for the first time since she had arrived at the mention of the campaign sabotage.

"I have to apologize for something else about your bag," Sadie said to her.

Helen glanced at her, surprised. "Oh, whatever it is, I'm sure it's all right," she said dismissively.

"Perhaps," Sadie said. "But as I was collecting it from below your seat, a few things almost fell out of it. And as I was putting them back in, I couldn't help noticing a somewhat strange receipt."

"A receipt?" Helen said, her expression quizzical.

Sadie nodded. "Yes. For salt. A very large quantity of it. Purchased on the day of James's campaign barbecue."

Helen's face blanched at this, and she leaned back into the circle of James's arm. For his part, James's expression, a moment ago so unusually open and friendly, suddenly turned to a dark glower.

"Now wait just a minute here," he said. "I'm not sure I understand what you're trying to say."

Even Edwin was giving Sadie a questioning glance with a hint of warning in it. But he still moved closer to her as the conversation turned heated, as if he wanted to shelter her the same way that James was sheltering Helen, but was restraining himself.

But now it was Helen who put a hand on James's arm, restraining him. "It's all right," she said. "It's not Sadie's fault."

As she said this, her voice broke. Tears sprang into her eyes, and then, as her husband looked on in shock, began to stream down her face.

"Helen?" James said. "What are you saying? What is going on?"

"I was just so tired of watching you try to prove that you're a good man to this old town," Helen burst out, her voice high with emotion. "You're the best man I know. You always have been. But ever since we've been married, there's a part of you that—I don't know if you didn't believe in yourself, or if you didn't think other people in town believed in you. But you've spent so much time fighting it. Not just you, we have. Because all the time you've spent fighting that battle, I've been right here beside you. It's been my time too. But we never seem to win," she said. "We've been fighting our whole lives, but we could never beat it."

"I had no idea that all this had affected you so much," James said quietly.

"Of course it did!" Helen said passionately. "Because it affected *you*. And there's nothing else I care about more in the world."

"So are you saying," James said haltingly, reasoning it out as he spoke, "that you're the person who ruined all our barbecue?"

Helen nodded almost fiercely. "And I ruined the signs in our yard. And I lit the Roman candles in our trunk."

"But why in the world would you ever do a thing like that?" James asked.

"I just couldn't stand it anymore," Helen repeated. "I'd been fighting alongside you all your life, thinking one day it might be enough, but it never was. And then, just as you were finally getting ready to lay down all your responsibilities at the bank, you got this idea of becoming mayor of Silver Peak. You never wanted to be mayor, honey. You weren't even really happy with the administrative work you had to do in leading the bank. You're happiest when you're out in the mountains, or just sitting with me on the back porch with a cup of coffee. You've been robbing yourself of those moments all your life, because of the crazy idea that you could prove to the town that you weren't your dad, if you were just good enough, responsible enough. And now you were getting ready to spend our golden years on the same losing battle. Our golden years. And pouring our savings into it too," she added. "Everything we'd built up through the years. I know the rest of the town thinks we must be made of money, since we own the bank, but I knew differently. And it scared me. Not even the big expense, but the thought that you might spend your whole life on this fight, instead of enjoying all the good things you have as well."

"Well, honey," James said. "Why didn't you tell me all of this?"

Helen gazed deeply into his eyes. "Would you have really listened to me?" she said. "Before Sadie had proven that your father was innocent, I mean? Do you really think you would have changed your mind about the campaign because of my objections?"

James took a long, remorseful breath. "Probably not," he said. "You know me pretty well."

"I didn't want you to think I didn't believe in you. Or that I'd given up and started believing the rumors about your family, just like you thought everybody else in town did," she said. "But I didn't want to see you running yourself ragged for the rest of your life in a battle I knew you could never really win. So I just started trying to—make trouble for the campaign," she said. She leaned against him, letting her head drop onto his shoulder. "I'm sorry," she said. "I shouldn't have lied to you."

"And it sounds like I should have listened better to you," James said. "Maybe a long time ago, for that matter. But don't worry. I don't have any intention of pressing charges. And I don't think Edwin does either."

Beside Sadie, Edwin grinned. "I'm just glad nobody's pressing charges against *me*," he said. "I wasn't too comfortable with the idea that people might think I had brought those hard-nosed campaign tactics with me from the big city."

"I'm so glad you're not angry with me," Helen said.

"Honestly?" James said. "I'm kind of touched you care about me so much."

"You should have known that already," Helen said. "I hope I've never given you reason to believe anything else."

"Well, sure," James said. "But where in the world did you get the paint for the signs?"

"It was left over from when we redid the dining room. In fact, I was afraid you might recognize it. But I never could get you to look very closely at those paint swatches," Helen said.

"And how did you ever get your hands on all those Roman candles?" James asked.

"I just saw somebody had put them out in the trash by the curb," Helen said. "I wasn't even sure they would work."

James shook his head in amazement. "You're quite a woman," he said.

"Well, you're quite a man," she told him. "And finally everyone in Silver Peak knows it."

James smiled and gave her a quick kiss. "So I guess it was never one of your dreams to become Mrs. Mayor?" he said.

Helen shook her head decisively.

James looked at Edwin. "You heard the lady," he said. "I'm not sure I can continue in this race without the support of my wife."

"Oh, don't pin it all on me," Helen said, patting his side.

James face took on a more serious expression. "Helen's right," he said. "I'm afraid I never really wanted the post of mayor. It was always about proving something personal. And now that I see it, I don't think that's a good reason to run for public office."

Edwin raised his eyebrows. "I guess I can understand that," he said.

James stuck out his hand. "So let me be the first to congratulate you. The way I see it, if I drop out of this race, that makes you the winner, de facto."

"I hate to jump the gun on that," Edwin said. "The people still need to go to the polls."

James grinned. "Yes, but with only one name on the ballot, I think I have a good idea of who they'll choose this Tuesday," he said. "And I can't think of a better man for the job, *Mayor* Marshall."

24

SADIE STOOD FOR A MOMENT OUTSIDE THE FESTIVE CIRCLE OF lights and bunting that ringed the Silver Peak town square, where Edwin's victory party was in full swing. The unseasonably warm late-autumn weather had remained, though Sadie knew it could change again without warning, and it seemed like just as many people had come out for it as it had come out for James's campaign event a week earlier, and for a similar reason: once again, Andi presided over the barbecue. This time, however, the sauce was a success: all around the square, Silver Peak's citizens celebrated the victory of their new mayor by munching happily on wings, ribs, or brisket.

Spike Harris's trio had taken the stage again, and with a pleased smile, Sadie could see Alice standing near the stage, watching him as he played. Nearby, in the crowd, she made out Theo's familiar form, as he swatted at Sara, who was making an attempt to steal bits of barbecue from his plate.

"So it looks like your boyfriend is mayor of the town now," Roz said, sidling up to Sadie.

Sadie gave her a quick hug. "He's not my boyfriend," she protested.

Roz's shoulders fell. "Sadie. Don't tell me you're going to turn him down. What does that poor man have to do to get your affection? He just became mayor of the town!"

"I didn't say that," Sadie said.

Roz's eyes widened. "So you're going to say *yes*?" she asked.

"I didn't say that either," Sadie said.

"You've got to make up your mind sometime," Roz admonished her.

"I know," Sadie said. "But I can't very well tell you before I tell him, can I?"

"I guess that's fair," Roz agreed, reluctantly. "Look! There he is!"

Sadie glanced into the crowd, but wherever Roz had seen Edwin, she didn't find him.

"And it's just time for me to be going!" Roz said, with a broad wink, as she vanished into the crowd.

With a satisfied smile, Sadie stepped into the party, still glancing around to see where Edwin might be. She didn't plan to make a beeline for him. After all, he would be the star of the evening, and she knew plenty of other people in town to talk with. But she just wanted to get her bearings. She knew she owed him an answer to his question about "going steady." As corny as that phrase might seem to a couple at their age, there was a serious question behind it. And she knew that he deserved a serious answer.

But before she caught sight of Edwin, Jesse Wilson strode up to her. To her surprise, he had a big, welcoming smile on his face—a big change from the furtive, almost suspicious way he had treated her before the election.

"Sadie," he said, clasping the hand she extended to him in both of his. "It's wonderful to see you. How have you been doing?"

"Well, just fine," she said. "I'm very pleased to see Edwin become mayor, of course. As I'm sure you must be as well."

"Pleased doesn't begin to cover it," Jesse said. "I think this is the best thing that's happened to this town in years."

Sadie smiled. Jesse still sounded like he was campaigning, even now that the campaign was won. It was a nice sign that he actually believed the things that he said, and that all of his enthusiasm, even if at times it had bordered on excessive, had actually been genuine.

"I'll certainly look forward to seeing how he leads as mayor," Sadie said.

"Listen, Sadie," Jesse said. "I wanted to talk with you. I feel like we had a few awkward moments during the course of the campaign."

"Oh," Sadie said waving her hand to show that all that was in the past, "there's nothing to worry about."

"No," Jesse said firmly. "I'd like to explain. I got the feeling a few times that you thought I might be up to no good. And I wish I'd been able to tell you at the time what I was really doing. But I knew Edwin wouldn't approve."

Sadie's smile faded. She appreciated Jesse's attempt at candor, but his tone had turned almost conspiratorial. And she didn't want to be part of any conspiracy that Jesse himself knew Edwin would object to.

"See," Jesse said, "there you go again. Sure I'm up to no good. But it's nothing shady, I promise. You see, I've always been certain that Edwin was going to win this campaign. Even before James dropped out. And I know that Edwin doesn't enjoy a big fuss, but I wanted to make sure he had a great party. Not just for him, but for Silver Peak. We need a little celebration around here, especially with all the ups and downs in this campaign. Something to replace all those memories with, and remind us why, at the end of the day, we're all neighbors and friends."

"It certainly is a lovely party," Sadie allowed.

"Thank you," Jesse said. "But you don't believe I just put it together since last night, when the election results came in. Do you?"

Sadie stared at him, the wheels in her mind turning. "I guess not," she said.

"That's what I've been doing," Jesse said. "When you've caught me skulking around Silver Peak, I was putting plans in place for Edwin's victory party. But I had to start doing it well in advance. You don't have any idea the kind of demand Andi's barbecue is in, for instance. And I knew Edwin would never approve of it."

Sadie's smile spread back over her face. "You're right about that," she said. "He would think it was the worst kind of arrogance."

"Well, if he ordered it, maybe it would have been," Jesse said. "But I figured, if I did it, it would just be a sign of my faith in him. And it would result in a much better party."

Sadie nodded, grinning. "I see," she said.

"So what do you say?" Jesse asked, sticking out his hand. "Friends?"

"Of course," Sadie said, giving a little yelp of surprise as he pulled her into a bear hug of his own. "I always thought we were."

Jesse raised his eyebrows as he released her. "But you weren't quite *sure*," he prodded. "Were you?"

Before Sadie could answer, Edwin strode up. "Very good," he said. "I see you've located Ms. Speers for me, just as I requested."

"Glad to be of service," Jesse said, giving a brisk nod as he backed away, then melted into the crowd.

Sadie looked askance at Edwin. "Did you really send your campaign manager out into the party looking for me?" she asked, not sure whether to be complimented or insulted. It was nice if Edwin had been thinking of her, but not so nice to feel like she was being summoned like some lackey in an old-time court.

Edwin laughed. "No," he said. "Nope, I didn't. Although I wish I had. It would be the best way I can think of to put a campaign manager to use."

"It seems to me that Jesse actually did a pretty good job running your campaign," Sadie told him.

"Well, as I always like to say," Edwin said. "It's much easier to win when you're running unopposed."

"Still," Sadie said. "Jesse didn't know that was coming. And he managed the campaign well until then."

"And since," Edwin added. "And you're right, as usual."

Sadie smiled.

"I've always loved your smile," Edwin said, his voice suddenly low with emotion.

Sadie's eyes met his. This time she didn't look away. "I know I owe you an answer to your question," she said.

"Only when you feel ready," Edwin said. "You take all the time you need. I figure, if you haven't told me yet, at least you haven't said no."

"I think I'm ready," Sadie said, with a little lump in her throat. But as she said it, she suddenly felt just as nervous and vulnerable as the teenage girl she had once been, standing with Edwin in this very same park. She looked around quickly at all the citizens of

Silver Peak, laughing and enjoying their barbecue. She wasn't sure she wanted all of them to be part of this moment with Edwin too. "I just don't know if this is the right place."

Instantly, Edwin took in the situation. Then he caught her hand. "I know," he said. "Do you realize where we're standing?"

Before Sadie could answer, he had led her through the crowd to the old clump of pines where she'd met him that night, years before. An instant later, he had led her inside. Immediately, Sadie remembered why it had been a favorite haunt of teenagers, even back in the day. Despite the fact that they could clearly hear the crowd around them, they were completely shielded from view by the thick evergreen branches—even more completely than they had been as teenagers, since the old trees had had years more to fill in and grow. Perhaps something like she and Edwin had had years to change and grow themselves, Sadie thought.

But then Edwin looked into her eyes, and all her thoughts fled. "So, Sadie Speers," he said gently, "what do you have on your mind?"

"Yes," Sadie said simply.

Edwin's eyebrows leapt, and a big grin spread across his face. "You realize I didn't actually ask you a yes-or-no question," he said.

Sadie, whose own smile was almost as wide as his, ducked her head in embarrassment, at a loss for a quick reply, for a change.

"So I'm just going to take that as an answer to the question I asked you earlier," Edwin added. "About whether or not you'd like to 'be my girl'."

Both of them cringed a bit at the corny language, but they were also so delighted that something felt right about it. After all these years, Sadie thought it was a gift to know someone who could still make her feel like a girl again.

"Is that fair?" Edwin asked.

Sadie nodded.

In Edwin's grin, Sadie could see both the boy she had once known, and all the history of the man he had become. For a long moment, he stared into her eyes. Then he leaned down and gave her a gentle kiss. In some ways, Sadie felt all the thrill she had at her very first kiss with him, so many years ago. In others, the feel of his lips on hers was deeply familiar, with a sense of coming home.

He wrapped his arms around her. For a while, they just stood there, enjoying the moment together, as the crowd chattered, unseen, around them, and the stars began to come out, high above the strings of lights that ringed the party. Finally, Edwin spoke. "I don't want to," he said. "But I suppose we're going to have to go back out there at some point."

"You're the mayor of the whole town now," Sadie said. "If they notice you've been gone too long, they're liable to send out an official search party. And just imagine what would happen if they found us here."

"I'm not sure how you'd feel about it," Edwin said. "But for my part, I'd be proud. It's one thing to win a political campaign. But it's quite another thing to have the affection of a good woman."

He gave her another kiss on the cheek before he released her with a final squeeze. "I'm honored to be the mayor of Silver Peak," he told her. "But you're the one who really makes me feel like a winner."

About the Author

Carole Jefferson is the pen name for a team of writers who have come together to create the series Mysteries of Silver Peak. *Silver Surprise* was written by Vera Dodge. Vera grew up in small towns in the Midwest. She lives and works in Brooklyn.

Read on for a sneak peek of another exciting book in Mysteries of Silver Peak!

Wildfire

SADIE SPEERS TURNED UP HER COLLAR AGAINST THE COLD SPRING rain and closed the car door.

"Come on, Hank."

Her golden retriever, who had stopped to sniff a pinecone, bounded after her, racing toward the house. Sadie moved a bit slower, picking her way carefully across the soggy yard toward the front door. Her work boots were caked with mud from Milo Henderson's horse farm, and she tried to keep her balance as another gust of wind blew.

For April, it sure felt like winter. The forecasters had called for rain mixed with sleet tonight, and it looked like they were right about that. It had been sunny and in the high sixties over the weekend, but that was life in Colorado, she supposed. You never knew what the weather was going to do.

Hank was pawing at the door when Sadie reached it, and she unlocked the door and stepped inside gratefully. Now that she'd checked on the horses and taken Hank for a walk, all she wanted to do was take a hot shower and settle in with a good book for the evening. She pulled off her boots and peeled off her wet coat and hung it in the closet by the door. Claribel had been here today, and the whole house smelled like the lemon and fresh pine soaps the housekeeper used. Sadie inhaled deeply, and then walked into the vaulted living room, eyeing the tall stone fireplace. It was the perfect night for a fire. First she would—

She jumped. Her cell phone was ringing. Where did she—oh yes. She rushed back to the coat closet and pulled it out of the pocket of her jacket. It was Virginia Radcliff calling.

"Hello?" Sadie said.

Sadie had always liked Virginia, a teacher at the high school who had taken over Sadie's history classes when Sadie retired. They'd been friendly through the years, and when Virginia asked Sadie if she'd be interested in helping her with a presentation for the big spring fundraiser at the high school, Sadie had been glad to help. As part of a gala event that would raise money to update the school's library, Sadie and Virginia would give a short multimedia presentation on the history of Silver Peak's first schoolhouse, a historic one-room structure that dated back to the early days of the mining town's boom years. Though the schoolhouse had burned down in 1965, when Sadie was still a child, it was a key piece of Silver Peak's history, and their presentation at the fundraiser next week would be one of several that traced the history of education in their beloved small town. Sadie had spent many happy hours at the Historical Society and library researching the old schoolhouse and had found some neat old photos and accounts of its early days.

"Sadie?" Virginia's voice sounded a bit muffled, like she was speaking into a headset, but Sadie could still hear the excitement in her voice, as well as some soft music playing in the background.

"Virginia. How are you? Where are you? What's going on?"

"I'm in my car. Let me-" There was a shrill noise, and then Virginia was back on the line. "There, is that better? I adjusted the headset."

"Much better."

"Oh good. Sadie, you'll never believe what I found."

"Oh?" In their research into the old schoolhouse, they had uncovered some old rumors and suspicions about the about schoolhouse fire. Though the blaze was determined to be an accident, the result of dated and shoddy electrical work, Virginia had come across some old newspaper articles that suggested that things might not have been so simple. Virginia had become fascinated by the idea that the fire had been set on purpose, and had spent much of the past few weeks digging through old town records, looking for clues to see if she could find any truth to the rumors. Sadie had been interested to see her conclusions, but she had been left doing the bulk of the work on the history of the schoolhouse itself. Sadie didn't mind—history was her passion, and as a former high school teacher, she could think of few subjects more fascinating.

"It's true," Virginia continued. "The fire was definitely not an accident. I know who—"

The reception cut out, as it often did on these twisty mountain roads.

"Virginia?"

There was some static, and then Virginia was back on the line. "—anyway, I'll tell you more when I get there. I should be there in just a few minutes."

"You're coming here?"

"Is that okay? I'm sorry, I shouldn't have assumed. I just thought—"

Sadie was used to the bad cell reception out here, but still felt herself growing frustrated.

"No, no, that's great," Sadie said. "Of course you're welcome. I just wanted to make sure I was hearing you right. I'm home, and I'm anxious to hear what you found."

"It's unbelievable, Sadie. All this time, it was right there, and no one thought to look for it." As she spoke, Virginia's voice lost the excitement Sadie had heard earlier, and something like hesitation entered.

"Is everything okay?"

"Yeah, it's fine, it's just—"

Sadie couldn't tell if the line cut out again or if Virginia had just hesitated again.

"This car has been behind me the whole way. It's weird."

Sadie knew seeing the same car behind you for miles was usually nothing to worry about on these old mountain roads. They were generally limited to one lane in either direction, and there weren't a lot of places to turn off. But Virginia knew that too.

"Where are you?"

"I was working in my classroom at the school, and when I figured out who set the fire, I came straight to the car and set off for your house. I'm close now, out on Country Rock Road."

Sadie heard the hum of Virginia's windshield wipers swishing across the smooth glass. She was surprised to hear that Virginia had been at her classroom at the school this late. She had a husband and two small boys at home. "Something about this car behind me is weird. It's far enough back that I can't really see it, but it slows down when I slow and has made every turn I've made."

Again, under most circumstances, this wouldn't seem strange at all. Of course the car behind her would slow down whenever Virginia did—she was no doubt braking for the curves in the road and stop signs, and other drivers would need to brake for the same reasons. But if Virginia was nervous, Sadie had reason to be as well.

"Maybe you should pull over and see if they pass," Sadie suggested.

"Good idea. Hang on." Virginia said, and Sadie heard the click of her blinker. "That's weird."

"What?"

"The other car slowed way down. It's—okay, now it's pulling over too."

Sadie's heart started racing. Was someone really following Virginia to her house? Why?

"What kind of car is it?"

"I can't really tell. It's far enough back that it just looks like a sedan of some kind, in some dark color. I don't recognize it, but it looks like any other car."

"Where on Country Rock Road are you?"

"I just passed Mickelson's Garage. Now I'm just before that big curve."

"You're close then." She wasn't more than a couple miles from Sadie's ranch house. "Why don't you get back on the road and come here, and we'll see if it follows you."

Sadie didn't know what she would do if the car did follow Virginia to her house, but they'd cross that bridge when they got there.

"Okay, I'm pulling out now." Again, Sadie heard the click of the blinker, and then the quiet hum of the car moving.

"Is the other car coming too?"

"It's hard to tell…" Virginia's voice trailed off. "Oh yes, now it's pulling out into the road again too…" the line went fuzzy. "—this is really weird."

The line cut out again, and Sadie held her breath.

Static again, and then "—getting closer to me. I don't know what it's doing. I can't—" The line cut out again, and Sadie wanted to throw her phone across the room, but then Virginia came back on. "—about the fire. Here, Sadie, write this down. I tracked down the old police ch—" Sadie scrambled to get a pen and paper, but just as she began writing, the line cut out again. *Old police what?* "—The Wilc—" Sadie copied it down even as Virginia's voice disappeared again. "5100—"

The line went dead again, but this time it came back quickly, and she heard Virginia yell, "He's coming at me!"

And then, all she heard was the screech of tires and then metal scraping against metal.

"Virginia!?" Sadie yelled into the phone, but the only answer was a loud thud and the sound of glass shattering.

"Virginia! Are you okay?" Sadie shouted again, but there was only silence, and then the line went dead.

A Note from the Editors

WE HOPE YOU ENJOYED *MYSTERIES OF SILVER PEAK*, PUBLISHED BY the Books and Inspirational Media Division of Guideposts, a non-profit organization that touches millions of lives every day through products and services that inspire, encourage, help you grow in your faith, and celebrate God's love.

Thank you for making a difference with your purchase of this book, which helps fund our many outreach programs to military personnel, prisons, hospitals, nursing homes, and educational institutions.

We also create many useful and uplifting online resources. Visit Guideposts.org to read true stories of hope and inspiration, access OurPrayer network, sign up for free newsletters, download free e-books, join our Facebook community, and follow our stimulating blogs.

To learn about other Guideposts publications, including the best-selling devotional *Daily Guideposts*, go to Guideposts.org/Shop, call (800) 932-2145, or write to Guideposts, PO Box 5815, Harlan, Iowa 51593.

Sign up for the
Guideposts Fiction Newsletter
and stay up-to-date on the fiction you love!

You'll get sneak peeks of new releases, recommendations from other Guideposts readers, and special offers just for you . . .

And it's FREE!

Just go to Guideposts.org/Newsletters today to sign up.

Guideposts

Visit Guideposts.org/Shop or call (800) 932-2145